A J Thomas

A J Thomas spent his early years in Nottinghamshire.
He has worked on projects around the world, in mining, oil,
gas, power and railways, and now lives in East London.
Young Lad on Old Street is his debut novel.

YOUNG LAD ON OLD STREET

A J Thomas

RED PAGE

First published in Great Britain by
RED PAGE PUBLISHING
PO Box 346, WARE,
Hertfordshire, SG12 4DX
Great Britain
www.redpagepublishing.co.uk
www.younglad.co.uk

The right of A J Thomas to be identified as the author of this Work
has been asserted by him in accordance with the
Copyright, Designs and Patents Act 1988.

Cover image © M T A Smith, 2015, all rights reserved.

ISBN (paperback edition) 978-0-9932904-2-8
ISBN (Kindle edition) 978-0-9932904-0-4
ISBN (EPub edition) 978-0-9932904-1-1

Production: Janson Woodall

Chapter 1

Harry looked up from the old guy's deflated penis and shrugged. 'I still need paying. It's not my fault you can't keep it up.'

'But it is your fault,' the old guy exclaimed. Earlier Harry had been curious how the old guy's voice had boomed so confidently down the phone, now it sounded cracked with bewilderment. 'The whole point of an escort is that he should indulge his client, play to his fantasies and satisfy his needs. You have done none of that. That's why I haven't been able to…' He turned away and gestured below.

Harry was unimpressed. 'Look, I've delivered what you ordered. You wanted a boy in your bed with no clothes on, and that's what you've got.' He stretched out across the bottom of the bed, propping up his head on his arm, naked except for his wristbands and rose tattoo. 'This isn't a magic wand, you know, I can't wave it to stop you being impotent.' He waved.

The old guy snorted. 'Rubbish. I have never been impotent.' He stole a glance at the wand all the same.

'Perhaps you're just nervous.'

'I most certainly am not!'

'Have you thought about seeing a doctor? They have pills for the older gentleman nowadays.'

'My sexual performance,' the old guy hissed, 'has never been anything but superlative.'

The old guy's body was not gym fit. It might have been muscular once but, as he sat there hunched, the skin was starting to flap from his upper arms and his abdominal muscles were lost in rolls of fat, heaped on top of each other like layers of a collapsed wedding cake. Looking at that first thing in the morning, or any other time of day, couldn't do much for his self-esteem. No wonder he resorted to escorts. In Harry's experience, it was this type of punter that was usually the easiest to please, the quickest to pay. The old guy pushed himself up off the bed and wrapped a silk dressing gown round himself. Harry sat up and brushed his hair away from his eyes.

'That's great. I'm glad you don't normally have any problems and I'm sorry that today's an exception but you still owe me a hundred and twenty quid. This is business, you know. I'm not here for fun.'

The old guy choked, gasping for breath like he had just finished a forced sprint. The capillaries on his cheeks blushed, the hairs of his moustache bristled.

'What do you mean, you're not here for fun? That's exactly what you're supposed to be here for! I pay you to come here and have fun. Or at least pretend to. You're supposed to look like you enjoy it! That's the whole point of an escort.'

'You sound like you go with a lot of escorts,' remarked Harry, wondering how long it would take to get his money. 'Look, we could try something else. How about you give me a blow job?'

'I'm not paying you one hundred and twenty pounds for that! That was not the deal. I don't give people "blow jobs".'

'OK. Well, since you can't fuck me, maybe I should fuck you instead. How does that sound?'

The old guy shook his head in disdain, maintaining stiffly that he would never submit himself to another man, let alone... he nodded towards Harry. He needed a drink, he said, then tugged the dressing gown chord to ensure it was firmly tied, checked his hair in the mirror, and strode off in a show of how vigorous he was. His hair was black with just a tell-tale hint of grey underneath suggesting it was dyed; and it might look full-bodied but Harry had spotted the bald patch on top. He probably bulked it up using some high end product. There was a call from the room at the other end of the corridor, asking whether Harry wanted his brandy medium or large. At five-thirty in the afternoon. Harry shouted back that he didn't want any, thanks all the same. He wondered whether to put his boxers back on, but decided this might send the wrong signal – he didn't want the guy thinking he'd given up on the money. The room was stuffy, the central heating was on too high.

The old guy came back into the bedroom with two heavy-bottomed tumblers a third full of what was presumably brandy. He thrust his hand out to Harry.

'Here you are.'

'No thanks, I don't really drink.' One thing Harry's parents did have in common was that neither of them liked alcohol - it stopped them doing more worthwhile and productive things - so Harry had grown up without that temptation to hand. He would go out on the lash with his mates, of course, but most of the time he would be drinking something soft. He didn't see the point. Even if his dad did say he got wasted.

'What do you mean, you don't drink? Yes, you do. It says so on your profile. It says you drink socially.'

'Well, I do, but only occasionally. I just thought it would look better on my profile if I bigged it up a bit.'

'Well, drink this.' The old guy pushed a tumbler into his hand abruptly. 'I would never select an escort who doesn't drink.'

Harry sniffed the glass before taking a sip. He wasn't going to finish that.

'So what else have you made up on your profile? If I'm to pay someone a hundred and twenty quid, I expect to get what I ordered. In fact, let's take a look.' The old guy yanked him up by the wrist, and Harry reluctantly let him lead him down the passage towards the reception room.

When he had first turned up, Harry had said he didn't drink and the old guy had not picked up on it then. Now, the old guy fiddled with his PC, Harry standing naked behind him. Up on the screen came his profile: Young Lad on Old Street aged 19.

'So you claim to be nineteen years old. I don't believe it. That photo's out of date. You're at least twenty-five.'

'No, I'm not. I'm just a bit over nineteen. Punters like to think they're going to bed with a nineteen year old. Anyway, your profile says you're fifty, and you're definitely not that. You're at least sixty.'

'I am nowhere near sixty. I'm in my mid-fifties.' The old guy grunted. 'But that's beside the point. You say you live on Old Street: I do believe that, though why anyone would want to live in such a god-forsaken area, I have no idea. You say you're a "single gay man looking for 1-to-1 Sex with gay or bi men aged 18 to 99". How old is the oldest man you've had sex with?'

'Mid fifties, supposedly.'

'Hm. Well, it certainly wasn't me. You describe yourself as "slim" – too slim, I'd say – and "5'10' / 180 cm" – half an inch less, I suspect – with "brown hair and grey eyes". Your eyes are blue, they're not grey.'

'They're grey-blue.'

The old guy read on. 'You're Out. And your profession is... Escort. Well, you've a sense of humour, even if it is a rather cynical one. You don't smoke, according to this you drink socially, and you'd "Rather not Say" when it comes to whether you take drugs or not. Well, do you take drugs or don't you?'

'Not really.'

'Then why do you say you'd "Rather not Say"? I'd always understood that "Rather not Say" is code for "I do, but I'm not going to say so online". Isn't that the case?'

'I'd rather not say.'

The old guy grunted again, apparently becoming more composed. 'And you don't do incalls. Why do you only do outcalls? Doesn't anyone want to go to Old Street?'

'I guess they do. But I don't do incalls because I share a flat.'

'Boyfriend?'

'No.'

'Girlfriend?'

'No. Just friends. They don't know I'm an escort.'

'Nor do I. Oh, and here's the service you offer. "New Boy in London. 19 years old. Educated, intelligent and well-dressed." Well, I don't know about the first two but I suppose well-dressed can mean different things to different people.' The old guy took a long look up and down at him before reverting to the PC. Harry, never normally self-conscious, found his hands covering himself. 'Carrying on. "Available for dinner, theatre, and other social occasions. Disease free. Friendly and discreet. If you are looking for a pleasing and relaxing time, you have found the right guy." And then finally, "A good time and fun guaranteed". Ha! So, apart from all the other embellishments and lies, you do actually guarantee a good time which you have most certainly failed to deliver. And, as we've both agreed, it undoubtedly wasn't fun. You have held yourself out as providing a service you don't deliver. I'm vindicated and fully justified in withholding payment!'

Now Harry was feeling the need to plead. 'Look, it's just a hundred and twenty quid.'

'And have you ever really accompanied a client to the theatre? Or to dinner? I don't see it.'

'I've been to the theatre.'

'To see what?'

'Er... *Jeremy Kyle the Opera*?'

'Never heard of it. I doubt it even exists. And I am adamant that you've never been to dinner either. In fact, you're not a real escort. This is probably your first time. That would explain everything.'

It was not his first time, second time or whatever time, but Harry was feeling frustrated and losing the will to argue. All he wanted was his hundred and twenty quid. From the clock on the wall, it was nearly 6 pm. He started working out how long it would take to get to Waterloo from – where was he? – Fulham. The walk from Fulham Broadway Tube had taken ten minutes. Catch the train back to Surbiton, change into something that would make him stand out less – why had the old guy insisted he wear something smart when the whole point was to take his clothes off? - and meet up with his mates as planned. He took a glug of brandy without thinking, the sudden taste of which brought him right back to looking at the old guy's face.

'I just want my money.'

'Well then, you shall have it. You shall have it. Wait here. I won't be a minute.' The old guy strode back towards the bedroom. At last, thought Harry. In five minutes time, he would be on his way back home with cash in hand. He relaxed back into the couch behind him, his back rubbing against the leather, his buttocks feeling the cracks where it had been split by age. The tumbler rested coolly on his crotch. Looking around, he could see the place was quite spacious, it was probably worth a fair bit. He wondered what you could get in Surbiton for this. When they had spoken on the phone, the old guy had called it an apartment. An apartment in a mansion block. The people round here would be minted, no doubt about that. There was probably a lift, but Harry had jogged up the two flights of stairs. He noticed a cluster of decanters on a corner table, the brandy presumably came from one of those. The ceiling was high and corniced, pine shelves went two-thirds up the wall. At home, they kept books out of the reception rooms and hid them upstairs in the study that his parents supposedly shared. Books were untidy, they said, and he agreed. Here, the books were lined up like conscripts on parade, uneven in height and size. There were photographs too on the shelves, some yellowed by age or maybe damp, pictures of boats in a harbour, a town climbing up behind it, a family round a table with a trellis of grapevines On a side table, a picture stood by itself, a photograph of a woman who looked quite elegant – Asian, Harry thought, probably Indian. She was looking out at him, at an angle. He studied her, conscious that his bum was starting to stick to the seat.

He could hear the old guy marching back with his money. When he entered the room, Harry realised that those were his clothes heaped together in the guy's arms, his check shirt, his bitter chocolate shoes. Next thing, they were dumped onto his lap, on top of the tumbler.

'Here you are. I believe this is all yours. And here's the fee for your services. Thirty pounds.' The notes drifted down, one slipping away to the left.

'But that's not what you owe me!' he protested.

'Well, that's all you're getting. Now, off you go!'

The old guy pulled him up by the arm and across to the door. Harry let the tumbler spill as he scrambled to keep his clothes bunched together and retrieve the stray banknote. He found himself bundled out into the corridor, the old guy stooping to toss the remaining shoe after him, then banging the door shut. He leant back against the wall, struggling to get into his trousers, scared that someone might come out and challenge him, wanting to know what he was doing there with no clothes on. Pulling on his jacket, he stuffed his boxers into the pocket and, shirt still hanging out, ran down the stairs and into the cold open air.

Chapter 2

Sunday afternoon, the next day, Harry had just come downstairs. He could hear Marianne out there in the autumn air, smoking one cigarette then another as she and Adele took their time saying goodbye. Marianne didn't care about the draught that ran through the open door and clicked on the radiators in spite of Steve's complaints about the rising cost of fuel. Inside, Harry watched his dad across the room pretending to focus on the paperwork he had brought back for the weekend, frowning over some technical legal issue. He had seen all this before. In less than an hour, Steve would be heading for the garage and burning through his frustration in his Maserati Gran Turismo S, 0-62 mph in 4.9 seconds, top speed 183 mph. Harry had a driving licence but not a licence to drive the Maserati.

Marianne was chatting about how Harry's mates were getting on - she'd moved on from the new wet room Adele had come round to admire and had just been explaining how Sam - who, of course, had been Harry's best friend since they'd started at school – had split up with Sophs. It was the same old story, going to college had taken the young sweethearts in different directions but they would soon find new partners. Sophs – Marianne's voice dropped, but he could still hear - got on very well with Harry. She went on to how another of the girls was blogging her way round Asia and had now arrived in Nepal. How exciting. And so on. Marianne hadn't heard any of this from Harry. She didn't need to. She didn't need to take time out for a chat with her son when she could find out everything she needed on social media. It was less complicated. And maybe showing an interest in his friends helped make up for the fact that, compared to them, Harry was going nowhere. Not college, not Nepal, and certainly not leaving that room just now. He was going to stay and listen in to what his parents had to say.

Closing the front door, Marianne slipped back into the living room, wrapped in her pale cardigan. She dropped her cigarette packet onto the table right by Harry and remarked to no-one in particular, but really for Steve's benefit, how it was always a pleasure to have Adele round. 'She's a breath of fresh air.'

'She's clumsy,' Steve retorted.

'OK, she spilt her coffee, but so what? It's not as if there's any lasting damage.'

'But she always has to make a mess, doesn't she? And you shouldn't have mentioned the central heating.' He smoothed down his weekend chinos as he awaited her response.

'What was that?' Marianne was searching for something. She found it, her mobile.

'You shouldn't have gone on about it, how I've turned down the heating. It was embarrassing.'

'Why?' She was checking her texts.

'Because it makes me look like I'm mean. Or run out of cash.'

Marianne was multi-tasking, regardless of Steve's wanting her attention. Absently, she said he was being oversensitive, that she'd had to explain why the room was so cold, it wasn't something anyone could ignore. It still was cold as far as Harry was concerned, bloody cold. He should have been wearing more than a T-shirt.

'It was rude of her to draw attention to it.'

14

'That's Adele. She speaks her mind, you know she does. And, from where she's standing, we're rich as Croesus.'

Steve had started scowling at her now, but Marianne was absorbed in her texts. 'Why,' he complained, 'does she always insist on wearing boots in the house? All that stomping around on the landing is bound to leave scratch marks on the floor.'

'She doesn't pay attention to petty rules, that's why. Like being told to take her shoes off at the door. Anyway, leave Adele alone. She's done nothing wrong.'

'She's put on more weight.' Steve wanted the last word on everything. 'Still, how do you know we're not short of cash? "Rich as Croesus." I might be going bankrupt for all you know.'

Harry thought his dad was bipolar when it came to finance. Either he was strutting round, telling everyone how he had outperformed the markets or he was neurosing about how those same markets could wipe out his savings on an impulse. Marianne, though, wasn't interested in money, meaning he could accuse her (as well as anyone else around) of being financially illiterate.

'It could all vanish, you know,' he carried on. 'There'd be no quantitative easing option.'

'I'm sure you're right. That's why you turned the heating down.' She fiddled with her hair, checking it was pulled back properly.

'No, it isn't. I turned the heating down because those bastards have put the price of gas up again.'

'Same difference, isn't it?' She was texting someone.

'No. It's not the same.'

'OK, it's not.'

'FUCKING LISTEN, WON'T YOU?'

Marianne looked up from her mobile, unimpressed. 'Look,' she said, 'you've just been telling Adele what a big swinging dick of a lawyer you are. And it's true, you are very successful. You're at the top of your game. You're committed to your clients, and I'm sure they love you back. So don't get so worked up. Chill out.'

So, he wasn't going bankrupt. Steve sat back and let Marianne get on with her texting. He resented it when she stepped in to reassure him and was looking restlessly round the room for something else to criticise. Harry wondered when that would be him; but, next thing, Steve leapt up to examine the shelves, drawing his finger along the surface to check for dust. Harry was safe for now.

'We should get rid of the cleaner. Whatever her name is.'

'Anna.' Marianne helped him out.

'Look.' Steve waved his finger in the air but Harry couldn't see any sign of dust. 'Get rid of her. She's useless. And when I leave her a note telling her to do something, she never does it. She probably can't read English.'

'She can understand English. She's reliable, she's trustworthy. OK, she's not Mrs Doubtfire, but who is? She does enough to keep the house under control.'

'She's not value for money.'

'Oh, money again. We pay her the going rate for Surbiton but it's hardly a match for a corporate solicitor's hourly charge-out rate.'

'Yes, but do we really need a cleaner?'

'Oh God, this isn't another of your haphazard budget cuts, is it? Isn't that something of a false economy? You're obsessed with hygiene, you can't bear anything being untidy or out of place, so someone has to keep the place clean. Who else is going to do it? I'm not, I have way too much on; and, anyway, as far as I'm concerned the place could be a pigsty. You certainly haven't the time. And I'm sure Harry has better things to do.'

Safe no longer. Steve turned on his son. 'Oh, yes, Harry. No, we wouldn't want to get in the way of whatever Harry's doing, would we? And what exactly is that when he's not cluttering the place up all day? I can't keep up with his motivation, his go get it attitude to life.' This was unusual. Normally, Steve didn't find time for sarcasm, he went straight to the abuse. 'Think of the tens of thousands I'd have pissed away if she'd let me put you through a private education. Well, maybe the housework is something he could just about manage.'

Harry laughed. He knew he had to say something. 'Actually, I've got a job in a bar at the moment. But I'm not sure it's any of your business what I do so long as I keep paying the rent. And I do pay you rent, don't I? I think I've got the right to expect you keep the house clean and tidy in return.' As it happened, Harry was pretty tidy-minded himself – it was in his DNA – so he would probably make a fair job of the housework, but now was not the time to offer.

Exasperated yet again, Steve asked if he was going to be doing anything that day other than hang round the house. He replied that he was due to meet someone later in the afternoon, around five-ish. He made a mental note to check the time.

'I'm sure he has loads of things on the go.' Harry didn't need Marianne defending him. 'He's always up in London with his mates.'

'Playing the lad, you mean. Going clubbing. Getting wasted. And wasting money.'

'They're young, that's what twenty year olds do - remember? They're entitled to have fun. And he's always liked dancing. Just like you used to. Anyway, he does help out round here. Only the other day, he was showing one of Adele's boys how to mend a puncture.'

'Actually, Mum, that was years ago. He must be old

enough to drive by now.'

'Those boys need a male role model,' she carried on, 'not having a dad around.'

'They "need a role model",' scoffed Steve, slumping back in his chair. 'And you give them Harry.' Harry could see where Steve was coming from, although he'd be the boys' role model if they wanted a so-called waster.

'So there we are,' said Marianne, 'we need a cleaner, no-one else is going to do it, and you're far too busy making your millions.'

That was when Steve lost it. Harry hadn't been prepared. He felt a jolt as Steve jumped to his feet, waving and shouting around. 'You've absolutely no fucking idea, have you? You think it just keeps on coming in.' Harry could see Marianne preparing to have her say. 'I've told you time and time again, there's no such thing as a secure job nowadays, at least not in the real world.' He leant forward to spit it out to her. 'You don't realise how I have to justify my existence every day. I have to tart myself round for business.'

'Lucky you.'

'Only to find my so-called colleagues then trying to nick it off me. You know, they'll put the knife in given half a chance.'

'What a martyr.'

'All that. The economy's cratering. And then, back here…back here, I've got you. You. Poncing off me all the time.'

Harry knew how Marianne would react. She snarled back from the chair. 'Oh shut the fuck up. You do talk such crap, don't you? Crap, crap, crap. "Poncing off you." I have my own career, thank you very much, as well you know. I have my own income stream, I don't need yours.'

'What? Your career? Oh yes!' They had had this argument more than once before, Harry knew the script even if it was the first time every time for his dad. 'Working three days a week constitutes a career, does it? Three days a week working in the public sector, pretending to have a job.'

'It's not "pretending", it's a highly responsible, service critical job in hospital management.'

'"Service critical"? You're just a parasite, coining it at the taxpayer's expense and sitting on an undeserved gold-plated pension. In fact, you screw me twice. First, through the taxes I pay to keep you in your non-job and, second, by leeching off me in my own home. Anyway, you're not a nurse, you're not a doctor, so what professional skills do you bring to a hospital administration job? Oh wait, yes, you're a qualified solicitor!'

'Not this again. I was a solicitor. I'm not now. That was years ago.'

'That's right. When you and I met, you were a solicitor. And you were going places. Trouble is, I didn't realise quite what places.'

'Yes you did.'

'I'd assumed you were going to build a career practising in law, you never told me differently.'

'I did.'

'You never told me of your plan to ditch it all as soon as you found some sucker...'

'Oh, do shut up. It's so boring. Every time.'

'... Some sad fucker to ponce off. I was young and naïve, I was there for the taking. It must have been obvious. You were three years senior to me...'

'Just shut up. No-one's listening anymore.' No-one apart from Harry.

'I'd never have married you if I'd known. You knew that. My life would have followed a completely different trajectory.'

'Oh, get over it, for god's sake!' Marianne looked really riled. 'It's my decision what career path I follow, I don't have to ask your permission, for fuck's sake, or anyone else's for that matter. And, anyway, you supported me at the time.'

'I had no choice!'

'You knew full well I needed to find something personally fulfilling. And I wasn't going to achieve that at Grant Matcham Rose, was I, not without a penis?'

'It's not like that.'

'The health sector offered equal treatment. It's vocational, it's stimulating, and it's actually very well paid by ordinary people's standards.'

'It might be well paid if you worked a full week, but I don't see what's so vocational about doing nothing two days a week.'

'I don't do nothing. It's my time for myself.'

'Your free time, at my expense.'

'Oh stop going on and on about money. You're obsessed. And it's boring.'

Steve choked as he spoke. 'You're so fucking middle class, don't you know? You've no idea what it's like to live hand to mouth.'

'Give it a rest! You're no more working class than I am. Not nowadays. This is the lifestyle you've created for yourself.' She waved her hand round from the comfort of her chair. 'Don't give me all that barricades stuff. Anyway, class means nothing anymore.'

'Means nothing? Listen to yourself. You live in a bubble, you and all the other *bien pensant* liberals. No-one in your family has the faintest idea what life's really like. I mean… look at that sister of yours, stuck in a ranch in the Cotswolds. And that lard arse husband of hers.'

'You mean Bob. You are pathetic. Just because he has more money than you. And, if this is now leading up to where we're spending Christmas, we're going there. End of story.'

This was news to Harry. No-one had told him they were going to the Cotswolds for Christmas. At least, not while he was listening.

'I don't care where I go for Christmas. Christmas doesn't mean anything to me. I couldn't care less where we spend it.'

'That's settled then. We're going. And you won't fuck it up for everyone else.'

Steve thought about that. 'Have you asked Harry where he wants to go?'

Harry was saying nothing. 'I'm saying nothing.'

'We're all going, Harry included. And you'll make a special effort with Mum and Dad please.'

'Those two are so pickled, they'll have trouble decomposing when the time comes.' Harry coughed, but Marianne ignored him.

'You only need to be on show at mealtimes. Most of the time, you can do your own thing. The house is big enough.'

'They are so ostentatious.'

'Oh right. And you eschew any public display of wealth, do you? Spending thousands on the fast car for the boy racer. What the hell's that for?'

'Look who's fucking talking?' Marianne had raised the stakes, the Maserati was supposed to be off limits. 'Look who's just splashed out £10,000 on a wet room? Ten thousand pounds down the drain. A wet room? I mean, what is the point of that? Why can't you just have an ordinary shower like everybody else? It's not as if it'll make you any better looking.'

'What are you talking about? I haven't the faintest idea. It didn't cost £10,000 and, anyway, I paid for it out of my own savings. It has nothing to do with you. I don't need you in there, leaving pubic hairs all over the place.' Harry could not recall ever having seen any of Steve's pubic hairs in the shower; and, as for other hairs, well, Steve was bald. He guessed

Marianne shaved. 'And, as it happens, wet rooms are not some absurd extravagance. They're par for the course round here. Every house has one.'

'"Every house has one." Listen to yourself. Have you any idea how bourgeois you've become? Just because everyone else has one, we have to have one too. Or, rather, you have to – as you say, it has nothing to do with me. I'm not going to use it. You know what, you fit perfectly in this brain dead suburb. All those airhead women wondering whether it should be macchiato or espresso.' Steve waved his hands above his head. 'And the numbskull husbands up at the golf course with their averages.'

'What on earth…? You have no idea what goes on round here. And why's that? Because everyone knows you as the psycho at the end of the road. In the ten or so years we've been here, you've alienated nearly everyone. New arrivals are told to cross the road to avoid you. And I'm left to get on by myself. Don't forget, it was you who wanted to come here in the first place, I was quite happy back in Old Street.'

'Old Street? Well, if you were so happy in Old Street, then why don't you fuck off back there? I could have the house to myself then. I'd be able to get rid of your sodding wet room.'

'Fine. But you'd have no-one to talk to. I don't mind where I live. I don't need possessions or status. I'm not so inadequate I need a fast car to show how virile I am.'

'Psychobabble. Typical psychobabble of an '80s feminist. With your dungarees, your head scarf, looking like a land girl.' Harry had never seen Marianne in dungarees and he didn't know what a land girl was.

'Oh, get lost!'

'You have enough stubble to give a guy a rash. I can't imagine how I ever brought myself to have sex with you!'

'If you're talking about the other night, I hardly think that rated as sex. A teenager could have done better.'

'You're just ugly. Gross and ugly.'

'Don't try and blame your lack of performance on me! Actually, have you ever thought you might be gay? That would make sense, wouldn't it? You're gay but you can't face up to it. You're a repressed gay.'

'A "repressed gay"? That just shows what an '80s mentality you're stuck in. There are no repressed gays any more, you stupid cunt. You're just a cunt. A useless cunt.'

Steve left the room for his Maserati. Marianne was searching round for her cigarettes. She spotted them near Harry and crossed the room with an empty laugh. 'Hey, Harry, whatever was I thinking when I married him?'

Chapter 3

Steve might be no great shakes in the sack but sex was one thing Harry always had been good at, right since Year 11 when he'd first made out with this older boy. Science, no. German, never. But knowing what a boy really wants and making it happen, that came easy. He took pride that this was a talent for which he owed his parents nothing - like his couldn't-be-arsedness except that, in this case, no-one had ever complained. Before now.

Earphones on and looking out of the window on the journey home later that day, he saw Raynes Park station pass by. He reflected on how Steve wasn't really any better looking than Marianne. Neither of them had the edge over the other in that department – in fact, they were quite a good match. He mused on whether he did actually look like either of them and glanced for reassurance into the window. An express train came rushing back down the next line to Waterloo, punching the air as it passed him. At least he wasn't going bald. His hair was thick and dark, cut so as to sweep over his forehead and ears. It was one of his better features. Marianne was starting to show signs of grey. He wondered if she'd bother having it coloured but, no, she wasn't personally vain that way. She was quite well-toned though, for someone her age. Steve's face was fatter than his and they were supposed to share the same snub nose. Harry knew he was never going to be particularly good looking but he didn't care. Some of his mates had grown somewhat narcissistic as they realised girls rated them hot.

They spent hours each week in the gym and probably believed that made them better in bed. Harry didn't exercise much. He wanted to be seen as more your average kind of guy, someone people liked having around but also found slightly intriguing. Anyway, Steve was gym fit and not much of a stud, not according to Marianne.

The old guy had been unfairly harsh about his online profile, but he had believed he lived on Old Street. Harry, of course, did not live on Old Street or share a flat with friends who didn't know he was an escort. Though none of his friends did know. Well, almost none. One reason he called himself Young Lad on Old Street was that he didn't think Young Lad in Surbiton would have the same pulling power. He reckoned there would be a market in Surbiton. Mostly, it would be middle-aged men who were publicly successful but bored and frustrated in private. Marianne used to say it was the stultifying dullness of the suburbs that made them such a breeding ground for punk in the '70s. These guys were modern day wannabe punks – only marriage, money and, worst of all, age, stopped them. Harry calculated that, bending over, he could be a vehicle for their frustration, their rage at getting old, their vengeance on youth.

No, the market would be too narrow. Of course, ruling out Surbiton didn't explain why he had chosen Old Street. He had spent the first years of his life there and, although he might since have been totally Surbitonised, he liked to think - watching those young lads on the streets - that there was still some inner city boy inside him. Old Street according to his parents had been the Wild West of east London when they lived there but now it was going vertically upmarket, leaving the locals behind. It wasn't attractive, the roundabout at its centre was topped by what looked like the frame of a dome-shaped tent that someone had erected before wandering off.

But the main reason he had chosen it as his escort tag was that, when he first found the website, all the guys seemed to live on Old Street or, at least, in EC1, the area round Old Street. There were thousands of guys who were members and he came to realise that not all of them lived in London EC1, but Old Street had stuck in his mind. One unexpected consequence of his pretending to live on Old Street was that he actually spent quite a lot of his professional time there because people would hit him up, writing 'Hey, I live just off Old Street...', etc, etc. So he ended up seeing inside quite a few Old Street flats belonging to others.

He didn't care if punters were punks or if they were just too lazy to get out of bed and find someone real. Some were in open relationships or felt like cheating on their fellas. Others lacked confidence. Many were just greedy. Wherever they came from, Harry gave them what they wanted and they wanted him back. It was a kind of relationship, a fantasy one; and, given his experience of his parents, that was as near to the real thing as he was prepared to get. It showed you could have feelings without getting hurt. There was plenty of sex but no risk, nothing to take away apart from the cash. It was romance without strings.

The money helped keep Steve off his back. So long as he could pay the rent and have enough cash to large it up, he didn't have to think about anything else, especially a 'career'. He could just do his own thing. Once, when he had been out all night, Marianne suggested that, if he ever wanted to bring someone back home, that would be fine by her (she wasn't speaking for Steve). She never asked directly about his love life. By someone, she meant a girl – gays were just guys out there who had rights. What sort of girlfriend would she like him to have? Someone emotionally intelligent. Someone who would encourage him to get involved in single issue politics and read all the post 9/11 fiction Marianne talked about. Someone like, oh, Sophs. And it was true, Sophs and he were close and they did have something in common sexually – they both liked men.

As it happened, there were times when he did ditch his escort identity and go online to see if there was anyone out there with something for him that he could return. Guys listed in their profiles what they were looking for. Was it Friends, Relationships, Group Sex, or just No Strings Attached? He wasn't comfortable about Friends, let alone Relationships, so he didn't highlight either; but, all too often when they realised this, guys who hit him up would message, 'Hey dude what's wrong with Friends and Relationships?', 'I'm not sure I ought to go with someone who's not prepared to look beyond the sex', 'After all, we may really connect'. Pretending to feel the same way, or not sure if he did, Harry would reply, 'Hey let's meet now!' And they would, they would share interests, talk about pretend past boyfriends and how hip Old Street was and where they went clubbing, have caring and mutually respectful sex, exchange contact details and embrace tightly on the doorstep, not caring who saw them. Then he would leave, wondering if he would ever see the guy again; but he didn't, dumping him the first time he saw the phone ring, never answering his calls, deleting his messages without hearing them. He despised these guys for their neediness and their interest in him. Some would try and reach him again online. One guy – quite cute, 5'9", slim but with a firm body – had messaged him beseeching that he understood what Harry was doing, he had known from the start what would happen but he always fell for bastards; and this had left Harry feeling awkward enough to reply, thanking him for his interest but suggesting he'd do better elsewhere. And then he put a block online, barring any more contact from him. So there were no Friends and no Relationships. Actually, he did have one

Friend, a young lad who had managed to break through using wit and cheek, but they were never going to meet.

Which, sitting on the train, brought him back to his profile. He thought it was well put together, even quite polished. The old guy was right that he hadn't been completely truthful, but that was just part of the marketing. The product was pretty much as packaged. He wasn't quite the age he claimed, but 'nineteen' was a cause for excitement in a certain class of punter. Anyway, everyone online, including the old guy, listed himself as younger than he was. The old guy had to be at least sixty. It was true that Harry didn't admit he never took drugs, but that was because he wanted to give the impression of being a nineteen year old with edge. And he really was available for dinner and other social occasions – even theatre – it was just that no-one had ever taken him up on the offer. The aim was to introduce an edge of refinement so that no-one would assume he was rent. Edgy but refined. Old Street. No, Harry didn't agree with the old guy and he wasn't going to change his profile. And he was still owed ninety quid.

*****

Two days later, his phone rang.

'Is that the young man from Old Street?' Harry had heard that same voice not long before, those same words. Deep and slightly grumpy, it sounded like one of his old teachers.

'Who's that?'

'You came to my apartment last Sunday afternoon.'

Apartment? 'Oh! You're the guy who kicked me out the door with no clothes on!' The guy who couldn't keep it up.

'I was too hasty.'

'Someone could have seen.'

'It was inconsiderate.' It sounded like he wanted to apologise.

28

'And you owe me ninety quid.'

*****

Harry had agreed to meet him at a champagne bar in St James's. On arrival, he checked inside. It was a converted bank, a few afternoon diners sat on high stools by the bar, the old guy not among them. He stood outside, uncertain whether he was dressed properly this time, shivering when the wind gusted round the corner. A waiter came to the door, presumably to shoo him away, a white cotton shirt stretched over his chest.

'Mr Adami is seated in the alcove at the back of the bar.' He had a German accent.

The waiter stood aside to hold the door open for him, and Harry could feel his eyes running down his back as he walked across the room. The old guy was sitting behind an ice bucket, acting the host but not looking very apologetic.

'Ah! You've arrived!' His eyes flitted for a moment onto Harry's Converse trainers. 'I have selected a vintage champagne.' He paused. 'You do drink champagne, don't you?'

Harry nodded and sat in the chair opposite. He supposed champagne was OK. The German waiter appeared from behind to fill his glass, his eyes not on the champagne but looking into Harry's via a mirror. Cool and in control. Harry broke away to pay attention to the old guy, who was asking his name.

'Harry? So, Harry,' his voice was gruff as when they had first spoken, 'I assume you are a student? At university?'

Ha, the old guy was so wrong. 'No. I don't see any point spending three years making myself unemployable when I can be out there getting cash now.'

'Quite right! All those degrees do nothing to prepare

young people for life, other than foster the illusion that they are better than they are. So, what is it you do?'

'I work as an escort.'

'Ah. Yes.'

'And, in my spare time, I do a bit of debt collecting.'

'Really? I expect you meet some disreputable characters in that line of work.'

Harry laughed. 'Ha! You're right, I do. You owe me ninety quid.'

'Ah. Indeed.' That didn't sound quite like an admission. The old guy topped up his own glass. Harry wondered if anyone ever admitted to not liking champagne. 'And this,' the old guy gestured towards the bucket, 'is meant by way of apology.'

'Cheers.' The bubbles fizzed up the back of Harry's nose. 'But you still owe me ninety quid.'

'And you shall have your money, Harry. It was quite improper of me not to have paid you in full at the time.' His eyes rested on Harry's torso, and Harry let them. It was obvious he was thinking back to the last time he had seen it. Harry had never doubted that the champagne bar was just a detour on the way back to the old guy's flat, his apartment. He slid down the chair and tilted it backwards so as to show the guy some arse.

'So,' Harry asked, 'now you know my name, what's yours?'

'My name's Frank.'

'Frank. Is that short for something? Like Harry?'

'It is. Francis, normally. But, in my case, Franġisk. It's a Maltese name.'

'Cool. Does that mean you're Maltese then?'

'I am Maltese British.'

'Wow. I've never met anyone from Malta. That is, before

now.'

The conversation wandered round the Mediterranean, stopping off at places Harry had visited until it returned to Malta.

'So, those pictures on the shelves, back at your apartment? Are they of Malta?'

The old guy looked surprised. 'They are. You're quite observant, Harry.'

'I like to take an interest in my surroundings.' In the mirror, he could see the waiter in the distance, watching what he was doing. 'And that picture on the side table, the one of the lady, that looks like it was taken by a professional.'

'It was. I had it commissioned.'

'Is she someone special?'

'She is indeed.'

But not that special, not just then. Harry spread his legs apart but Frank stayed looking at Harry's face, playing it cool. 'So, Frank,' Harry stretched his arms behind him, 'are you a regular here?'

'You might say that.' Frank seemed to sigh, then reached inside his breast pocket. 'Now, to business, Harry. The money I owe you.' Whoa! Harry had expected a bit more chat, more foreplay over the champagne. Still, Frank was the client, and now he was counting out the notes from his wallet onto the table. 'There you are. Ninety pounds.'

'Cheers. And now it's back to yours.'

'I'm sorry?' Frank sounded surprised.

'You know.' Frank might want to play games but Harry had him hooked. 'Back to yours. Your apartment.'

'My apartment?'

'Yeah. You still want to have sex with me, but you knew that first of all you had to pay me what you owe and admit I'm a proper escort.'

'A proper escort?'

'Yes. "Available for dinner, theatre and other social occasions." Like now. Right?'

Frank put his glass down on the table. 'Young man, I am sorry if you are under any misapprehension but my purpose in inviting you here was purely to pay you money that is contractually yours. Nothing more. As to your being a "proper escort", no proper escort would arrive here and spread himself over the furniture in the way you have, exhibiting himself with such indecent "come and get it" vulgarity. Especially not in an establishment of this calibre. I have a reputation here and you might as well still have no clothes on. So no, my original judgment still stands. Proper escort, no. Dinner, theatre and other social occasions, no.'

On his way out, Harry passed the German waiter, who just shrugged. Harry felt himself blush. They both knew the waiter could have him whenever he wanted. Harry would have no say in the matter.

He walked down the street, past St James's Palace and on towards Victoria. Halfway there, his phone rang. It was Frank. It was an invitation to dinner. Tomorrow. In a restaurant in Soho. Yay! So, he was a proper escort after all!

Chapter 4

'And you're sure she won't mind you bringing an escort?'

'There's no reason she should assume you're an escort. Anyway, she has always had an eye for the younger man. There'll be no objection on her part.'

'I'm your escort, though, not hers. Right?'

On the phone that afternoon, Frank had explained they were to meet a lady for dinner that evening, the widow of an old friend of his who had died the previous year. Harry's presence would mean there was less chance of the meal turning into a wake. Now they were standing in the middle of the restaurant, caught between the cramped tables. The walls were roughly painted egg yolk yellow and the air swirled with the heat of the grill and the smell of oil. The diners seated around them seemed mainly tourists, Europeans with backpacks and Brits giving up on their kids being co-operative. Two young waiters in black tie leant over the tables to help. Frank was wearing a green cravat. Harry couldn't imagine Steve ever wearing a cravat. Steve dressed too young, he was in denial about being middle aged. Looking round, Harry could see that Portofino was not at the celebrity end of Italian restaurants - and he did feel self-conscious in his suit - but he liked the sense of occasion that being with Frank seemed to bring.

From behind the till, another man, grey-haired and grander than the waiters, strode solemnly towards them.

'Mr Adami, Mr Adami,' he intoned solemnly, 'it is always such a privilege.'

'Stefano!' Frank boomed back. 'The privilege is, as ever, mine!'

The exchange of civilities continued while Stefano slipped Frank's coat from off his shoulders and draped it over the counter. He was clearly higher up the food chain than those younger guys.

'And Lady Dahlia, Stefano? Has Lady Dahlia arrived yet?'

'The Lady Dahlia? Lady Dahlia is joining you? Marvellous. What a lovely lady. We don't see her since Mr Nick passed away. So sad.' He shook his head at the same slow pace as his speech.

'It is indeed. In what should have been the prime of his life. He was scarcely older than I am now. Imagine, Stefano, it could have been you or me.'

'I will find a discreet table, Mr Adami, for you and the Lady Dahlia. In the back. It is quieter.' He cast his arms around apologetically.

'That would be excellent. But we are three this evening, Stefano, not two. This is Harold,' Frank stepped aside to reveal Harry, 'a young friend of mine, new to London. I've promised to look after him.'

Stefano bowed and said it was a privilege to meet him. He called for one of the waiters to find them a table. Harry thought he would let the name thing drop for now.

'And a glass of Prosecco for you and your young man, Mr Adami? On the house, of course.'

'That sounds just about perfect.'

When they sat down, a waiter brought glasses over, together with bread and olive oil. Portofino was unlike the Italians Harry was used to eating at, those tended to be chains where he met with his mates and you knew what you were getting before you turned up. This was different, this was more of a stand for the real Italy in the middle of a foreign land. Frank poured oil into a white saucer, dabbing pieces of bread into it and gesturing to Harry to follow. Harry had seen this done. It was all very communal and tasted OK. Stefano stood over them and Frank asked how business was doing.

'Business is good,' said Stefano, as if surprised that was the case. 'Business is good, even with all these wretched Tube strikes. But the Tube is one thing – there are always other ways of getting around, the city keeps going. Just imagine if all the restaurants in London decided to go on strike. Then there really would be a problem. I shouldn't say this but many of our regulars - not you, of course, Mr Adami, but many others - they have no idea how to cook. They have these big swanky kitchens but they can't even chop an onion! They'd starve.'

Harry's house had a big swanky kitchen but only Steve really took advantage of it. He'd spend thousands on a new model NEFF oven that looked no different to the last one. It was his wet room.

After Stefano had left to attend to an adjoining table, Harry summoned a waiter over to order some tap water. He could see Frank looking at him approvingly. Harry had known he'd have no problem doing 'Available for dinner'. He could be urbane and sophisticated. He twiddled the buttons on his cuff and asked if Lady Dahlia was a real Lady.

'Aristocracy, Harold, is a matter of character, not of birth. So, yes, she is a real Lady.'

'I don't believe in class divisions. I think everyone should get the same chances in life.'

'You're white and middle class, Harold, it's your privilege to say that.'

'Stop calling me Harold. It's Harry, not Harold.'

'Harold suits an escort better. Besides, he was a king of England.'

'So was Harry. At least, I think he was. Anyway, I'm a republican.'

'You're too *contraire*, Harold. An escort – a proper escort, that is - should admire his client's intellect, not challenge it. And, in his body language, he should show how he finds it somewhat appealing. Tilt your head to one side.' Harry gave up on the name thing and did as he was told. Frank adjusted the angle, tweaking his chin with his fingers. 'That's better. And republicanism is a treasonable offence. In better times, you would have lost your head for such talk.'

It was time for Lady Dahlia to arrive, Harry could hear Stefano slowly fussing over her in the front. There would presumably be commiserations followed by talk of happier times. When she was escorted in, Frank tried to get to his feet but his knees were constrained by the table. Harry stayed sitting as Lady Dahlia leant forward and Frank made a fuss of kissing her on the cheek. He found himself introduced again as Harold, Frank's new protégé. As he rose, she shook his hand, looking him briefly up and down and leaving him feeling a touch awkward.

'Ah, the suit, Dahlia?' Frank said. 'You've noticed his suit? Very good quality material, don't you think?' Frank brushed down Harry's jacket.

Lady Dahlia nodded slightly. Frank, from his hunched position, waved towards the empty chair; but Lady Dahlia searched round, saying they needed a further chair. A fourth person would be joining them. Harry had not noticed the guy next to her. Fair haired, well-built, quite masculine at first glance. Not wanting to seem interested, Harry shook his hand briskly, then studied the ceramic floor tiles. His name was Arthur.

Being introduced to Arthur, Frank displayed what Harry guessed was a customary look of irritated bafflement. After they sat down, he behaved like a gentleman in attending closely to Lady Dahlia, but he tried to ignore her surprise guest who, unfortunately, didn't seem to notice and kept butting in.

With the others engrossed in conversation, Harry thought he could check out this Arthur unnoticed. Possibly thirty, he looked the outdoors type. There was no denying he was quite good looking, but there was something quirky and unstylish about him too. He had thick eyebrows that made him look like he was constantly frowning. Maybe he was, as he listened respectfully to Frank. His sideboards were seriously misconceived, they were far too long. And that chin should have seen a plastic surgeon. His eyes flashed towards Harry, spotting he was showing an interest. Harry switched to look at the couple behind him. The eyes were a curious shade of green. Arthur tried to bring him into the conversation, asking whether he thought the same as Frank. Harry replied that he agreed with everything Frank was saying. Then he remembered to tilt his head. When Arthur turned back towards the others, Harry tried to make sense of his and Lady Dahlia's body language. Her lower arm was brushing against his and he let it – or maybe he just didn't notice. Her hair was jet black streaked with grey. He wondered if Arthur was her toy boy. Frank had said that she had an eye for younger guys, although not apparently for him after that first once over. She spoke in a considered, refined manner, with a nasal hint of some London accent or other. She talked of how pleasant it was to visit Portofino again and how Frank must agree that Italian cuisine surpassed any other in the Mediterranean, including Maltese and Greek. She must come from Greece. Actually, she didn't call him Frank, she seemed to know him as Frankie; though, when she talked to him, it wasn't with much warmth. She clearly valued having Arthur at her side, as if for protection. It struck Harry that Arthur must be her escort, not for sex but as company and support. He would observe and see if there was anything he could learn from him. There they were, Frank and Lady Dahlia, each with an escort, like duellists with their seconds.

Frank was very good at acting the host. He ordered a bottle of red wine called Dolcetto and, at his direction, they all drunk a toast in memory of Nick. Stefano brought the menus and more bread. He called it *focaccia*. Now the others were tearing pieces off and dabbing them in the same saucer. Like the others, Harry opened his menu. Stefano recommended a selection of *torte salata* as starters. These turned out to be cheese and vegetable pies, nothing too unusual. Harry scrolled down the list of mains. He could always have *pansotti* – described as huge ravioli stuffed with vegetables and served with a walnut sauce. Then there were *tomaselle*, veal roulades filled with meat, eggs and herbs. Explaining that something was a roulade didn't help much. Ditto a lamb stew with *carcrofio*. There were plenty of fish dishes - something he generally avoided. He couldn't see any lasagne on the menu. Lasagne was his standard fall-back position when eating in Italian restaurants. Lasagne or pasta carbonara. There was no carbonara either, but there was pasta with pesto. And more red wine.

Frank was chatting to Lady Dahlia, recalling how Nick and he – indeed, the three of them – had shared many a meal at Portofino, ever full of conversation as well as fine food and wine. They had always meant to pay a visit to the actual Portofino, the harbour near Genoa, but sadly the opportunity had never materialised. Stefano had used to sing its praises like a classical lyricist. Lady Dahlia said she was minded to have some meat, some *tomaselle*. Frank praised her choice, and turned to ask Harry what took his fancy. Something not too weird. Harry tilted his head and said he quite fancied some meat too – had Frank any suggestions? Frank nodded, gratified to be asked for advice.

'If meat it is you want, Harold, then I suggest you follow our esteemed guest. *Tomaselle* would be a fine selection.' Harry nodded in return, realising that he was about to find out what a roulade was. 'He is very discerning, Dahlia,' Frank sought to draw her attention back to his new protégé. 'Very discerning, don't you think?' Frank put his hand on top of Harry's for just a moment.

When Stefano returned, Frank ordered for Lady Dahlia and Harry, then leant towards Arthur to ask with pained concern if he needed any assistance. Arthur said he would go with the flow and have meat too, but the lamb stew rather than the *tomaselle*. 'And lamb stew for Lady Dahlia's gentleman too, Stefano. Do you recommend the lamb stew?' Frank asked doubtfully, but he didn't delay in proudly shutting his menu. 'I myself will have the *fritto misto*. Seeing how Genoa is the finest place in Italy for seafood, how could I do otherwise?' *Fritto misto*. Deep-fried seafood, according to Harry's menu.

Stefano beamed lugubriously. 'An excellent choice, Mr Adami.'

Harry listened as Frank reminisced how Nick and he had met some twenty-five years ago at a club, quite nearby as it happened. The club had long since closed. Nick and he had shared the odd drink there. Of course, Nick and Dahlia had had two young children back then, so Nick never stayed late.

'Alex and Anika,' he declared.

'That's right, Frankie, you always did have a very good memory.'

'It seems like yesterday, Dahlia, it seems like yesterday. And they're both well, I trust?'

'Oh, they're both very well, thank you. Alex has been qualified as a doctor for some years now, he's working in Vancouver. And Anika's in Australia! She's a tour guide.

Getting married next year. At last. So, they are at the opposite ends of the Earth, and I'm stuck here in the middle.'

'What a shame! You're not tempted to join either of them then? Not persuaded by a change of climate?'

'No, Frankie. Home is here.'

'Indeed it is, Dahlia, indeed it is. This country has taken us to her bosom and we should never forget that.' He paused, searching for the right question. 'And you're still in that lovely house of yours? Not thinking of finding somewhere a little smaller now that you're more on your own?'

'No, at least not yet. It would feel like a betrayal of Nick. I know that may sound a bit OTT, but I don't care. I'm staying put. The house is full of memories. And, come the day I ever need to go into a home, well I'll cross that bridge then.'

'A bridge too far, Dahlia,' Frank assured her, 'a bridge too far.'

The table fell quiet. Harry became aware of some rowdy music playing over the speakers. Opera, he guessed.

'Death's never easy, is it?' mused Frank, pondering over his *fritto misto*. 'And never predictable. You cannot foretell what surprises it may bring.' He glanced up at Dahlia with concern. 'Have you not found that?'

'Oh, you're right, Frankie, quite right. Nick was very good at planning, doing his best to make sure we were in the most advantageous position financially. And I left him to it, I was never involved in that side of things. Besides, I've no head for figures. Which is why it's so very kind of Arthur here to help me out now.'

Frank looked sharply towards Arthur, who said by way of explanation, 'Dahlia was a rock to my mum while she was alive. It's not a favour I could ever repay in full.'

'Such Christian charity,' applauded Frank, 'is rare to find in today's society.' He re-charged their glasses and made a toast to those who devoted themselves to caring for others. Harry tried to count back the number of glasses he'd had.

'And he has a first rate brain, Frankie,' Dahlia said, as if he needed warning. 'Nobody could get anything past him.'

'Indeed?'

Arthur wasn't paying close attention, he was holding his glass up to the light and scrutinising it. 'This is a very fine wine, Frankie, if I may say so.' He took a mouthful that he rolled round contemplatively before swallowing it. 'Firm but youthful.'

Firm but youthful, thought Harry. That was probably how Lady Dahlia saw Arthur. Harry himself was starting to feel more blurry than firm.

'Arthur has a good nose for wines, Frankie. He picks them out for me.'

'He picks his what? Oh, the Dolcetto? Firm but youthful? I suppose so,' Frank conceded, unimpressed, then brightened up. 'The nose is a curious protuberance, isn't it? I once read that slugs have four of them.'

'That's amazing,' cried Harry, tilting his head. 'I never knew that.'

'And on the subject of noses,' Frank continued, addressing Arthur in particular, 'did you know the story of Pinocchio originates from a Turkish myth that a man's member increases in size when he lies?'

Harry thought it was the other way round, that the more a man lied about the size of his member, the smaller it became. That was his experience, anyway.

'Oh, I think someone's been having you on there, Frankie,' observed Arthur, frowning intently. 'Although they were being quite witty. But have you ever heard of the Pinocchio paradox? It goes like this. Pinocchio's nose grows when he lies. But, if he claims that his nose will grow and it does, then he can't have been lying. An interesting conundrum, don't you think?'

Arthur sat back, apparently assuming that Frank would find this puzzle as intriguing as he did. Harry had spotted from the start that he was clever. Lady Dahlia wasn't paying attention to the conversation, she was looking down at her *tomaselle*. Harry had finished his roulades and quite enjoyed them. He wondered what Frank would have to say next.

'It doesn't say his nose grows only when he lies,' retorted Frank.

Arthur nodded earnestly into his lamb stew as if in agreement, although Harry suspected Frank had missed the point. Arthur was clever. 'And by the way, Frankie, may I say how much I admire your not being hidebound by petty conventions?' Harry had no more idea than Frank. 'I know some of your generation can be very old school,' Arthur continued, 'when it comes to red wine and think it's not done to drink it with fish, but I'm glad you don't pay any attention to such outdated social niceties.'

Frank placed his glass flatly down onto the tablecloth. 'Old School', he echoed. 'Social Niceties. Is that so?' He turned to Lady Dahlia, raising his voice to draw her back into the conversation. 'Now, Dahlia, do you still manage to go to the theatre much nowadays? I recall it was a pastime you and Nick very much enjoyed. I'm sure there is many a gentleman who is more than happy to lend you his arm.'

'I go when I can, Frankie. There is a group of us girls who like to take trips down to the West End. The National's very good nowadays, you can get £10 Travelex tickets there, you know. We saw *Hamlet*. Of course, that's the South Bank. But there was also a very beautiful production of the *Nutcracker* at the Coliseum. Matthew Bourne, it was.'

'How marvellous. I don't see as much as I would like, I'm

afraid, I never have enough time. But don't you find it disappointing there are so many musicals on these days? It all seems so targeted at the youth end of the market.'

'Oh, I rather like musicals…'

Harry was getting bored. Theatre bored him. He never went, at least he hadn't been since he was sixteen and school trips ended. Marianne did go regularly. There were some very good theatres in Kingston and Richmond, she would say - getting no response from him or Steve. It would make him feel self-conscious, sitting in the middle of a crowd of people, most of whom would be old. The seats were too close together. His personal space would be invaded. There was no privacy, not like in the cinema where you could be who you wanted and do what you wanted once the lights went down. Actually, his personal space was being invaded just now, and it was Frank who was doing what he wanted. His hand had been wandering up and down Harry's thigh on and off throughout the meal. Harry didn't think he had much to learn from Arthur about being an escort. Arthur had been somewhat *contraire* with Frank. He had been dismissive about Frank's Pinocchio theory and then come up with a story of his own that was a bit too smart. He had embarrassed Frank over the wine he was drinking. He was definitely intelligent though, and quite good looking. Almost fit. Now, he was trying to engage in the conversation between Frank and Dahlia about the theatre, or whatever subject they had moved on to, but with Frank determined to cut him out. He seemed confident and at ease with himself. He probably played a lot of sport. Squash, perhaps. Mountaineering, or even white water rafting. Harry could see him kitted out for karate. Of course, he wasn't Frank's escort, he was Lady Dahlia's, so it didn't matter if he was *contraire* with Frank so long as Lady Dahlia was cool about it. That was far enough. Under the table, Harry wrenched

Frank's hand off him. The conversation stopped.

'So, Harold,' asked Arthur, 'how long have you and Frankie been an item?'

Harry jumped inside. 'Pardon?'

'You and Frankie. The two of you.' His finger flicked between the two of them.

'Er... well... it all happened very quickly, as it happens.' His throat felt dry, some more wine might help.

'Cool. You obviously rub along well together. Which is great. When we first came in, I thought you might be an escort.'

Harry choked, his wine spurted down his jacket. Arthur frowned, as if surprised. Lady Dahlia turned to peruse the table alongside. Frank dabbed the jacket. 'Allow me,' he snapped, 'to clarify. Harold and I work together. We are business partners. That is all there is to it. Nothing more. Whatsoever.' Still frowning, Arthur started to apologise but Frank raised his hand. 'Enough. Now, Dahlia, my dear, the food has been lovely, the wine perhaps more so. But is there any particular matter you wish to discuss? I'd understood this evening was going to be an intimate catch up of old friends, but I sense there is something more to it than that.'

'You're right, Frankie, there is.' Lady Dahlia seemed to be steeling herself. 'There is more to it than that. It's about those properties on Regent's Row.'

'Regent's Row?'

'Yes. As I said, Arthur is helping me out with my investments. I want to sell them. That's what I needed to tell you.'

'Sell them?'

'Yes. Nick did his best but, as you say yourself, the future is never predictable. The markets haven't helped. Nick could never have known what was going to happen and things haven't gone as well as they might. So now I need to liquidate some assets.'

'On whose advice?' Frank's gaze stayed on Lady Dahlia, but his finger was waggling at Arthur. 'His?'

'Arthur has been very helpful.'

'So, what is he?' demanded Frank. 'A stockbroker? An investment banker?'

'Actually, he's training to be an osteopath.'

'An osteopath? An osteopath advising on an investment portfolio?'

'No, Frankie, I have my professional advisors to do that. But I can trust Arthur to take an overview.'

'I trust in God, Dahlia, but not to make business decisions for me.'

'I get lots of advice, Frankie, from all sides, but everyone is out to get a slice. Everyone but Arthur, that is.' She put her hand, clustered with rings, over his.

'No doubt. But do your professional advisors have any idea how valuable an asset the Regent's Row properties are? Does this Arthur? Do they not recognise that those properties provide us – that is, you and me, Dalia,' Frank's finger flitted between the two of them, like Arthur's had, 'with a steady rental income? And that there's the prospect of a cash windfall if a developer comes along?'

'I know. But they've weighed up the options and this is the best one for me. I'm told those leases don't generate as much rent as they should do. I'll grant you there's the potential redevelopment value, but that could be a long time in coming, if at all. A buyer now will pay me a premium and take the risk of any downside.'

'Or, more likely, the benefit of any upside if he knows his onions.'

'That may be so, Frankie, I don't know, I'm only going on

what I've been told. I'm not Nick. I'm not comfortable dealing with money matters. But I know the market's not good, which is why I'm offering you first refusal on my half.'

Frank closed his eyes, presumably so he could concentrate on some mental calculations. He opened them, declaring, 'No, I couldn't afford it. I couldn't finance that sort of purchase on the back of the rentals. It wouldn't wash its face. Like you, Dahlia, I'm not as well provided for as I might be. I couldn't manage it, not unless... not unless the price on the table contained some kind acknowledgement of our long and mutually beneficial relationship.'

'I thought you might say that, Frankie. If only I was in a position to help. Look, as I said, I don't have the head for all this, or the heart. So Arthur's going to act as my agent on the sale. You'll need to liaise with him.'

'And Harold's my agent,' Frank rebounded, his hand firmly back on Harry's thigh. 'It's just his sort of thing!'

'I'm planning to go and look at these properties some time in the next few days,' Arthur told Harry. 'Kick some tyres.'

'He'll go with you,' charged Frank.

Confused, Harry exchanged contact details with Arthur.

*****

Frank was outraged. Harry was trying to do outrage through an alcoholic fuddle.

'That anyone should choose to suggest,' Frank carried on, 'that I would take an escort to dinner with one of my oldest and dearest friends. How dare he? The impertinence!'

'It was totally out of order,' echoed Harry.

'The very insinuation that a man of my reputation would ever associate with an escort.'

'Who the fuck does he think I am?'

Frank was stressing, striding up and down the length of

46

the same room in which he had dissected his escort profile, while Harry was now sat upright on the couch displaying his own indignation. He tried counting Frank's steps in each direction, from underneath the print of a foxhunt on the far wall, past the table with the photo, and along to the doorway leading into the kitchen. This time, though, Frank continued through the doorway and returned with the brandy bottle. No bothering with the decanter. His seething had boiled over as soon as their cab left the restaurant, straight after a glass of grappa shared by Stefano with his customers. Following Frank, Harry had downed his in one. Grappa tasted like he imagined petrol did. Now he tried to focus on what Frank was saying.

'That Arthur has no manners, no breeding whatsoever.'

'He's no aristocrat.'

'To suggest that I am not familiar with matters of social etiquette.'

'Fucking Arthur. 'King Arthur.'

'He had no conversation, nothing of interest to contribute.' Frank splashed the brandy into the tumblers and thrust a glass towards him, expecting him to take it. Harry, mindful of the last time he had been sitting on that couch with a tumbler, accepted. 'He had not even taken the trouble to dress appropriately. No tie! Not even a collar!'

Harry had not taken any notice of what Arthur had been wearing. Now he recalled a white T-shirt under a blue V-neck sweater. He looked down at his own jacket, wondering if that stain would ever come out. Frank's cravat was probably a little looser than he realised. 'To be honest,' he declared, 'I just thought he was a geek. He had these really uncool sideboards. And eyebrows that made him look like a Vulcan. And a pointy chin like a wizard's.'

Frank shook his head distractedly. 'What is an osteopath anyway?'

'It's a bit like a physio.'

'I know what an osteopath is. But what has an osteopath got to contribute in circumstances like these?'

'He said you can't drink red wine with your fish.'

'People like him, with their university degrees, think they can run rings round you and me, Harold. And what experience of life does he have? How old was he? No more than twenty-five, I'd say.'

'Oh no, he was definitely older than that, Frank. I'd say…'

'It doesn't matter. How rude of him to interrupt a fellow diner and, what's more, one his senior. How supercilious to try and show people up with a silly riddle.'

Harry looked down into his tumbler. He was not going to drink that, he might have to start pouring it down the back of the couch. Seeing Frank about to go off on one again, he butted in. 'Funnily enough, when I first saw him, I thought he was her escort. Not as in a having-sex sort of escort – that did cross my mind but I just couldn't picture them together in that way. No, more of an escort as in "Available to go to dinner, theatre or other social occasions" – that sort of escort.'

'That's it. An escort. Nothing more. She has always had a weakness for younger men - even when Nick was alive. He'll have spotted that – this Arthur – and be seeking to exploit it. People like him make their living by seeking out such people and exploiting their vulnerability. Vultures. Take my word for it, Harold.'

'My name's Harry, not Harold. If you want me to stick around, it's Harry.'

'Harry, Harold. Whatever.' Frank stood in the middle of the room, waving the bottle around. Harry left to go to the toilet, the tumbler hidden behind his hand. He emptied it into the bowl, his urine the same colour as the brandy. On his return, he found Frank sitting on the couch, next to where he had just been. He decided to stay standing.

'What is it with these properties anyway, Frank? What's the story there?'

'The Regent's Row properties? Regent's Row, Harry, is one of the jewels in my crown.' Frank paused to swallow a mouthful of brandy. 'At least, that's the idea. The story, as you put it, is this. Regent's Row is a market, way up in north London.' He stopped, swallowed again, and choked, taking time to recover.

'And?' Harry prompted him.

Frank cleared his throat. 'And there are properties there I owned jointly with Nick. So, now he is dead, his fifty per cent share has passed to the widow.'

'You were more than just mates then, you and Nick?'

'We were mates, Harry, we were very good mates. But we also used to do some deals, on the side.'

'And what was he like, this Nick?'

'What was he like? Very canny financially, he will no doubt have left Dahlia well provided for, whatever she's now being told. There can be no sensible reason to sell those properties, not as the market is now. Which must mean this Arthur is trying to fleece her. He will have spotted that she has no-one to look after her interests, he will have reckoned on her family staying far away. He may even be part of some crime syndicate. But,' he pulled himself up from the couch, 'what we do know is that he - this Arthur - is at the centre of it all.'

''King Arthur.'

'Your glass is empty, Harry! It needs re-filling.'

'No thanks, Frank, I don't really drink alcohol. So what's so important about these properties? Why would these guys be so keen to get their hands on them?'

'I shall tell you why, Harry. Presently, the market is a

horrible area, filthy. I would never go there out of choice, it is full of immigrants. But there is a parade of buildings that Nick got wind of – some years ago - that was up for sale, going for a song. It was a speculative opportunity. The owner had died and his daughter wanted nothing to do with them, she had moved out of London. So Nick and I decided to make her an offer, before anyone else showed an interest. Three shops, each with a flat above it. The Regent's Row properties. There were tenants in place, and no shortage of new ones to replace them. The buildings were in good nick, no dilapidations. And they have turned a tidy profit for us over the years. But that is not what is important, Harry. What is important is that, in due course over the years, the area has improved. There has been government money. With house prices rocketing, those lower down the ladder with aspirations to buy round here have been pushed out to areas like that. You may even have seen it in Old Street.' Harry nodded like he knew. 'So the area is changing, it has even been described as fashionable; and, sooner or later, that market will start to attract the attention of those newly arrived middle classes. It will adapt to cater for them - there will be a farmers' market on the street every Sunday. And, crucially, as part of it all, there will come a time when developers start stepping in, offering cash premiums for buildings such as mine which they can then turn into smart cafes and restaurants. That will be my time to make a killing.'

'Amazing,' said Harry.

'So you see, Harry, that's why we need to protect dear Dahlia's interests from these rapacious rogues and cheats.'

'And how are you going to do that?'

'Well, she can't sell in the short term, not without my say-so, but that won't keep them at bay for ever. So you, Harry,' he waved his glass in salute, 'you must keep track of Arthur. Make sure you know everything he's doing.'

'Me?' blurted Harry. 'Why me?'

'Because I said you would, of course.' Frank was looking perplexed again. 'Why not?'

'Because I'm just an escort. You didn't mean what you said. You were just trying to cover up.'

'Of course I meant it, Harry. Please understand, I never say anything I don't mean.'

'What? So you really expect me to go up and visit this Regent's Row with Arthur?'

'I certainly do, Harry. As I said at Portofino, we're business partners now. You have a fine mind. It's clear you're entrepreneurial. I have no doubt you'll rise to the challenge.'

Harry thought about it. Did he want to get caught up in some plot to swindle this old woman out of her money? Did he care? Was Arthur really like Frank made him out?

'What would it involve?'

'Well, we must find out what Arthur plans to do. You must ring him first thing in the morning.'

'I don't know about this.'

'We shall sleep on it.'

*****

Harry slept on the couch. When he woke, his head now clearer, he wondered how much he could charge Frank for this new line of business, assuming he wanted to get involved. It wouldn't have to interfere with his escorting duties. Frank would have to pay him up front though - no more stunts like the first time. Actually, Frank still owed him for the evening just gone. It was 9:10 am, he went to get himself a glass of water. The room stank of brandy.

By 9:45 Frank was still not up and about. Harry dropped his phone onto the couch. Restless, he went into the kitchen, looking for something to eat. There was some salami in the fridge, along with an open tin of some sort of liver sausage, but nothing normal for breakfast. No cereal. No bread. He gulped down some milk from a container. There had been plenty of food at the restaurant but that had been ages ago. There was no mess in the kitchen, it was almost clean enough to meet Steve's standards.

It was coming up to 10 am and he was getting bored but couldn't leave. He held his phone in the palm of his hand and dwelt on Arthur's number. He rang it. At first there was no answer but then it defaulted to voicemail. Arthur's voice came over very matter of fact. 'Hallo, this is Arthur. Thanks for calling. I'm not available right now but, if you leave a short message,' etc etc.

'Hi, Arthur, this is, er, Harold, Frankie's business partner. I was just ringing to touch base about when you were going to visit these properties... and kick some tyres. Give us a call when you can.'

The phone rang back, hardly sixty seconds later.

'Sorry, Harold, I was at the door saying goodbye to my partner. Yes, I was planning on going up soon but I need to liaise with the managing agent first. Is that OK by you? Are there any dates you can't make?'

Harry swallowed. 'Er, my schedule's pretty busy at the moment, but I'm sure I can fit something in. Just so we're on the same page though, what exactly is it you have in mind?'

'Well, I would like to get a feel for the area. Check the condition of the buildings, talk to the tenants, that sort of thing. Is that what you were thinking?'

'Yeah. Pretty much.'

Arthur said he would let him know when he had heard back from the managing agent. He suggested the two of them meet up at Kings Cross on the day, so they could travel up together.

*****

From then on, Harry saw himself as officially a proper escort, available for dinner, theatre, and other social occasions. He had already got to meet a wide range of people in the course of his work. It wasn't just the regular in Willesden aged 44 (or whatever) who needed to be dominated. And there was the back of that car in Highgate, though he wasn't going to get caught doing that again. There had been more picturesque settings, such as on his knees among the pot plants of a Shoreditch roof terrace. He had probably seen more areas of London than many real Londoners. It was true that there was a risk of violence. In fact, it was a statistical certainty that an escort would get murdered by a punter sooner or later. A new Jack the Ripper perhaps. There were horrific stories of that sort of thing happening elsewhere in the sex industry, but the chances were that it wouldn't happen to him. Anyway, he wasn't meeting punters on the street, he had prior opportunity to screen their profiles and check them out on the phone before deciding whether to meet up. He wasn't obliged to go with anyone. But now that he was a proper escort, he could target the higher end of the market, literally in the case of an investment banker's office on the thirty-fourth floor of a Canary Wharf tower. Standing there while the client sucked him off, he had time to reflect how he would never have got to see this view otherwise. These clients came not only with champagne and cash on tap, Harry could be assured of his personal safety with them. On one occasion, this guy passing through London booked him for the whole night at a five star hotel in Park Lane. Harry turned up late as planned and was met with a glass of fizz, but that was as far as the social niceties went. What started out as playful roughing up quickly turned into something way less consensual and the client smothered Harry's head in case his crying out attracted attention. There was the occasional break. It was 8 am when Harry was told he could go. He got quietly dressed and left, without any thanks but with the consolation that he was a few hundred quid better off.

Chapter 5

It was trying to sleet as he walked up the drive to the house. The beech hedges, leaves now bronzed, gave some cover to the pale lawns either side. From time to time, Steve had ideas about redesigning the gardens, plans that usually got ripped up. Harry had joined in when he was younger, when he was in his landscape gardener phase. Marianne had left them to it. Anyway, it was no time for a garden show now, it was too cold. It was December, Thursday and not much after 9 am. Marianne's Golf parked randomly outside the garage. Thursday was one of her days for doing her own thing, undistracted by work or anything else. She would be upstairs in the study. Steve would be at his office. Steve's routine was the same every weekday. Before anyone else was up and around, he was off for a run in the park. A perfunctory shower on his return, he had breakfast standing up before making tracks for the station and an early train. That meant Harry would have the place pretty much to himself; which was good, because he wanted to forget about last night and that guy in the hotel.

Not thinking, he pushed the front door gently open, slipped inside, then pushed it shut behind him. It slammed. Even wrapped up in her study, Marianne would have heard that. He waited for her to come out onto the landing. But it wasn't Marianne who showed up, it was Steve, Steve who should have been at the office at 9 am on a Thursday, Steve who shuffled in from the direction of the kitchen in a T-shirt, jeans and bare feet.

'Hey, Harry.'

'Hey, Dad.'

'How's tricks?'

'Not bad.' He used his feet to ease off his shoes. 'Shouldn't you be at the office?'

'Well,' Steve was acting chatty, 'there's a Tube strike, see, so I thought I'd take the opportunity to work from home. I didn't want to get caught up in all the hassle.'

Harry thought that was a bit lame. All Steve had to do was to walk ten / fifteen minutes from Waterloo to his office, he didn't need to use the Tube and supposedly never did. Harry, though, had just walked from Park Lane to Victoria and witnessed the confusion of commuters being directed by Underground staff outside the station.

'Does Mum know you're here?'

'I think she's upstairs. I'm making sure I don't get in the way.' Harry couldn't get his head round – and didn't want to – why he was sounding so considerate. 'You look knackered.' Now he was the dad whose son has just come off after a hard game of football. Harry might have used to kick a ball around, but that was as far as it went.

A door opened above them and Marianne appeared, looking over the bannister.

'Oh, I thought it was going to be Anna. What are you doing down there?'

Harry didn't know who the question was aimed at. He and Steve just stayed there while Marianne picked her way down the stairs, peering through her varifocals, and checked out her son.

'You look knackered, sweetheart.' A cardigan, her trademark sky blue, was draped round her shoulders.

'That's what Dad's just said.'

'Didn't you get any sleep?'

'Sort of. I ended up on a bed in a five star hotel in Park Lane.'

'As if. Is it really shit out there?'

'It's not too bad.'

'I was just getting some coffee. I take it you don't want any?'

'No, thanks. I really need a shower.'

'Use the wet room. There's nothing like it.'

The wet room wasn't normally spoken of in polite conversation. Harry dipped in there occasionally, but he had regular showers as well.

'What about you, Steve?' She acknowledged him at last. 'A cup of coffee?'

'That would be great!' That was a bit too keen. It was a cup of coffee, not a school prize.

'I hadn't twigged you were still here. You haven't seen Anna, have you?'

'Anna? No. I was just telling Harry, there's a Tube strike on, so I thought I'd work from home. For a change.'

'Oh, right.' Marianne didn't buy it either.

'Actually,' Steve was shifting from one foot to the other, 'I've had an idea. I was planning on fixing some lunch later. How about I make something for the three of us? Since we're all here. It's been a long time since we sat down together.'

There was a reason they didn't eat together and it wasn't just that neither Marianne nor he shared Steve's interest in food. Harry was tired, he wanted some shut-eye; and he didn't want to deal with why Steve was behaving like this.

'Oh, I dunno,' Marianne sounded unconvinced. 'I'm in the middle of something at the moment.'

'Oh, go on. Sometimes a break can help. Like your having a coffee. Hey, Harry, what about you?' Apparently, Steve was looking for some father / son support. 'You look like you could do with something inside you.'

Not right then, he couldn't. But Harry realised he was hungry, he hadn't eaten anything for ages. Maybe it was time to give Steve's cuisine a chance. After all, since he'd met Frank, his taste buds had flourished; and anyway, he would probably just lie on his bed in a torpor otherwise.

'I'm not sure,' he said, sounding as doubtful as he could. 'What are you thinking of having?'

'Well,' replied Steve, cooking up some ideas in his head, 'how about lasagne? You like lasagne, don't you? I know there are some in the freezer.'

Defrosted lasagne. So much for *haute cuisine*, Steve was trading down to his level. 'Don't suppose there's any chance of something a bit more Nigella, is there?'

'Ha ha, very funny. Great, that's settled, then. How about it, Maz? You'll join us, won't you?'

'Oh, I dunno. I'm supposed to be having a meat free week.'

'I'm sure I saw some veggie lasagnes there too.'

'Well, OK then. Since Harry is.' Like him, she would be wondering what this was all about, how it would turn out. Steve's ideas might start OK but they did tend to get out of control.

'Excellent. So, Harry, you're on your way upstairs. How about we meet up at…' he looked at his watch, '…half-twelve? No, make that one o'clock.'

So lunch it was going to be. For some reason or another. Harry climbed the stairs, the hems of his smart trousers dragging under his feet. Anna was coming out of Steve's room. She waved hello. Anna was OK. She had cleaned his room too. He flicked on the radio and lay on his back on the bed, knees flexed, looking up at the ceiling. He thought about the guy the night before and then decided he didn't want to think about him anymore. He had been American – mid thirties, quite good looking, masculine, loaded of course – he had seemed OK at first, but later Harry realised he must have been chemmed up from the start. He hadn't spotted it in time. He felt inside his trouser pocket and pulled out a reassuringly thick roll of ten and twenty pound notes, which he kissed. Reading through his messages, he saw that everyone was going to a bar in Kingston that night.

Eighteen people had checked out his escort profile. The chances were that they were just being nosey and not seriously interested. Anyway, he was going into Kingston that night. He searched to see if his one Friend was online but he wasn't. Not surprising, it was 9.30 on a Thursday morning.

He stripped off carefully, put on his bathrobe, and padded quietly off to the wet room. Marianne's towel was on the rail, he hung his next to hers. The jets of water drove against his body, feeling their way round those bruises. Marianne was right, there was no point setting foot in the old shower after this. After a while, he decided he was as clean as he was going to get. He towelled himself down in front of the mirror. Back in his room, he lay on the bed.

When he woke, the radio announced it was five minutes past one. He was running late for Steve's lunch. He picked out a top and slipped on a clean pair of trousers, put the roll of cash in his pocket, and went downstairs. Marianne was at the kitchen table, reading a book. Steve was at the other end, washing up at the butler sink. Harry didn't appear to have interrupted any conversation. It was a big room, the Jam were playing in the background.

'Hey there,' he said. 'Anything need doing?'

'Well,' Steve called over his shoulder, 'I've got my hands full. It would really help if you could lay the table.'

'Lay the table?'

'Yeah. The mats are in the second drawer from the left.'

Harry knew where the mats were. 'These brown leather ones?'

'That's the one.'

Over at the table, he stood by Marianne who didn't notice and kept reading her book.

'Mum?'

'Oh, sorry, darling.' She clutched the book, leaving him room to lay the mats.

'You were far away.'

'Was I?'

Most of what Marianne did in her own time was a closed book so far as Harry was concerned. She didn't talk about it unless pushed, she just assumed neither Steve nor he was interested. Her own family were always engaged in cultural self-improvement; at least, Harry's grandparents were – Auntie Sarah really was a bit ditsy but Gran and Grampa would sit round, discussing their latest books and expecting everyone else to be as well-informed as they were. Marianne had a particular interest in art history but she also worked hard on her language skills. Not that it was all academic. She had recently been involved in an on-line petition to Downing Street against faith schools. And she had once raised the topic of sponsoring a child in Botswana – Harry didn't know what had happened there. There was always something on the go. Mostly though, it was art history, that was her private passion. Learning Italian and Spanish helped her find her way into those countries and round them. So, whatever Steve claimed, her two days off work each week were not spent doing nothing; they were employed in hard work for no financial reward. Steve couldn't get his head round that; and Harry, in her shoes, would have put his feet up.

'Is it another course?'

'Yes, it's another course. Anyway,' she slipped the book on to the chair beside her, next to her bag, 'is it time for lunch yet?'

Cutlery. When Harry asked whether it should be knives or spoons, he got contradictory replies.

Steve had the double oven gloves on and, crouching down, pulled the lasagnes out of the oven where he'd been keeping them warm. Each portion would have come in its own microwave-friendly tub and Harry would have eaten his out of that; but, for lunch today, Steve had got out the best china.

'Mind the plates, they're hot.' He brought two over before returning for his own. 'So, Harry,' he called out over his shoulder, 'were you out clubbing last night?'

'Yeah.' Harry thought he might as well play along.

'Anywhere good?'

'Yeah, it was as it happens. Somewhere in Kingsland. Just opened.' Harry had never been to Kingsland and wasn't sure where it was, but he'd heard that that was where things were happening.

'Kingsland? Blimey, that's a bit rough, isn't it?'

Harry had no idea. 'Not if you know your way round.'

'I'd heard,' Marianne joined in, 'that Dalston's the really in place these days. Or is that old hat now?' She'd been using social media again.

'You've always got your finger on the pulse, Mum.'

'In our day,' Steve pulled up a chair and sat down, 'Soho was where it was at. Everyone drank at the Spice of Life, the Admiral Duncan and there was one other place. Do you remember, Maz?'

'Not me. I never really did pubs in Soho. It must have been one of your other girlfriends.'

'Really? But we did used to go clubbing in Soho, didn't we? You, me, a whole crowd of us?'

'It feels a bit embarrassing talking about that now.'

'There was the Wag. Do you remember the Wag Club? On Wardour Street?'

'It's starting to come back.'

'That was really hip. And what about the one on the corner of Charing Cross Road and Shaftesbury Avenue? You know, the one in the converted church?'

'You're thinking of Limelight.'

'That's right, Limelight! I knew you'd remember.'

'It is a long time ago.'

'Not that long.' Steve had forgotten the water. He called out as he went to fetch a jug. 'Clubbing was really taking off back then, Harry. It was just before Ecstasy came on the scene. Isn't that right, Maz?'

'I guess so.'

'And then there were the raves. Mum went on a few raves in her time, Harry.'

'Oh, that was another life.' She turned to Harry. 'So, did you stop over with Sophs last night?'

'Sorry?' Harry knew his mother had hopes for him and Sophs, but this was a bit blatant.

'She's got a new flat share, hasn't she?' Oh, more social media.

'Has she? No, I told you, I stayed in a five star hotel.'

'You must have some very rich friends. Is she OK about it?'

'About what? You've lost me, Mum.'

'Her and Sam breaking up. Is she OK about it?'

'Oh yeah, she's fine.'

'She's not found anyone else yet?'

'Not as far as I'm aware. She may have done.'

'Oh, I see. And what about Sam?'

'Sam? We haven't been in contact for ages.'

'And then it all turned gay.' Steve hadn't been following the train of conversation, he was still back in the twentieth century. 'Is Soho still gay, Harry?'

'I don't know. There were loads of gay clubs up near Tottenham Court Road, but they got bulldozed.'

'That's a shame.'

'Nice lasagne, Dad.'

'Cheers. It would have been better if I'd made it myself.'

The conversation dropped off as they ate.

'So, Maz,' Steve chopped a corner neatly off his lasagne, 'did I hear you say you are doing another course?'

'Yes, yet another course.'

'What is it? Art history?'

'Yep.' She paused to swallow a mouthful. 'And since you're going to ask, it's on art in Germany and the Netherlands in the early sixteenth century.'

'Not Italy or Spain?'

'No.'

'Interesting. So, what was happening back then?'

'Steve, you know you're not interested really. I'd just be boring you.'

'How do you know? I don't know anything about art. If I did, maybe I'd find it as absorbing as you do.'

'OK. If you really want to know. The artists back then were concerned with the state of the human soul. They had broken away from what was happening in Italy. They weren't interested in idealising beauty.' She gazed coolly at Steve.

'That's cool. Who were the main players?'

Marianne sounded reluctant as she gave up the names. 'Durer, Grünewald, Mabuse, Hieronymus Bosch.'

Harry had heard of the last one. 'Hieronymus Bosch was a freak, Dad. He painted visions of devils torturing human beings. Scary stuff. Trust me, you wouldn't have liked him at all.'

'Thanks, Harry. So, Maz, is that art really still relevant today? I mean, all those devils and that religious stuff?'

'Of course it is. It's the form of expression that's relevant, not the subject-matter. I mean, I'm a republican but I can still appreciate portraits of the Royal Family.' She prodded her lasagne, then put down her knife and fork. 'So, how are things at Grant Matcham Rose?'

'They're busy, really busy. Much the same as usual.'

'Glad to hear it. It's just we don't normally see you back home on a work day. Especially not when it's busy.'

Marianne was right. Steve lived for his job and never liked being away from work. Grant Matcham Rose and he had been part of each other since before Harry was born. In fact, Harry pretty much owed his life to it. As Steve would say, the law firm had fed him, clothed him, housed him, taught him how to drive. So far as Steve was concerned, GMR had been his and Marianne's dating agency, the witness and registrar at their wedding, and the place where their son had been conceived. He still could not understand how Marianne could have chosen to turn her back on it. And yet, since she had, he had reacted by becoming more and more drawn into his work life so that often it seemed nothing outside it much mattered.

'I just wanted some time out. I felt it would be good to put some distance between me and the office. You understand.'

'Not really. It doesn't sound like you. Is there anything you want to share?'

'Yeah, Dad, what's going on?

Steve paused for a moment, then announced, 'Godfrey's stepping down as managing partner. He has decided to retire.'

'Wow,' remarked Marianne. 'Good old GPH. That will be an end of an era. He has always looked after you. So, who stands to gain?'

'Well, Andy is tipped to step into his shoes.'

'You've always got on OK with Andy, right? Since you both started?'

'I'm going to stand against him.'

So this was the news that demanded three frozen lasagnes.

'Wow again.' Marianne sat quietly back in her chair, taking in what Steve had said. 'That's quite a big decision. Have you given it a lot of thought?'

'You don't sound too convinced.'

'It's not that. I just wondered how long you'd been planning it.'

'Actually, it was Andy's suggestion. He and I were shooting the breeze the other day, talking about the future direction of the firm. We all know we need to be more international in outlook. Well, his plan is to build up links with firms in Europe so that we can work with them on the big cross-border transactions but, at the same time, keep our independence. That's Andy's response to globalisation.'

'Gosh,' said Marianne, still cautious. 'It does sound very ambitious. But you're not convinced?'

'It's total bollocks!' Steve pushed his plate away. 'It doesn't go nearly far enough. We'll never be able to compete with the big City firms if we carry on thinking small. What we need is a merger with a major US law firm. They're the ones with the real muscle and there are plenty of them out there looking to hook up with people just like us.'

'Well, I can see where you're coming from.' Marianne still sounded doubtful though. 'But Andy doesn't agree?'

'No, he just doesn't get it. He's too tied to the old order. He doesn't grasp that, if we get into bed with a US law firm, we'll have the reach to set up offices all over Europe and beyond.'

'Fair enough. But wouldn't that be more of a takeover

than a merger?'

'No! That's exactly what he says! I don't agree at all. It would be the same people, it's just we would be part of a bigger outfit. There'd be much higher profile as well as the opportunity to earn a shed load more. And there's nothing wrong in wanting to be financially secure.'

Steve sat back, satisfied he had made his case, but Marianne had another question. 'And are there other people in GMR who think the same way as you?'

'There must be. Which is why Andy suggested I stand as well.'

'That's very good of him. So you've made your mind up?'

'Yep. What do you reckon?'

'It would certainly shake things up.'

Harry thought it was time he contributed something. 'So, Dad, if this merger of yours goes ahead, does that mean you'll be making loads of trips to the States?'

'I hadn't really thought about that. I suppose it would.' Then Steve laughed, apparently he had seen through Harry. 'But don't go getting your hopes up, there won't be any jollies in it for you. No room for freeloaders!'

Harry had been right not to trust Steve's matiness, it had been simply a ploy to help get Marianne to the table. Now he was just a spectator. 'I wasn't thinking about me,' he retaliated. 'I was thinking of Mum. Maybe she'd like to go.'

'Well,' Steve searched for an answer, 'if she wanted. But she doesn't really like Americans.'

'I do if they're paying,' quipped Marianne.

Everyone finished eating, but no-one left the table. Marianne had still not given a decision on Steve's career move.

'Speaking of trips, Maz, where would you like to go on holiday next?' Now he was trying to buy her support.

'Wherever you decide, I suppose. That's what always

happens.'

'No, it isn't.'

'Yes, it is. You always choose somewhere hot and expensive. Then, when we get there, you can't cope with the sun and have to spend all day indoors. Like some vampire.'

'That's so true, Dad,' Harry laughed at him. 'We only go these places so you can tell people we've been somewhere flash.'

Steve grumbled that he couldn't remember Harry ever complaining. Harry announced that next time he would be making his own plans. Marianne and Steve looked at each other.

Marianne got up, saying she was going to make some coffee. Filling the kettle, she remarked that it wasn't long until Christmas. 'I could do with the break. And it'll be nice having everyone around. Did I tell you Emma's going to be there with the baby? And the father, Ben?' Ah, this was her price, or part of it.

'Really?' Steve replied, 'that'll be nice.'

'I hope you won't find it all rather overwhelming?'

'Why should I? Anyway, I'll always have Harry to chat to.'

'Don't count on me!' Harry wasn't going to give him a way out now, not after that stuff about freeloaders. 'I'll be doing my own thing. Anyway, Mum, we've heard all about Dad's job? How's yours going? You hardly ever talk about it.'

'Oh, there's nothing to report. Just politics.' Her answer stayed hanging in the air.

'Oh, come on, Mum, don't leave it at that.'

Marianne glanced at Steve, presumably wondering whether it was worth going on. 'It's a case of same old same old. All about politics, nothing about health.'

'Go on. Sounds interesting.'

'Well, every time a new Government comes in, it looks with horror at the health service, digs it up to inspect the roots, re-pots it, and then leaves it to the little people down below to spend all their time trying to embed some new regime. And that's where we are now.'

'And you're one of the people whose job is to do the embedding?'

'That's me.'

'Sounds harsh. Don't you think, Dad?'

Steve looked awkward. 'I guess it does. Anyway, that's enough about the two of us. What about you? Got any more work? I assume not, given you're loafing around here on a weekday?'

Well, so are you - loafing around here on a weekday - but you've still got a job. As it happens, I do have some new work on.' He reached inside his trouser pocket but was interrupted by Anna walking in and handing Marianne a receipt. Marianne searched vaguely inside her bag for her purse but she couldn't put her hands on it. Harry stepped in. 'Don't worry!' He pulled out his cash. 'I'll pay!'

He enjoyed seeing Steve knocked back at the sight of his freeloading son holding a roll of banknotes in his fist. Marianne seemed confused but just handed him the invoice. £27.97. For cleaning materials. He licked his finger and peeled off thirty quid. Anna left, unconcerned who paid so long as she got her money.

'How did you get hold of that?' demanded Steve, disbelievingly. 'It's like something out of a fairy tale. That or serious crime.'

Harry liked the reaction. 'Well, I said I had a job, didn't I? And, as you can see, it's cash in hand.'

'It looks like quite a lot of cash in hand. You're suddenly sounding rather streetwise, Harry. What's the story – or wouldn't we want to know?'

Marianne sat back down at the table along with her coffee, waiting for him to explain. 'First things first,' he said, 'here's next week's rent.' He counted the notes out onto the table in front of Steve.

Of course, Harry wasn't going to mention the main source of the cash; but he did want to talk about his new job with Frank, even if the story would need some editing. He recounted how he had met Frank when working at a bar. The old guy had clearly felt comfortable confiding in him; he had talked about how he was an entrepreneur whose junior partner – very sussed, apparently – had just been headhunted by some City outfit. Harry had started helping out on a couple of deals. Frank had said he had a good head commercially. The work had expanded, so the two of them had sat down and agreed a package. They hit it off OK. He knew that there was a lot he could learn from Frank about business. When Marianne asked him to give them an idea of what Frank was like, he described him as being about sixty, British Maltese, very savvy and with loads of experience. Liked to stand on ceremony and could be rather volatile, but nothing Harry couldn't handle. And possibly a bit of a drink problem. But very successful. Steve wanted to know if he was gay, and Harry answered that he had no idea.

Steve wanted more details of Frank's business. Harry said he had a variety of commercial interests. He himself was handling the real estate. Frank owned a portfolio of properties across London, commercial and residential. Harry dealt with the tenants, checking the rent came in on time, that sort of thing. He also kept an eye on the managing agents. Harry liked getting an insight into the tenants' lives; they were all sorts, old-timers, immigrants, students. But helping out on the property side wasn't all he did. One of the perks was that he got to drive

Frank round London in a Mercedes, an A300 saloon from around 1990. Steve looked impressed but wondered if it was in good nick since, historically, not many cars in that range had been well-maintained. Harry didn't care. Steve remarked that it couldn't be that much fun driving a car like that round central London. Harry still didn't care, he knew Steve was still impressed.

Marianne wasn't interested in cars. She wanted to know more about the office environment and the other people with whom Harry was working. Actually, there wasn't anyone else apart from an accountant who dropped in from time to time, an old friend of Frank's, and the office was just a room in Frank's apartment; but Harry brushed over all that. He described how Frank liked conducting business on a mobile from the back of a coffee shop in Fulham Broadway. Harry joined him there for lunch. In fact, talking of food, Frank had taken him to an upmarket Italian in Soho to introduce him to some business contacts. The food was very fancy, and Frank had splashed the wine about.

'He does sound very old school,' remarked Steve, doubtfully.

'I guess he is. But, as I said, he has loads of experience, and he knows a few tricks.'

'I'm not sure I want to know.'

'And he pays you cash in hand, this man?' ventured Marianne.

'Yep. As you can see.'

'So there's no job security.'

'No, there's no job security, Mum, but, if it all goes up in smoke, at least it will have been good experience. Anyway, there was something else I wanted to ask you. I'd like to go and see a play. Is there anything worth seeing?'

As expected, Marianne was non-plussed. 'A play? What's

brought this on? You don't like the theatre.'

'I know. It was just something Frank mentioned. He said that going to the theatre was good for the soul.'

'Oh, Frank again. He does appear to be a bit of a character.' She brightened up. 'Actually, Sheridan's *The Rivals* is coming on at the Rose soon. I was planning to go with Adele and the boys. Now the five of us can go.'

Lunch was at an end. Marianne said she needed to get back to the study. After she left, Steve suggested that it might be good if the two of them - father and son – did something together some time.

'Like what, Dad? Go for a run?'

*****

Harry woke up, concerned about what to wear. He wondered what Arthur would choose. It was nearly three weeks since the two of them had met. Harry had texted a couple of times and on each occasion Arthur had apologised, texting back that he was having inexplicable trouble getting hold of the managing agent. Then, two days ago, he had rung. The trip was arranged. Harry decided Arthur would be wearing a suit. He himself wanted to appear credible business-wise but he didn't want to look like Arthur – in case he came across as some geeky junior – and, not knowing the area, he was also thinking streetwise. He opted for Diesel jeans, Converse trainers, and a leather jacket with a dark grey hoodie tucked inside. He looked in the mirror, brushed his hair across his forehead, watched his eyes stare palely back, and wished he could grow a bit more stubble. Still, he felt quite cool, walking down the street to Surbiton station.

Standing outside King's Cross Tube, Arthur was also wearing jeans but there they parted company. Backpack, thick check jacket, and climbing boots into which his trousers were tucked, laces threaded round hooks. Arthur was very practical but not too stylish. He had probably been a Boy Scout.

'Hi, Harold.' It was a cloudy day but his hair caught the light.

'Hi, Arthur. Actually, it's Harry, not Harold.'

'Oh. I thought it was Harold.'

'I know. It was a joke. Frank started it. But it's Harry really.'

'Cool. Hi then, Harry.'

'Hi.'

The two of them took the Tube going north. Arthur said that, as a rule, he didn't use the Underground. He travelled round London on a bicycle, saving money and keeping himself fit in the process. When asked why then was he was taking the Tube this time, Arthur replied that it was so Harry didn't have to travel up on his own. Harry thought that was a bit of a twatty comment. He didn't need accompanying like a child. And he knew his way round London. Arthur was a bit of a twat. He wondered where he lived. Mindful of Frank's instructions that he should shadow Arthur and find out everything about him, he decided to ask. Arthur answered that he had just moved into a new flat in Brockley; it was not as large as his last place and he rather regretted the move, but finances had necessitated it. He was renting, he couldn't afford a mortgage. Brockley was somewhere between Peckham and Greenwich. Harry recalled that Arthur had been saying goodbye to his partner when he first phoned. On probing, he discovered this partner was female. Yes, she lived with him. Her name was Jane, they had been going out for three years and living together for just under one. No, they were not about to get married. Harry thought that he probably did not need to know more about Jane at this stage. Arthur didn't mind answering his questions, he volunteered that he had been born and brought up in Twickenham. He was, he said, genetically suburban. Harry contrasted this with his own background, born and brought up in Hackney, though he had to correct Arthur's assumption that he still lived with his parents and explain that he shared a flat with friends. He accepted that that must be expensive but said he needed his independence. Arthur told him he should get a bike, it would save him loads of money.

Harry thought he had managed to get quite a good profile of Arthur so far. Still, he felt sure Frank would be intrigued to know more about the connection between Arthur and Lady Dahlia. It transpired that Arthur's mother and Lady Dahlia had attended the same church and that, when his mother had become terminally ill, Lady Dahlia had been assiduous in visiting her. No, Arthur did not believe in a god. He asked if Harry had any further questions.

The train rumbled through the blackened tunnel, one wall of which was threaded with differently coloured cables that gave Harry a sense of their momentum. Arthur and he were sitting side by side, with no-one else nearby. He summed up Arthur as being very self-sufficient, not too bad looking. Fit, but still a bit of a twat.

The train arrived at their stop and Arthur led the way out. While they had been on the Tube, it had been raining, presumably quite heavily since the pavements were liquid. Now, the air had cleared and people were out on the street. Arthur's shoulders rolled muscularly as they strolled along; even so, Harry would have preferred a faster pace. There was a cute Japanese guy, a mass of spiky hair brushing the collar of his blue-black suede jacket, who was looking intently down the road they'd just come up. Harry glanced back to see a bus approaching. A massive African woman in a white dress patterned with birds, a tangled shawl and a green and white head-dress, was carrying a fake designer handbag. Louis Vuitton. At least, he assumed it was fake. He found it difficult to make out where the different layers of her clothing started and finished. He was looking too intently. He became conscious that Arthur had been talking to him and was now awaiting a reply. He played back to himself what he had been saying. Arthur had been asking if he was Frank's business partner across the piece or just on the property side. Harry didn't take seriously Frank's theory that Arthur was some master criminal; but, still, he didn't want to give away something by mistake, so he said that he dipped into this and that. 'And I'm handling Regent's Row now,' he added, 'so as to free him up to focus on his other interests.'

'Oh? What other interests has Frank got?'

'I don't think I should be talking too much about Frank's commercial dealings. I'm sure you understand.'

'Not really, Harry. But that's cool.' They walked on in silence.

Now they were in a high street milling with shoppers getting ready for the weekend. Harry remembered something else about Arthur he should check out. 'Hey, talking of jobs, aren't you a bit old to be training to be an osteopath? If you don't mind me asking.'

'I don't mind your asking at all, Harry. In fact, that's exactly what Dad says, that I'm too old. I guess it's an early mid-life crisis. I did some postgraduate stuff after Uni and, ever since, I've been employed doing research at Imperial. But the trouble with academia is that it's very bitchy, all office politics, and I'm no good at that. So I've been looking for a change of scene; and, as it happens, I've always been interested in osteopathy, so it was an easy decision to make. My hope is that, practising as an osteopath, I can just be my own man. Independent. Like you, Harry.'

Harry stayed quiet, unsure whether Arthur was taking the piss. He wanted to find out more about the research that Arthur had been involved in, but then they turned a corner and found themselves in Regent's Row, facing the market.

He didn't go to - or know of - any regular market back home in Surbiton although he had sometimes seen signs stuck to lamp posts advertising a farmers' market somewhere behind the high street. He recalled that Frank had aspirations for a farmers' market here. Back home, there were just Waitrose and Sainsbury's and Harry did occasionally pass through the fresh produce aisles there, usually on his way to fetch something ready-made. Here in the market, the vegetables looked more authentic in their soiled grubbiness than the polished supermarket products that were cleaned at extra cost. Perhaps one day, well-off supermarket consumers would want to pay that extra cost for the genuine grubby look. Arthur was inspecting cauliflowers, cabbages, other vegetables Harry didn't recognise, telling him what good value they were and how they should both stock up on their way back to the Tube. Harry said he would text his flatmates to see if there was anything they needed. He pulled out his phone.

They pushed their way up through the market between the stalls, Arthur taking the lead. He turned back to remark that it was a good idea for them to get a feel for the place. Vegetables weren't all that was on offer. There was jewellery, Harry thought of checking out that stall for a gift for Marianne or his Gran; it was, after all, the run up to Christmas. Silver tinsel, wrapping paper, cards. Bags, bags were clearly a big thing up here, bags and cases of all kinds. The Family Butcher was not so much a stall as a mobile van. Arthur stopped at the fishmonger's alongside it, there must have been five times as many fish there as on a supermarket counter. Perhaps the supermarket strategy was to show that it didn't want to be party to depleting North Sea stocks but that, if the no doubt environmentally guilty customers wanted cod, then they could feel absolved if they paid five times the market price. Arthur wanted to see if there was anything Jane and he might like for supper. Harry had limited interest in fish. He looked round and saw burkas, and a woman in a hijab with a nose ring. There were older white people, probably longer resident, moving uncomfortably down the road, perhaps held back by arthritis and back problems. Maybe these were the sort of people Arthur would treat when he was a fully qualified osteopath. He saw hoodies, black, white and mixed race, using the market as a forum for meeting up. One had an ugly dog on a lead. Arthur was now engaging with the fishmonger. Facing onto the pavement on either side behind the stalls was a row of shops that presumably extended to Frank's properties, numbers 41, 43 and 45.

Bored with waiting for Arthur and whatever he and Jane were going to be eating that evening, Harry left and stepped onto the pavement. He walked past an optician's, a chemist's, a Nail / Beauty / Tattoo shop, and a hairdresser's offering 20% off all colour services. On top of its usual business, a dry cleaner's washed and ironed five shirts for only £4.99. In fact, there were bargain deals everywhere, plus a 'Cash Converter' that turned out to be a pawnbroker's. There was a yellow and green jerk curry house with a Rasta logo, advertising rice 'n peas with beef or chicken. Two doors down, a bright new deli was serving lattes and pastries to the first wave of the newly colonising middle classes. He could see Marianne in there. But elsewhere there were shops shuttered up with To Let signs hanging from the second storeys; while proliferating at ground level were the transparently thin blue plastic bags carried by shoppers in either hand, filled with vegetables, packs of cut price batteries, newspapers. The stalls had petered out by now.

He reflected that this market wasn't really the pulsating heart of the neighbourhood that it should be, it could do with a pacemaker. Newspapers. Now he had arrived at the newsagent's at number 41 and the white guy talking with the Asian shopkeeper was presumably the managing agent Arthur had arranged to meet.

He went inside and asked the white guy if he was Colin Broadbent. The man, too broad and tall for the shop, hovered over him, shaking his hand enthusiastically and saying he must be Arthur. He had a big hand but a soft grip. Harry corrected him, he wasn't Arthur. The man apologised painfully. Of course not, he was Harry, Mr Adami had rung to explain. He peered quizzically over his shoulder looking, Harry realised, for the real Arthur. He explained he had lost him somewhere in the market. Colin introduced Mr Rai, the grey-haired shopkeeper who had been standing motionless behind one of the tills up to now and whose slightness of frame was emphasised by Colin's jumbo size. Mr Rai, fastidiously turned out in his soft cotton shirt and light tan cardigan, shook Harry's hand with a reserved courtesy. He had a red string bracelet round his wrist, not too different from Harry's.

Short of anything else to say, Harry remarked how full the shelves were; but then Arthur strode in, declaring how he had been worried Harry might have got lost. Harry replied that he had just been saying the same thing about Arthur, but no-one was listening. Arthur was the centre of attention now. Harry looked back down the narrow aisle. One customer, wanting to get up to the till, was finding it tricky to squeeze past another who was bent over the cold display unit and scanning the range of lunchtime snacks. Mr Rai called through to the room at the back and a young woman came out. Mr Rai motioned to her with quiet authority to serve the customers. Then he led Harry and the others to the rear from where Harry could see into the back room, windowless and bulb-lit but the source of aromas of tea mixed with spices. They didn't go in there, Mr Rai wanted to keep an eye on his assistant.

Making sure he included Harry, Colin relayed how he had been explaining to Mr Rai the purpose of his and Arthur's visit. Mr Rai told them how Mr Adami and Mr Mundis had been very good landlords over the years he had been there – facilitated, of course, by Colin towards whom he now nodded – and that he had never had cause, or given cause, for complaint. He continued that, consequently, regrettable as it was that a sale was now contemplated, he appreciated that things were likely to change following Mr Mundis' unfortunate death. Mr Rai was quietly spoken and self-consciously dignified. Speaking directly to him, Arthur acknowledged that Mr Mundis' death had been a great shame. Mr Rai winced in response; but Arthur didn't notice, he got out a notebook and said he had some questions. He started by asking what the square footage of the retail area was, then moved on to whether the cellar was used for storage and, if so, what condition it was in, then whether Mr Rai had ever considered adding Pay Point or the Lottery to the services he provided and, finally, what the competition in the area was. Although obviously somewhat put out – at least, obviously to Harry - Mr Rai answered each question in turn but concluded by observing stiffly that he thought that it was just the freehold that was being sold, that he still had fifteen years left on his lease, and that the rent was increased annually on the basis of changes to RPI rather than by some measure linked to turnover. Nodding eagerly, Arthur stressed that he fully agreed, adding that he was just trying to get a sense of the fundamentals. Harry felt confirmed in his opinion that Arthur was a bit of a twat, and he suspected that Mr Rai thought the same.

Colin was now explaining that the flat upstairs was vacant

but Mr Rai coughed, as if to clear his throat. He declared that he was aware of certain gentlemen going in and out of the flat on occasion. He didn't believe anyone actually lived there, but he was quite sure he had heard noise upstairs on a number of occasions. One or two would turn up every other day or so, typically mid to late afternoon. There were maybe three or four of them in all. Colin intervened to explain that it was a bog standard two bedroom property, pleasant enough really, although possibly due a lick of paint. Mr Rai described how, mid-afternoon the other day, one of these men had come into his shop and bought some cigarettes. Very charming and polite, not to mention well attired, he had apologised to Mr Rai for the van blocking his frontage and said it would be out of the way in no time; but it had still been there the next morning. Arthur sympathised and asked Colin if he had known any of this. Colin – uncomfortable, just as Mr Rai had been in front of Arthur's questioning – replied that he had gone upstairs when Mr Rai had first mentioned it but that there had been nothing evidently out of order, no sign at all that anyone else had been up there. It was all a bit of a mystery. Arthur suggested that Colin get the locks changed for a start and then start thinking about having the flat decorated with a view to letting it on a proper footing to reliable tenants. Colin assured him he was on to it.

'And, if there are any guys and there is any trouble,' Arthur ruled, 'we can get them evicted'.

Colin reiterated awkwardly that, notwithstanding his great respect for Mr Rai, there really wasn't any tangible evidence that there had been any people using the flat. It was possible that there had just been a misunderstanding, maybe they had been using another property in the vicinity. And, as for eviction proceedings, his experience was that those could turn nasty and that it was often quicker and cheaper to sort things out informally. In the absence of any reply from Arthur, Harry assured him on behalf of both of them, 'We hear what you say'.

On their way out of the shop, they were blocked in the aisle by an Asian guy coming in, wheeling a stack of the local paper on a trolley, poorly dressed with an ornamental mark on his forehead.

Next door, at number 43, was a fast food store. Southern Fries was a chain, so Colin said that the manager there would not be the right person for them to speak to. The coffee, however, he did recommend as not being too bad. Looking at the menu on the wall, Arthur asked Harry if he fancied anything. Harry replied, no, it looked gross. He wasn't going to be seen as some sort of fast food kid. Arthur went ahead and ordered a double-sized portion of chicken for himself, with brown sauce. Harry hadn't eaten since breakfast, it was now past one o'clock and he was hungry. The three of them sat there, Arthur eating his lunch in Harry's face and running over what Mr Rai had been telling them. Although Colin was keen to reassure him that there really wasn't any problem, Arthur was concerned in between mouthfuls that the situation might complicate the sale.

The flat above Southern Fries was lawfully occupied, let on a six month tenancy to two students who, Colin said, were pleasant enough fellows. The property was ideal for students who weren't that fussy. These lads had agreed with him that one or other of them would be in; but, when Colin pressed the buzzer, no-one answered. He searched for their mobile numbers, but the first call went straight through to voicemail. The second of the students did reply, Colin relayed the conversation over his shoulder. It seemed the dozy bugger thought the visit had been arranged for the next day. He wouldn't be able to be back at the flat until 6 pm at the earliest.

Colin shook his head and shrugged at Arthur. It was half past one and starting to feel chilly.

The tenant living at the top of the number 45 - the third and last building - was away, something that Colin had found out only that morning. It transpired that she had broken her wrist and gone to recuperate with her daughter in Essex. The daughter had taken the phone from her mother while Colin had been talking to her and said he would just have to wait until she was fully better and back at home.

Below this old lady's flat was a shop selling a wide range of phones. Three Asian guys in their mid-twenties were bouncing with energy behind the counter. When Colin asked if Mr Aziz was around, the guys laughed, saying 'Have you come to buy a phone, man? Take a look at our phones'. Mr Aziz, Harry deduced, was not available. The latest gear was on sale there, although actually the range was limited. A poster on the wall offered cheap deals on calls to Islamabad, Delhi, Mumbai, Chennai, Dubai. Arthur chatted to the guys about the package available for one phone and said he might buy it for his girlfriend for Christmas.

'We don't celebrate Christmas!' they chanted in chorus.

Outside, Harry and Arthur shook hands with Colin who said he was sure the visit had been well worth making, even though they had only met one tenant. Never mind, he said. Arthur requested he keep them updated with any news on the flat above Mr Rai's. Harry followed Arthur back into the market where Arthur stuffed his backpack with vegetables bought from the stalls, and some fish on top. Harry joined him, buying carrots and an inexplicably large number of onions, all of which he put in one of those thin blue plastic bags and lost on the Tube somewhere south of King's Cross.

Chapter 6

Santa Claus was coming to town; and, in the opposite direction, Steve, Marianne and Harry were on their way to spend Christmas in the country as guests of Sarah and Bob. It was Christmas Day morning; they had left Surbiton at half past eight, having promised to arrive before eleven. Harry was driving the family Audi. Marianne was in the passenger seat so that she could navigate - once they left the A40, he would need some guidance; but, for now, she was telling him how Adele was having to have Martin, her ex, round for lunch that day. It was for the sake of the boys. Steve was flat out in the back, IPod on and eyes shut. Looking at him in the rear view mirror, Harry judged that he was probably awake but incommunicado, building himself up for what was to come. Harry had been to this house just once before. Sarah and Bob lived in the Cotswolds, in a recently converted barn outside Burford. Burford would have been perfect without the tourists, what with the limestone buildings piling down the hill towards the river. Harry had listened to Marianne, sat in a teashop with a scone in her upturned hand, rhapsodising about life there. She would not accept that she was no way cut out for Barbours and muddy walks. Dismissing Bob and Sarah as phoneys pretending to be country gentry, Steve had stayed back in Surbiton that time but he had glanced at Marianne's photos. Sarah's house lay a mile or so away from the town, carved out of the surrounding farmland. The Barn, as she and Bob had decided to christen it, had twice as much floor space as back home, give or take. Five years older than Steve, Bob had been a fund manager in the City who had made his pile before the financial collapse and then chosen to retire to the country. This was the first Christmas they had invited family to the Barn. The time came to leave the main road, Marianne pulled out the map, and soon Harry was guiding the car down the flint drive towards the circle in front of the house.

Car doors slammed, Marianne led the way through the front door and into the hall. There was a vision of a Christmas tree. A hairy little dog scurried across the floor towards them, its feet invisible under its coat. Marianne leant forward, calming its yapping with her most poochy voice. There were cries of 'They're here! They're here!' and Sarah came to greet them, dressed up in a cook's apron, hands - mucky with food - held high in the air. The two sisters embraced amid mini-shrieks of excitement, Marianne the taller and bonier one. Sarah rubbed noses with Harry, he was her 'special nephew'. Nor did she forget Steve, she searched into his eyes intently and, brushing herself down and clutching his arms to his sides, earnestly wished him his own 'Very Merry Christmas, Steve'. Steve smiled back.

She beckoned them through to the kitchen. The baby was asleep upstairs but Emma had just gone to check on him. Marianne moaned that she still hadn't come to terms with being a great-aunt, but she brightened up to ask where everyone else was. Their hostess furrowed her brow. Ben, she thought, was upstairs with Emma but he had been watching television earlier, over in… she gestured into the distance… the Snug. The others had gone to church but would be back by eleven. In the meantime, Sarah was claiming chef's privileges and had dipped into some of the sherry they had bought in for the old folk. Marianne wanted to know how Gran and Grampa were coping. Gran, Sarah said, had been very helpful in directing Ben where to put the decorations while Grampa and Bob had been spending time discussing such seasonal topics as why Islam has no Pope. They both tended to find their way to bed by ten o'clock as a rule; but, as everyone would know, the radio would then be switched on sometime after 2 am so that they could listen to the World Service throughout the rest of the night. Each of them needed a hearing aid, so the radio was not kept at a discreet level and blared at anyone passing by, but Sarah said that the walls within the Barn would smother it. They were staying a full week.

The baby arrived wrapped in the arms of Emma, flush-faced and hair uncombed, with a guy smirking behind her who Harry presumed was Ben. Everybody gathered round to take a look, even Steve joined in at first. Marianne, scrutinising through her glasses, adopted her poochy voice again in addressing the child, who was lucky enough not to care. Six weeks old, he was gazing bluey-eyed into the empty distance while wearing a specially selected Christmas bonnet and socks. There was ritual discussion of who he looked like and Emma, speaking for the first time, said she thought he had Ben's nose. Ben wrinkled his own. Ben was unshaven, hair messed up.

While the rest remained thronged round Emma and the baby, Steve had slipped away to fetch the suitcases. Now he was standing in the kitchen doorway, hands stretched up to the lintel, waiting for an opportunity to ask what the sleeping arrangements were. Sarah took him by the elbow and pointed him up the open staircase to the far end of the landing where, she said, there was a twin room with life-affirming views towards Lechlade. Harry was to have the room opposite, his cousin's who was away for Christmas. He went to help Steve with the luggage.

Looking out of the window upstairs, Steve said Sarah was right, the view did give some reassurance that there was life

84

beyond the Barn. On the horizon was a line of leafless trees which, he told Harry, were beeches. Steve retained a fondness for the country from growing up in Sherwood Forest, although he used to say that, like Robin Hood, you never quite knew where the forest was or if it really existed. Looking down, he remarked how crass it was to carve a garden out of the countryside and then populate it with silly topiary. That hedge, he said, shaped as a giant cockerel would be one of Bob's 'jokes'.

'I bet there's an amplifier in there,' said Harry, 'that plays cock-a-doodle-do.'

There were more signs of Bob's wit on the wall. In a print, a tweed-capped gent waded knee deep in a river, trying to fish while widely smiling salmon weaved past him on either side. Next along, the same man was caught with a netted fish, startled in the light of a gamekeeper's lantern.

'He doesn't even look like a poacher.'

'I wonder what Mum would make of it. It's not exactly Hieronymus Bosch.'

Steve suggested they check out Harry's room. An off-white duvet covered the double bed while, over on the bedside table, there was a photo of Harry's cousin in his graduation robes.

'Jeez, Harry, how sad he wants to wake up looking at that.'

'That'll be me tomorrow.'

On the wall was another photo, this one from his time in Cambridge, rowing in stroke seat. All the crew members had signed it. Opposite the bed was a pencil drawing of him signed '*Amelia xxx*'.

'Do you think that's his girlfriend?'

'Doesn't exactly leap out at you, does it?' Steve was the art critic now.

Inside a wardrobe, they found a silk dressing gown that they tried on in turn. Harry told Steve it suited him.

'It's so pretentious. Anyway, you're just as good as he is. Don't ever think otherwise.'

'Cheers, Dad.'

Steve looked back at the drawing. 'And I've never heard anything about him having a girlfriend... Not that there's something wrong with not having one.'

Hearing the roll of a car below, they spied down. A crimson Jaguar pulled up. Out of the driver's side rose the mighty figure of Bob who charged round to open the passenger door with ceremony. The small person who got out unaided was Harry's grandmother. Grampa climbed out of the back. Steve and Harry stood back as boom and crackle rose up to the window. Shortly after, they heard Marianne calling up the stairs for them.

As they came down into the hall, they saw Bob in a chunky red sweater, laughing, champagne bottle in hand – 'Father Bloody Christmas,' muttered Steve – and two expectant pensioners in front of him with glasses tremulously held out, waiting to toast the day.

'Don't spoil it, Dad.'

'Of course, I won't.'

Bob roared that Steve and Harry had been holding things up, hiding away while the rest of them were ready to rock. Moving to the Cotswolds was something of a return home for Bob, he had been brought up a West Country lad and still retained that burr. The corks popped and Bob toasted Christmas, Sarah's and his guests, and especially the joyous new arrival, Baby. The dog raced round under them all. Sarah called Steve and Harry over so that she could take a picture of them in front of the log fire with Marianne, Emma, Ben and the Baby. Harry teased Steve that he was a great-uncle now.

Photo session over, Steve placed his glass high up on the mantelpiece and moved to the edge of the circle. He would no doubt have liked someone to come over and ask about his work but no-one, except Harry, seemed to notice. The fire faced two ways, heating both the hall and the next door living room, smoke rising up a common chimney. Grampa was chatting to Sarah about the church and how some Levellers had been shot there during Cromwell's time. Sarah was nodding attentively but there were evidently other things that needed seeing to. Marianne stole her away, telling their father that both his daughters were needed in the kitchen. Harry had nothing to add about churches, the only service he could remember ever attending was his other grandmother's funeral. Instead, he asked Grampa if he and Gran were going to ignore him now that he was no longer the youngest member of the family. Grampa tapped Gran on the elbow and told her that Harry thought they were neglecting him. Gran left Bob who turned to engage Steve and, clenching Harry's forearm, proclaimed through the champagne, 'You'll always be my baby boy'. Grampa contradicted her grandly, 'Nonsense! He's a young man now!' and followed up by asking – somewhat lasciviously – whether Harry had any lady friends on the go at the moment. Harry told him to ask Marianne, she always knew what he was up to better than he did.

He could see Steve wilting by the fireplace in front of Bob's unceasing glad tidings of retired life, the statement he'd planned on his future at GMR remaining unbroadcast. Bob's elbow leant on the mantelpiece, Steve stared up into his armpit. Pellets of sweat were starting to show on his polished scalp. Noticing that Gran was without a glass, Harry mischievously asked if that was her champagne up on the mantelpiece. Looking over uncertainly, she hazarded it might. Reaching out for it, he attracted Bob's attention. 'Ah, Harry!

Can I grab you?' And he did, he grabbed him round the neck and led him off, apologising to Steve for leaving him on his own. Looking back, Harry saw Steve seemingly in two minds as to whether he should be outraged at his son's kidnapping or thankful for his own release. The latter, it seemed. Gran went for the glass. Harry had counted fifteen paces before Bob opened a side door leading out onto the unsheltered winter landscape and pushed him outside, pointing to a truckload's worth of chopped wood piled high next to the garage. He was being given the great responsibility, so Bob instructed him, of keeping an eye on the log fire during his stay and ensuring it was kept fuelled. Since there wasn't much storage space by the fireplace itself, this would entail him making regular journeys ferrying logs over from the pile. Bob showed how it was done. The two of them crossed the yard and, Bob paying no attention to the grit and grime rubbing up against his own Aran sweater or Harry's black urban shirt, gathered as many logs as possible in their arms and conveyed them back into the hall, Harry trailing in Bob's steps.

· All was ready in the kitchen for the Christmas lunch, tucked up and warm in the oven; so now Sarah could ditch her apron and join everyone else for Presents. All were assembled by the Christmas tree. The fire - Harry observed – was crackling. Emma and Baby were composed in a chair that had been brought specially in. Gran and Grampa went first, with Grampa announcing that they had decided not to give each other presents that Christmas. They had everything they wanted in each other and that sufficed. Sarah said she felt like crying, she hoped Bob and she could say the same when they were Gran's and Grampa's age. Bob, standing cosily behind her, wrapped his arms round her shoulders. Gran and Grampa hadn't forgotten everyone else though; they had cash for Harry 'because we know young people can always do with a little bit extra'. Sarah had bought Bob a series of riding lessons, a present that he protested took him quite by surprise. 'The thing about women is you can never tell what they're thinking. Eh Steve?' 'Listen up, Harry.' He had commissioned a drawing of Sarah's favourite horse at the local stables which, now framed, he showed round as if he were an auctioneer's assistant. Gran and Grampa got books, a political biography for him, a history of Carthage for her. There were clothes for Marianne and Steve. More cash for Harry. Marianne had been to John Lewis for a selection of babywear for Baby. Sarah and Gran hushed over how cute he would look in them. Harry cradled him for a photo and Gran said it would be his turn soon. 'He's a young man now!' declared Grampa. Marianne was rooting round under the tree for her presents to give. Harry had made sure his were opened at home and stayed there; but she had one for Steve and it looked from its shape like a book. Harry reflected that Steve didn't normally read books, hadn't last year's gift been a microlight flight? She handed the wrapped up present to him. Steve weighed it in his hands, wondering with Harry what it might be. Harry said the idea was to open it and find out. It was indeed a book. Marianne had given Steve *The Story of Art* by L.H. Gombrich.

'Well,' said Marianne, with an edge of defensiveness, 'you said you wanted educating in art history. This is the definitive guide. It's very readable.'

'What is it?' Gran nosed her way in. 'Oh, Gombrich! That's very good, you'll like that, Steve. But haven't you already got a copy, Marianne? I thought everyone had Gombrich.'

'Well, Mum, this one is for Steve.'

Steve declared himself thrilled. Harry watched out for any eye contact between his parents. Gran asked Marianne what Steve had given her. He presented her with a bulky package, the size of a pillow, Marianne squeezed it, and said it was certainly soft. She unwrapped it and out dropped a white bath robe. Sarah checked the label and announced it was from the White Company. She stroked it, saying it was velour cotton, it was lovely and, look, it had a hood. Harry, reflecting that this probably signalled Steve's tacit acceptance of the wet room, joked that his mother was a hoody now. Marianne put a hand on Steve's shoulder and stole a light kiss. Bob wanted to see - 'Bob coming through! Bob coming through!' – and, observing the gown, said that he could imagine what had been going through Steve's mind when he had picked that up.

'Probably not, Bob.' Harry could feel Steve's urgency.

'Something for when you're both feeling frisky of an evening.'

'Not really.'

'Admit it, Steve, you were fantasising about what Marianne would look like, curled up in that robe.'

'Fuck off, Bob,' urged Steve, under his breath. Harry shook his head, this was hopeless.

'I know what you were thinking, you dirty dog.' Bob's West Country burr was coming to the fore. 'There's nothing Sarah and I like doing more last thing in the day, when we're washed and ready for bed, than snuggling up on the rug in front of the fire, a bit of smoochy music in the background. That's the idea, isn't it, Stevie boy? It's all part of a master plan to get her in the mood before you have your wicked way.'

Wait for it, thought Harry.

'Fuck off, Bob!' Steve burst out. 'Shut the fuck up! It's a bathrobe, OK? Anyway, I'm sure the last thing anyone wants to think about right now is you and Sarah rutting away on a rug like a couple of goats!'

Everybody stopped. Pictures of Sarah and Bob, naked and together, passed unwanted through Harry's mind.

*****

Sarah had asked Steve to help out with carving the turkey in the kitchen, which kept him occupied and out of the way. Meanwhile, Bob had appointed Harry as butler, his job being to ensure that no glass remained more than half-empty. Here in the dining room, Bob announced that, despite the name being misleading, Cheval Blanc was a red wine, a premier grand cru from one of the best years. He recommended everyone to stick with it; but, for those who wanted white, there was Macon Lugny. Harry apparently also needed reminding to keep an eye on the fire. Marianne wanted to help ferry plates from the kitchen but Sarah told her to sit down and relax. She deserved a break. Gran was attending to Ben, asking about his job, his background, getting some insight into the DNA of her first great-grandchild. Marianne patted the back of Harry's thighs as he poured her some Macon, acknowledgement of the good job he was doing and that she hadn't forgotten him. Bob and Grampa were weighing up the merits of that morning's sermon. After the rutting goats, Harry had retired to his bedroom, texting the outside world and wishing it a happy Christmas. Then, flipping on to his escort profile, someone had popped up to say he looked horny and offer him triple time for a shag that night in Berkhampstead. Lonely place, Berkhampstead. He had wished this guy too a happy Christmas. Now most people were sitting down. Gran broke off from talking to Ben. 'Where's Steve sitting? You haven't forgotten a place for Steve, have you, Sarah?' Grampa toasted the splendour of spending Christmas in the company of his two lovely daughters – not forgetting Gran's and his first great-grandchild! – and, on behalf of all their guests, told Sarah and Bob how much they appreciated their hospitality. 'Well done, everybody!' called out Bob in response. Perched next to Harry, Gran twittered on to him about how she had the appetite of a sparrow and asked if he could help by smuggling some sprouts from her plate onto his. He conspired with her. She announced to the table that they were going to be playing charades later on. It was a family tradition. Harry glanced towards Steve, wondering how he was taking the good news. With a slightly crazed smile. Gran asked if Harry had reconsidered his decision not to go to college; she herself was always exploring new avenues of study, Carthage and the Punic Wars being the latest. He replied that he would bear it in mind but his grades had been shit. Gran muttered over her turkey breast. He asked her to tell him about Carthage.

Later on, one further lap round the table with the wine, Harry sat down to hear Bob boasting about how his absent son, working in Shanghai for a German engineering combine, was taking great strides career-wise.

'Harry's got a new job,' volunteered Steve to an apparently baffled audience. Harry supposed that none of them had realised he had had a job in the first place, let alone a new one. 'Hasn't he, Marianne?'

'Ye-es,' agreed Marianne, cautiously. Like her, Harry would have preferred they'd stayed in Shanghai.

'Why don't you tell everyone about it, Harry?'

Harry drew a breath and started telling his family how he was renting out his body and that, if they knew anyone who might be interested, he was available 24/7. Photos available on request. Mates rates. No, of course, not. He told them how he was working in Fulham for a businessman with diverse interests ranging from real estate in the UK to investments in import-export businesses. He was being taught the ropes, how to cook the books, that sort of thing.

'Well it sounds as if it might be quite interesting for him,' observed Gran, 'but is it a real job?'

Grampa assured him they were both very proud of him,

no matter what he did. Harry said he wouldn't forget that. Gran, touched, now wanted to know from Steve what his family were doing that Christmas and whether his parents had any great-grandchildren yet. Steve, taking a straightforward approach, reminded his mother-in-law that his own mum was dead and elaborated on how, that day, his dad would have walked round to Steve's brother's for his Christmas lunch, his sister-in-law would have done the cooking, the grandkids would now be parked in front of the TV with their new games, the adults would be bickering with each other, and shortly his dad would be stomping back home. A typical British family Christmas, no charades. Ben obviously found it all very funny.

In due course, the meal wound up, the plates and glasses packed into the dishwasher, the silver plate cutlery was washed and dried by hand. It had been dark outside for some time. The Christmas cake was wheeled out and taken with tea into the other room served by Harry's fire, the White Room with its unblemished sofas, carpets and walls. No longer able to avoid Bob's blatant nods in the direction of the fire, Harry left the room and, pulling on a jacket hanging by the back door, went out into the December night, security lights switching on automatically to guide him to the woodpile, and picked up a batch of gritty logs that on his return he allowed to spill out of his arms and roll across the now infamous rug in front of the fireplace, helped onto the adjoining carpet by an accidental tap of his heel. After a clean-up that regrettably left the rug still a little off-white, the time came to play charades. Baby was asleep upstairs, looked over by Emma, and at some stage Ben had managed to slip away from the party, meaning that there were seven of them left available to play, a number deemed just about quorate by Gran until Steve declared that he was going to bow out.

'Oh, but Steve,' Gran was as upset as a disappointed

child, 'you can't. That will spoil it for everyone else. There won't be enough people.'

'Of course there will,' Steve was doing reasonable, showing how he had thought about everyone else before making his decision. 'Usually, you don't get to play with more than five.'

'But having more makes it so much better!'

'Well, perhaps Ben would like to play. You could ask him.'

Ben, it appeared, had a free pass that Christmas.

'Oh, give it a rest, Mum,' Marianne interrupted her mother. 'This is supposed to be a game, it makes a nonsense of it if people are made to play. If Steve doesn't want to join in, that's fine.' Harry spotted Steve avoid her sharp glance at him.

Marianne's judgment was accepted in silence by her mother, mouth downturned in grimace; and Steve walked off without a further word, presumably in search of the television that could be heard in the distance and the isolation that watching it could bring.

For Harry, playing charades was like being back in the theatre he had never enjoyed; except, of course, that this time there was the risk of taking the leading role as well. His strategy would be to play to his uncultured, uneducated stereotype and let the grown-ups battle it out for the prizes. Sarah and Marianne would be best, they had both done Am Dram well into their thirties. As it happened, he didn't have to pretend to be uncultured and uneducated; his knowledge of Gilbert and Sullivan did have gaps, and he hadn't ever heard of *Samson Agonistes*. Even Bob did better. Only when Marianne primed Grampa to act out *Hollyoaks* did he get one right. Grampa made him do *It's a Wonderful Life*, which no-one got until he mouthed the answer. Then he gave Gran *Harry Potter and the Half Blood Prince* which, except for the first word, was beyond the team's reach until Sarah finally twigged.

It was late on in the evening in the White Room. Gran and Grampa had gone upstairs together, sleep beckoning them. There was no sound of Emma and the baby nor sight of Steve or Ben, and Bob was lying on the floor snoring with his pewter tankard beside him. Harry had his IPod on, and Sarah and Marianne were wrapped up on a sofa, talking. Actually, his IPod was turned off, but he had no qualms about that – he knew what they would be talking about.

'Why, Maz, do you put up with it? He's so fucked up. I dunno, maybe he did have some god awful childhood, but that's no excuse.'

Marianne was defensive. 'He had a very happy childhood… except his father never talked to him. His mother was lovely, it's such a shame. This fire's really gorgeous, you know, it's so atmospheric…'

'Don't be evasive. He's incapable of behaving properly in a social situation. He couldn't even be arsed to play charades, although he will have known Mum wanted it so much.'

'Well, that's hardly a crime. Mind you, he did promise to behave this Christmas.'

'Not much sign of that. He's emotionally retarded. And he is so screwed up about sex. When was the last time the two of you even had a hug?'

'He has never been very touchy-feely.'

'And what was that about me and Bob? Making out that we're at it like animals?'

'It's just his sense of humour.'

'It's just his sense of inadequacy, more like.'

'Well, you may have a point there.'

'He has always had an inferiority complex, Maz. That may have been what drove him to succeed at first, but now it's all gone bitter and twisted.'

'He's got a lot of complexes all of a sudden. Inferiority complex, emotionally retarded. You've missed out anally retentive – now that he really is.'

'You're being evasive again.'

'He has a lot on his plate at the moment. There are big changes going on at work and they're bound to have an impact.'

'He should be thinking of you.'

'He does. He works really hard so we can have the quality of life we do.'

'You don't have any quality of life.'

'Oh, rubbish, Sarah. We may not have the Barn, and we haven't earned enough to retire on, but we're doing all right. Anyway, Bob has his faults too.'

'He has loads of faults, but he's a good husband and father.'

'Steve's a good father.'

'Now who's talking rubbish? Just look at the boy.'

'Harry's OK. Maybe it's me. Maybe I'm simply a bad wife and a rubbish mother."

'You're a brilliant wife and mum, Maz, but now it's time to put yourself first. You should leave him. There's nothing to keep you there.'

'Oh no, I couldn't do that. Apart from anything else, I wouldn't want to give him the satisfaction. He'd say he'd won.'

'I knew you'd say that. There's something wrong in your head too. Well, I know we've talked about it before, but what about the alternative – an affair? It's not the same as a loving relationship within marriage, but you're entitled to some sort of emotional outlet. Some TLC.'

'I've thought about it, of course, but I don't think it would solve anything. Even if I did find someone who was interested. Actually, it would more likely remind me just what I've been missing.'

'You're soft. And I don't mean that in a nice way. He's emotionally abusive and you just soak it up.'

'Oh, get real. Get things in proportion.'

'Do you think he's had any affairs?'

'No. He's not capable.'

'You mean he's gay?'

'I have sometimes wondered; but no.'

'Tarts?'

'No way.'

Sarah patted her sister's thigh. 'Men, eh?'

'Yes, men. We'd be better off without them, wouldn't we?'

'Maybe you should think about going with a woman.'

'Euwww.'

The conversation moved off in another direction. Harry unplugged his IPod and stood up, stretching his arms and yawning, and said he was off to bed.

'Night, sweetheart.'

'Night, night, babe.'

*****

Upstairs in the bedroom, Harry logged on, curious to see if Mr Berkhampstead was still in need of festive cheer; but, before he could check, a message popped up on his screen. "hey dude!" It was Jake, his one Friend. Harry wished him a happy Christmas and asked what he was doing online just then. Jake typed back, what was HE doing, did people really think about escorts on xmas day lol? Harry told him about Mr Berkhampstead but explained that he was online now just for some distraction, he wasn't looking for punters. When Jake asked if he was having a shit Christmas, Harry wrote back, no, just boring, had Jake ever played charades? Jake was having a shit Christmas ☹. His dad had come round for the day so that they could all pretend they were a real family, and he had been such a twat. He'd started giving Jake and his bro orders even though it was their house and not his. Their Mum had smoothed things over but he had made Jake propr look like a well child. Harry laughed, Jake was a child, he wasn't even allowed on this site, it was for 18+ only. After some deliberation, Jake wrote back that everyone had something to hide. What did that mean??? Jake asked what Old Street was like. Well good. Jake wanted to see harry's flat on old street. Why? cos i want u to fuck me:) No you don't, you're not even gay; and, anyway, Harry's age range was strictly 18-99. Jake wrote back that he was 16, that meant legal, he wasn't jail bait – and, anyway, if Harry fucked him, he might find out if he was gay :P Harry replied that, for all he knew, Jake was a 90 year old perv masquerading as a 16 year old boy – after all, he had never posted a facepic. Jake's riposte was that he could post a pic of a 16 year old and still be a 90 y.o. perv. Touché. Jake said he had the cash now, so Harry couldn't say no. No. Jake asked, well, could he see a cockpic of Harry then? Harry laughed out loud again. They stayed chatting online until past 2 am, which was round about the time when Gran and Grampa would be switching on their radio and starting to listen to the World Service.

Chapter 7

It was late afternoon as Frank looked in the mirror, the toilet flushed and the cistern refilled behind him. Not for the first time, he assured himself that he had no desire to sleep with Harry, no interest in doing so whatsoever. Harry was a pleasant enough lad, it was just that he didn't have the attributes required of an escort. There was too little artifice, there would be no way of pretending he was anyone but Harry. Frank thought back to his online profile, that opening photo. The camera was uniformly kind to people of Harry's age and he did smile engagingly out at the viewer; but his skin was slightly pocked, although Frank supposed that would become less noticeable as he grew to shave more. He should be using skin lotion. His hair was quite fetching, the way he let it sweep over his forehead and hide his ears and collar; he had to brush it with his hand to stop it getting into his eyes. Frank reflected for a moment on his own full head of hair, scarcely grey and evidence of his continuing virility. Where physique was concerned, however, Frank preferred someone better built than Harry. His torso needed expanding – as it was, his head and neck looked outsized. Generally, he was too skinny even if he did have a perfectly flat abdomen; and one could tell from the seat of his trousers that he had a nicely filled out backside.

Clothes were another department in which Harry quite failed. He looked too much the teenager in his scuffed jeans and his untidily hanging out shirts; and, while he was right that there might be a certain *frisson* for some customers in choosing a nineteen year old escort, the packaging was all. He needed to show some urbanity, a well-judged taste in Ralph Lauren shirts, suitably pleated trousers from The Collezione, a linen jacket on hand when called for. The alternative would be something more rent boyish - a tracksuit look – but, while that might be to the taste of some, it was not something Harry could ever carry off, even if he did come from Old Street. He needed to reflect back to the customer the latter's good taste in choosing him. The teenager could wait till later.

Of course, urbanity required some cultural awareness and sophistication and, on those scores too, Harry was misselling himself. Frank had felt him drifting away in the restaurant at the mention of theatre. He had taken too literally Frank's instructions on how an escort should behave, he had contributed nothing to the conversation at the table. He had spent too much time gawping at Dahlia's gigolo. Then look at the way he had flapped in front of the fellow's questioning, leaving it to Frank to rescue him. None of these flaws Harry would be able to remedy by himself. However, since by way of fate he had come across his path, Frank was prepared to lend him some guidance. This would be in no way for his own benefit. Regardless of Harry's innuendos to the contrary, he held no torch for him as could be evidenced no better than by his own lack of reaction when first faced with the boy naked. No, his efforts with Harry would be for the boy's benefit albeit at his own cost, made in part payment of his own debt to pleasure.

The best means by which Frank could keep track of Harry, inform his behaviour and monitor his progress was, of course, by employing him to help out here and there. In fact, there was a genuine need to take someone on since his last assistant had left him for a job with a competitor (a mistake on both their parts). Frank's work was a mixed bag of speculative ventures. He would invest in one enterprise or another on the calculation that one out of ten would make money. He would typically sell at a premium in the start-up phase to someone more interested in taking on long term development risk. While most of his investments did fail, that was a risk that an entrepreneur built into his model. The aim was to find the occasional oyster with a pearl; and, although the pearls had been modest in size, they kept him comfortable enough and they gave him a certain reputation he enjoyed. In fact, work was central to Frank's life, he was root and branch an entrepreneur and never regarded himself as having a day off. He did sometimes suspect though that he engaged in life with a touch less zest than of old; and, while Harry might have little or nothing to offer by way of experience, his presence did give him a boost. Harry disrupted things, stirring them up when others wanted them kept as they were, a useful talent in business. Besides, he did amuse him, the way he looked at the world askance with youthful cynicism, taking little at face value. The two of them laughed at the same things. And, if the majority of Frank's work was too technical for him, there was always the property portfolio which could bear some light supervision; in which context, it was quite opportune that his appearance had coincided with the matter in Regent's Row, since it meant that he could leave Harry to deal with this Arthur.

One of the first tasks Harry undertook, on his own initiative albeit at Frank's cost, was a review of the IT, meaning first of all the computer through which they had first met. Frank found himself uncomfortable at Harry's dexterity in finding his way through the details of his personal and business lives. He kept a concerned eye over his shoulder, watching out for what might pop up on screen. Apart from him, old Anthony the accountant was the only person who usually had access to his records and Anthony was unshakeably discreet. So, when the time came for his mid-morning stroll to Fabrizio's, Frank was adamant that the boy should stop working and accompany him. Harry laughed, assuring him that he wasn't interested in any of Frank's secrets, commercial or otherwise. To prove his point, he showed how to encrypt documents and password-protect them although, cheekily, he gave no guarantee that he didn't know how to hack through any security Frank might set up. At Fabrizio's, he wasn't tempted by any of the coffee on offer – not espresso, cappuccino, not even latte – saying he only drank instant. He did however show an interest in the *panettone*. Fabrizio broke off a corner for Harry to taste; and Harry, with the proprietor looking keenly on, gave it a considered seven out of ten. The upshot was that Harry replaced the existing IT with a system that had many more functions than its predecessor but could still be used, as he demonstrated, to access Frank's favourite escort's online profile. More pertinent, Frank was pleased that Harry had struck quite a good deal financially. His administrative talents did not stop there. He upgraded Frank's phone. Next, he announced that the 'office' was to become 'paperless', meaning there was to be no printing and that all paper that had not been printed should be recycled. Frank conducted most of his business from elsewhere, and then mainly out of a notebook; so he agreed, paperless was the order of the day. Next on the list, Harry wanted an adjustable chair for use at the desk, he said the existing one would be bad for his posture.

There was, regrettably, a flipside to Harry's enthusiasm that Frank in no way appreciated, and that was his unreliability. There were times when, in need of his services, Frank phoned him, only to be brushed off with a reply that he wasn't available then, that day, or indeed the next, a response absent of any sense of regret or apology. The first time that happened, Frank rang back to leave an irritable message that he trusted Harry the escort did not treat his other customers quite so casually. Harry texted in return – he didn't bother to speak to him in person - that, unlike Frank, punters were paying top dollar and deserved premium treatment; but, if Frank wanted to pay him escort rates, then he'd get the same quality service. As a businessman, Frank was supposed to understand this. On another occasion, he challenged him that he didn't believe Harry was spending two to three days in a row fully booked up as an escort; but Harry, rather flippantly, told him to keep his mind on his own work. Frank was not used to people talking back to him. Once or twice, Harry would even let him down when there was a firm appointment in the diary, sometimes giving just a few minutes' warning; and, when that happened, Frank would declare that he had had enough of his irresponsible attitude, that he would find someone more competent and deserving in whom to invest his efforts, and that Harry was no longer welcome in Fulham. Harry would turn up the next day, searching round for things to do.

*****

For Harry, working with Frank took him far away from the college life that everyone else seemed to want him to lead. When Frank mentioned one day that he had business interests in Kingston - next door to Surbiton - he amused himself by dissing the place and saying he could never see himself living somewhere like that. When Frank suggested he accompany him to a meeting there, he thought of the kick he could get out of being Young Lad on Old Street so close to home. When Frank told him he wanted driving there in his Mercedes A300 saloon, he reached for his shades. Frank sat in the back, looking grandly out of the window like he was some town mayor. Driving through Kingston, Harry realised he should have been asking for directions rather than heading for the industrial estate on autopilot; so he took one wrong turn, then another, until Frank started slapping the back of the driving seat with his rolled up FT. Now directed by Frank, he took the slip road. Businesses advertised their presence on the estate drably. Spraytechnic Garage Services. Next Level Up loft conversions. There were signs of units for sale. Frank told him to steer left past Store Ur Own; and then there it was, Dordogne Delights, identified by a small green sign. A single storey breeze block building, painted white. Harry stood there looking at it, ignoring Frank who remained in the rear of the car, waiting for the door to be opened. After a while, Frank pulled himself out and, looking testily around, led the way in.

There was little natural light in the corridor inside. Partitioned off to the right was a makeshift reception area with a hatch through which Frank poked his head like a chicken. He announced that they were there to see Dominique. A young black woman - African, Harry guessed - had been preoccupied with some figures on screen but now rose from her chair and, inclining her head to one side in greeting, quietly said that she would go and find her.

Dominique allowed Frank to shadow kiss her on each cheek. They chatted to one another in French, Harry pretending to listen in and understand. Her hair was pulled back, showing off her neckline above a simple black top. In silhouette, she looked like a gymnast. He heard his name and Dominique shook him by the hand, starting to talk to him rapidly. Frank broke in to explain that Harry's French was not quite fluent and that it would be easier to converse in English. She told him Frank had been explaining how he was his new protégé and a fine entrepreneur in the making.

She led them through a large store room that comprised

104

most of the building's floor space, crates piled up at the far end. Harry felt the cold, the narrow rectangular windows high up let in hardly any light. Through the door at the end was an office, brightened by its own wide window. Dominique sat on her desk, casually showing off her ankles. Her English was fluent, her native accent folded into it.

Frank had already explained that Dordogne Delights was a mail order business. Dominique had moved to the UK from south-west France when she married her husband, an English cookery writer. Bored in her day job and searching for something more challenging, she hit on the idea of using sources back home to import French food to Kingston, which she could then sell online. Encouraged by her husband, she judged that the Brits were a little more daring with food than she had first found as a student. All this potentially helped her husband's work too, since each parcel they sent out included a flysheet advertising his work to their food-savvy customers. Now she brought the website up on screen. It marketed fine French food, promoting rillettes, cassoulet and confits among other Dordogne delights. Harry looked at the pictures, trying to decipher the contents of each jar. Goose and duck cropped up a lot, goose and duck and foie gras. Steve and Marianne had had an argument about foie gras once, even though they were both on the same side. Anyway, Dominique was recapping, the aim was to get people to buy hampers, although items were also available individually subject to a minimum postage charge. The business had grown well in its first three or four years and made a fairly good return, building up a regular client base that had expanded through word of mouth and social networking. The recession had hit them hard though, and that was what prompted her update now. Where Frank came into the picture was that he had an equity stake in the business. When Dominique had drawn up her initial business plan, banks had blown hot and cold about funding it and she hadn't been too keen on them either, which had been a good call given how they were behaving to small businesses now. She had been more attracted to finding an equity investor, one who – she had never made any bones about this – would take a back seat and leave her to get on with things so long as she delivered a good return on their investment. Someone back in France had known someone who knew Frank, and the rest – as she told Harry - was history; except that the difficulty now was that the business wasn't delivering a good return. Even with the rally over Christmas, orders had dropped eight per cent in value year on year, which certainly wiped out any margin. Rolling the English round in her mouth, she said it was a no-brainer that Dordogne Delights was one of those first things people forgot about as they tightened their belts. On top of that, increases in the wholesale cost of grain meant that suppliers were starting to squeal and wanting to pass on their extra costs to her. Plus – there was more – the rising price of oil meant that transportation costs had ramped up. Quite bluntly, she needed Frank's views on what they should do about it.

Frank mused that they could always put the business in cold storage and open up again when the worst was over; but Dominique dismissed that, saying it didn't address the problem of how to cover their fixed costs, the rent on the building in particular. Frank should know that. Also, it would be difficult to retain the remaining customer base, even though that had been pretty resilient to date. She surmised that those left were probably all bankers, no-one else had any money. And suppliers could be fickle too. No, she had a proposal, it was a case of diversify or die. She had contacts in Limoges who could supply her with porcelain figurines and she thought that could be a nice fit with what Dordogne Delights already supplied.

But, Dominique, Limoges isn't in Dordogne.'

'Don't be pedantic, Frank. Nor is champagne, but we still sell that. The way I see it, it's shit or bust. I wholly see the rationale for closing, but this may be a way round our problems. It would mean both of us putting our hands in our pockets but the outlay's not that great. It's your call, Frank.'

They debated the proposal for the next ten fifteen minutes, drinking coffee brought in by the woman at reception. Harry thought they were both quite relaxed given that they stood to lose their investment, her livelihood in Dominique's case. He didn't imagine a cookery writer's earnings put much on the table. Not unless they were Nigella. Frank drew him into the discussion, explaining the money side by way of a graph he sketched on the back of an invoice. His principal concerns were, one, whether anyone was interested in china nowadays and, two, the quality of the porcelain – he didn't want seconds. Dominique couldn't give him an assurance on either. The deal struck was that she would procure a consignment of porcelain at her own cost and risk which Frank would then use to test the market.

On the way back to Fulham, Frank opined that Dominique had guts and wasn't foolhardy, but that he didn't think her plan was going to have any legs.

*****

Now that he was kept busy trying to fit in his two careers – professional escort and trainee entrepreneur – with his residual lifestyle as lazy twenty-something, Harry reflected on how his own career path compared with his parents'.

Steve's was a no-no. He might have been frustrated at Harry's lack of conventional success and he had once joked that his son hadn't won any prizes since he was five years old at a fair, but there needed to be boundaries to how far career success should be pursued. Granted, Steve made more money than most of his friends' parents, but that money came at a price and not one Harry would pay. Frank didn't work 24/7, and Harry could get what he wanted from working as an escort with a lot less effort than Steve made tarting himself round his own clients. Still, Harry did respect Steve's ambitions at Grant Matcham. That took some balls.

Tarting aside, Harry's work seemed more aligned with Marianne's. Most of her women friends worked part-time for a number of reasons, ranging from childcare and housekeeping to (in Marianne's case) having a life. Of a kind. Adele and Marianne had become friends in a job share, the aim where Adele was concerned being to see more of her boys. In what she did inside and outside of her job, Marianne set great store by social benefit. A career in other people's healthcare was obviously very worthy. In her view, Harry's working in a charity shop was to his credit, but she was less sure about his bar work and didn't seem comfortable with his entrepreneurialism - she didn't understand that, unlike healthcare or law, that was something that could be genuinely productive socially. As to his other work, had she known he was a tart, she would have had trouble arguing that he was providing no social benefit. Come to think of it, where was the social benefit in studying art history? That was more like self-indulgence or masturbation, the ultimate in self-indulgence. In any event, healthcare wasn't all upside. Marianne was currently in the business of imposing work-life balances like her own onto other people. She was in charge of a 'change process' at her health authority, which was code for reducing the number of jobs. This did not have to mean an equal cut in the number of people employed, although some losses were inevitable; but it did mean some people being forced to take a drop in pay and share their jobs with others – as Marianne and Adele had done, only not out of choice. Marianne, whose role over the previous years had been to grow the hospitals and find the right places to allocate new resources, was now – as she wryly put it - Marianne the Enforcer, like some ascendant revolutionary during the French Terror. So, all in all, Harry decided, he won out on who provided more social benefit.

It was early Sunday evening and he was lazing about downstairs – in residual lifestyle mode but off to see a client soon. Stretched out over the corner unit, he didn't feel like getting up. Duck egg blue was what Marianne had said the walls were painted when she'd had the room redecorated the previous year. It was a dreamy colour that washed well with the off-white linen of the furniture. In the middle of the coffee table was a North African ceramic bowl – shallow but wide – that Marianne had picked up at the weekend. Its inside was decorated with an intricate apricot-coloured pattern. Marianne and Steve divided the house between them. She spent money on internal furnishings while he was responsible for bricks and mortar, meaning mostly the mortgage. That was part of the reason the wet room had turned into an incident; it was bricks and mortar, not furnishings. His parents were locked together in that house. Soon after he started escorting, Harry realised he could make enough cash to rent a place of his own and he thought he would manage pretty well by himself; but somehow he could never be arsed. Besides, the rent Steve was charging was well below market. Harry preferred to save his earnings, spread across a number of accounts. And, now that his son was starting out on his own career, Steve seemed keen to share how things were going with his. Steve was more and more adamant that his was the right path for GMR but, acknowledging that Andy had a head start, had adopted a controversial strategy. Unbeknownst to his colleagues, he had already approached a US law firm about a possible merger. The Americans had a small forward base office in London, and Steve had received a courteous welcome there, a keen interest in the figures he had produced, and an offer to visit the States to talk with senior management. He had flown in from New York that afternoon.

When he had arrived back from Heathrow, two of Harry's mates had been round. Steve had shared with them how exasperating the whole process of getting through US security had been. The mates hadn't been convinced, they said he was lucky he hadn't been flying cattle class. When Steve started to debate the point, the mates looked at their watches and realised they should be off. Everyone knew Steve was trying to be friendly, but he could lack sophistication when dealing with people. After they left, he gave Harry some feedback on how well the meetings Stateside had gone, how the personal chemistry was starting to produce a reaction. Now he was coming downstairs, freshened up in his beige chinos and nicely tucked in Polo shirt.

'You feel at all jet-lagged?'

'Just a bit. An overnight flight would have been cleverer. Next time.' He nodded towards Marianne's ceramic bowl. 'What's that?'

'It's a bowl. Mum bought it yesterday.'

'I bet she paid too much for it.'

'Dunno. You'll have to ask her.'

'What's it for?'

'Dunno. You'll have to ask her. It's just a bowl. Oh yeah, I meant to tell you. I've decided to become a lawyer.'

'What?'

'Frank thinks it would be a good idea if he turns up at this meeting with a lawyer; but, instead of paying for one, we've decided I'll act as his brief.'

'What will you say? You don't know the first thing about the law.'

'What? After twenty years of living with you? No, I'll just

110

be there to take notes. Like one of your trainees.'

'It's a criminal offence, you know, falsely holding yourself out to be a solicitor.'

Harry laughed. 'I'll let you know when I get caught.'

Steve tutted, nothing more. Through the double-glazing, Marianne's car could be heard revving up the drive. She came into the room, still holding her keys, and said she couldn't stay as she was running late for her Pilates class. She had just stopped off to pick up her kit.

'So,' she asked Steve in an awkward jaunty manner, 'when did you get back?'

'An hour or so ago.'

'The flight was OK?'

'Apart from some difficulty getting through security at JFK.'

'I've heard it's a nightmare... I hope the weather there's better than it has been here. It's been crap.' Steve didn't reply; by saying nothing, he was trying to make her stop being evasive. Marianne cracked. 'Go on then, how did it go with the big boys? Did the Americans get their cheque books out?'

'I told you, it's a merger. They're not going to buy us out.'

'Sorry, it was just the mental picture that popped up. So you think they're going to be interested?'

'I know they're going to be interested. They wouldn't have invited me to New York otherwise.'

'That's great! So, when are you going to break the news back home?'

'I'm going to save it to the end.'

'Oh. Is that a good idea?'

'If I tell people now, Andy might find a way to take the credit.'

'OK. Did Harry tell you about our trip to the theatre last night?'

'No, but he showed me the bowl you bought.'

'Pretty, isn't it? And yes, I probably did pay too much.' Steve made no further comment, he didn't need to. 'Talking of money, my car's phut. I'm going to need a new one.'

'That isn't a problem, is it?'

'I suppose not. It's just it doesn't feel like a good time, what with the cuts and everything.'

'Well, you need your own car.'

'Yes, it wouldn't send the right signal, driving up to the hospital in the Maserati, would it? You know what I heard last week? We're having to shut down an outreach unit that provides support to disadvantaged teenagers. It will mean more teenage pregnancies which will be left to the midwifery unit to deal with even though the midwifery unit is itself taking a cut.'

'I suppose there are other ways to avoid getting pregnant.'

Comments like that never went down well with Marianne. 'These youngsters have very little to look forward to, you know? No jobs, a life on shrinking benefits.'

'OK. Fair enough.' Steve wasn't planning on starting an argument this time. 'Hey, did you hear Harry has decided to become a lawyer?'

'What?' Her irritation switched direction.

'It seems he's masquerading as a lawyer for this guy Frank.'

'Really?' That was a cheap trick, Steve getting back on side with Marianne at his expense. She talked at Harry while finding a place in her bag for her keys. 'I wish you were doing something more socially useful… Mind you, who am I to talk? I'm actively promoting childhood pregnancies.' She left the room to get her gym kit.

'So, was this play last night any good?' Having dropped him in it with Marianne, Steve was now trying to buddy up.

'I just don't get it. Why do people go through the pain of

performing live on stage when they could be on TV instead?'

Marianne returned with her kit. 'Has Harry been telling you about the play? He helped out with the boys. They were kicking off before the start and grumbling about how the seats were uncomfortable; but Harry said it would be good for their souls and that, if they didn't take opportunities like this now, they'd end up like him. They both laughed at first but it did the trick. Adele gave you a big kiss at the end, didn't she?'

'You see, Mum, I can be socially useful.'

Steve said he had to prepare for tomorrow. Marianne's Pilates class was about to start. Harry asked if she could give him a lift to the station.

*****

After his and Arthur's first trip to Regent's Row, Harry had gone straight round to Fabrizio's to brief Frank on how it had gone. He was becoming a regular there. He walked smartly in, nodded to Fab, climbed up on to the stool next to Frank's, landing heavily, and gave his report. They had found their way to the market. There were plenty of cool dudes around there. Harry had looked like he fitted in, but Arthur was another story. Arthur lived in Brockley – Frank, mouth frothy with cappuccino, hadn't heard of it either – and he had a girlfriend called... Harry couldn't remember her name, but it didn't really matter. He had a girlfriend. Frank didn't seem that interested. Before training to be an osteopath – something he was doing against his father's wishes – he had been an academic, although Harry hadn't had the chance to find out what his specialist subject was. Economics probably, that would fit with his advising Lady Dahlia. Frank didn't seem to care about that either. Arthur had spent most of his time in the market checking out the fish stall. His foot swinging, Harry rapped Frank's shin under the table, causing him to spill his coffee and splutter, but he paid no attention and just carried on. They had linked up with Colin as planned except that Colin had thought he was Arthur, something Harry still didn't appreciate. They had talked to some of the tenants – at last, he saw Frank perk up. Mr Rai had been full of respect for Frank, but had definitely thought Arthur was a bit of a twat. Frank nodded, dabbing the table with a tissue to clean up the splatterings of coffee. Harry had been thinking about the students on his way back. Colin had treated it as a mix-up that neither of them was there, but he himself suspected that was what Colin had been expecting. What did Frank think? Frank shrugged. The lady above the Mobiles shop was also away, she had broken her wrist apparently and Harry did believe that. As for the guys selling the mobiles, they had seemed cool and quite fit as it happened.

'Well,' concluded Frank, downing his coffee and wiping his moustache, 'a successful visit by all accounts. And some interesting information on Arthur - who will no doubt be reporting back to his co-conspirators.'

'C'mon, Frank, you don't really believe all that crap about Arthur being a master criminal, do you?'

'Things are rarely what they seem, Harry,' Frank's tone was ominous, 'rarely what they seem.'

'Yeah right. Anyway,' he watched Frank closely for his response, 'did it all go as you planned?'

'Planned? What do you mean, planned?'

'There wasn't anything else you were expecting to hear?'

'Such as?'

'Such as… something that might turn out to be a problem for Arthur and Lady Dahlia if they still want to sell?'

'What sort of problem?'

'You mean you don't know?'

'Know what? For God's sake, Harry, get on with it!'

'Keep your hair on. I was just checking. Mr Rai thinks

there is a problem, but Colin says everything is OK.'

'What are you talking about?'

'Mr Rai says there are people living in the flat above him, even though it's supposed to be empty.'

'And what about Colin?'

'He says he has checked it out. He says there's no-one there. Do you think he's on the fiddle – you know, letting it and pocketing the rent? I think he may be.'

'I am sure Colin would never dream of doing such a thing. Not to me.'

'Well, Mr Rai's convinced there are squatters. He says he heard some banging about. And he has met one of them! He sounded kinda worried.'

'And who are these squatters supposed to be?'

'I dunno. There are three or four of them apparently. And a 4x4. So what are you going to do about it?'

Frank looked into the bottom of his cup, searching for any remaining coffee. 'I will think about it. Thank you, Harry.'

'It really weirded Arthur out. He told Colin to sort it.'

Frank sighed. 'Then I suppose I will have to phone Colin. He is such a nuisance, this Arthur, always in the way. You're supposed to be keeping him in check, you know.'

'You're too hard on him,' Harry laughed. 'Arthur's not so bad.'

'You don't mean that. What was that you called him?'

'A twat. But only a bit of one. Underneath, he's not so bad.' Harry laughed again.

*****

Frank put off calling Colin Broadbent. He decided that Harry had been overexcited by the supposed mystery and that there was really nothing to it. And, in any event, Colin would sort it out, he was a reliable fellow. And so, as the days passed and the New Year arrived, he let it slip his mind until one evening he found himself having dinner with Amita.

Some might say that theirs was a remote relationship, first in that she spent much of the year in Malaysia, and second in that her residence when in London was in Kensington rather than Fulham. But it was not remote emotionally, it was bound together by years of familiarity and kept fresh by romance. He would never know when she might fly in to London, as she had done that early January evening, ringing on arrival and demanding he take her out to dinner at such and such; and, while he did not share her taste in a cuisine that was designed for habitual international travellers so that they could eat from the same menu the world over regardless of what city they might find themselves in, he would indulge her over the dining table as she talked in wonderment of the pashminas she had brought over this time from KL for her girlfriends – not including the one she was now wearing, which she had saved for herself – and of how Europe had nothing to compare, while he observed the detail of her make-up and the ochre glow of her skin seemingly unblemished by her years and impossible to capture in the portrait he kept of her in the apartment. He could not deny that he had always felt privileged in her attention to him. Hers was an affluent background. Albeit they had had to leave their home in Punjab on Partition, her family had had the presence of mind to plan ahead and leave little behind. He, in contrast, had turned up in London as Frankie in his early twenties – much the same age as Harry now – looking for cash, finding work at first through contacts in the Maltese community. Keen to get as far away from the breadline as possible, he had had few youthful scruples about where money came from. He had been employed principally for his wits but had never felt queasy if someone needed stamping on. All that, of course, was long past but it was difficult to disassociate himself from it entirely. Nowadays, Amita and he indulged each other. She knew of his occasional resorts to young male company – in fact, she did not discourage it, she took the view that, if it kept him distracted in her absence, then that was fine. 'Boys will be boys' was her view. But Frank was always conscious that Amita's leniency was predicated on one thing, and that was that she didn't have to have anything to do with the earlier Frank, with Frankie. So, suddenly remembering as he sat opposite her that his phone conversation with Colin was long overdue, he started to feel ill at ease.

*****

The second time they went up to Regent's Row, it was without Colin. Frank, who had planned to come, had cancelled on them earlier that morning. When Harry told him so over the phone, Arthur was disconcerted, wondering whether old Mrs Tate would let them through the door without him. Harry said not to worry, he would schmooze their way in. After Mrs Tate, they might try and look in on the students; but Harry said they should steer clear of the flat above the newsagent's for now. That had been Frank's direction. After a pause, Arthur suggested that they could at least drop by and say hello to Mr Rai. Harry said he was sure Mr Rai would like that.

It was some time since their earlier visit. Harry had insisted Arthur travel by bike but, on the way up, he realised he'd missed out on the chance of a chat, them sitting side by side. Now, first to arrive at Southern Fries and clutching a weak cup of coffee, he watched out of the window as Arthur disassembled his bike and chained it to the lamp post outside. When he came in, wiping his hands down the front of his trousers, Harry asked if there was anything he could get him from the menu. Arthur, looking at the board, recalled how excellent the chicken and chips had been. Harry had meant a coffee but he paid up all the same. It was ten forty-five in the morning. Harry observed him, fair-haired and slightly tanned, earnest-looking and expectant, not seeming at all knackered by the ride up from Brockley but refuelling on chicken and chips at his expense. He decided he would ask.

'Arthur?'

'Yes, Harry?'

'What colour would you say your eyes are?'

'Green. Why do you ask? There's nothing wrong with them, is there?' He rubbed them as if to check.

'No, nothing at all. It's just that they're an unusual shade.'

'Oh! They're jade, apparently.'

Jade. Harry liked jade.

They chatted, Arthur's hands getting stickier with the chicken, until Harry caught sight of the clock on the wall. It was five to eleven, almost time for their appointment with Mrs Tate. Arthur got up to wash his hands.

'Arthur?'

'Yes, Harry?'

'What do you want to get out of this visit?'

'Another good question. A clearer picture, I suppose. I mean… the old lady. We'd get more if we could sell the place without her, so it would be useful to know if she was about to pop her clogs.'

'That's a bit harsh, isn't it?'

'Only kidding. To return the question, Harry, what are you hoping to get out of it?'

'Oh, I just want to keep an eye on you.'

Arthur rang the bell and, speaking loudly into the intercom, enunciating every syllable, announced that it was Arthur and Harry from the landlords. A pause followed, as if there was a different time zone up there, and then the voice at the other end crackled that they were early and wanted to know where Mr Adami was. Harry nudged Arthur aside and, pressing his lips up to the speaker like an old style crooner, promised that Mr Adami was right behind them. The door buzzed open.

The old lady who opened the door at the top of the stairs was stooped, her wrist still bound in gauze. Short and round, she wore elasticated trousers and a blue top. She looked past them, insisting she'd heard them say Mr Adami was right behind. Harry assured her that he was, he was five minutes down the road and had just texted to say they shouldn't wait for him. Unimpressed, Mrs Tate let them in before carefully closing the door and making her way to a brown-upholstered chair by a half-glowing gas fire. The chair had a slight rocking motion. She gestured to them to sit in a smaller two-seater sofa with antimacassars over its back, just like the ones at Steve's parents'.

Arthur opened, asking after Mrs Tate's health and hoping she was firmly back on the road to recovery. Defiant, Mrs Tate replied that she was fit and well, she was not about to fall off her perch. It was as if she had been listening in on them five minutes before. Arthur nodded sincerely, reiterating how glad they both were. Mrs Tate silently reserved judgment, then asked what they wanted. Arthur explained that, sadly, Mr Mounis had died and so Mrs Mounis needed to sell her interest in the flat. Looking round, Harry could see that the room was dusty, there was fluff piled up where the carpet met the skirting board; Steve would have had a sneezing fit in there. Mrs Tate said she had no intention of moving. Arthur carried on nodding. Mrs Tate asked again where Mr Adami was and what he thought of all this. Harry piped up that he'd just received another text, saying he was on his way. He held up his phone. She looked at him nastily, observing that she knew how texts worked and hadn't seen him receive any. Arthur sought to assure her that there was no suggestion she be made homeless, to which Mrs Tate retorted that she wasn't senile, she knew her rights. Harry wondered if offering to make her a cup of tea would help but, instead, found himself saying in a sympathetic tone that she couldn't find the stairs easy in her condition. Mrs Tate decreed that this was her home and that she wasn't going to be conned out of it by a couple of young spivs. Arthur said that there was no intention to con her, they just wanted to take a look round. Mrs Tate's voice got louder. If the landlords wanted a valuation, she said, they would have sent a valuer round. She didn't believe Arthur had any connection with Mr Adami, and she wasn't going to be intimidated by anyone. Arthur insisted there was no need to be alarmed, there just appeared to have been a bit of a misunderstanding. Mrs Tate disagreed. Arthur conceded it was probably best if Harry and he left for now. First, he asked if he could pop and use her bathroom and, without waiting, dashed up the stairs to the rear. The toilet flushed and, when he returned, Mrs Tate rose, said something about him getting lost, and told him to take his boyfriend with him.

Some ten minutes later, Mrs Tate would receive a phone call from a very apologetic Mr Adami, saying that he wouldn't be able to make the appointment scheduled for 11:30 am and hoping he hadn't put her to any trouble. He was shocked to hear that Mrs Mounis' representatives had been discourteous in arriving early without apology and then continued to behave so disgracefully.

*****

They had arranged to meet at the Anchor Bankside, a pub on the South Bank. Initially, George had wanted to convene at St Pancras Station, to experience the grand Champagne Bar he had been reading about. His line was that, if he had to come to London, which was something he would only do reluctantly these days, then he should at least be able to combine it with visiting one of these new sights in the capital that everyone was talking about. The Champagne Bar, though, was out of the question as far as Frank was concerned: it would be teeming with people, meaning there would be no place for a discreet conversation. How about the Shard then? They decided on the Anchor Bankside, an old haunt of theirs in Southwark, for a quiet drink. Except that it was no longer their old haunt. At some stage over the past fifteen years, it had changed from a sedate eighteenth century tavern into a brawl of unwashed human beings spitting and shouting into the face of whoever was opposite. So Frank had chosen to wait outside on the river front in the winter chill, but now George was late. Frank texted him and then rang his mobile but there was no reply. He was getting impatient, there were things that needed seeing to, he was due to meet Amita later and there was always Harry to check up on. Frank rubbed his hands together. Then George did appear in the lamplight, strolling down the front one slow pace at a time in that familiar chestnut brown overcoat, fists in pockets, grey hair elegantly cropped, eyes kind but weary. In that familiar voice, gentle but infuriatingly slow, he apologised for being on the late side.

'I've just been to Tate Modern.'

'We can't stay here.' Frank was feeling the cold.

'No, I can see that. Let's try round Borough Market. The beer at the Market Porter was always kept well.'

They walked eastwards towards London Bridge, picking their way over the humped cobbles.

'I've never been there before,' remarked George.

'Where?'

'Tate Modern. There's no "the" apparently.'

'Really.'

'Do you remember when the power station was still operating?'

'No.' Frank counted the seconds between George's paces.

'Me neither… It's a bit characterless.'

'What is?'

'Tate Modern. Apparently, galleries should be characterless. Did you know that? They distract from what's on show otherwise.'

'Is that so?'

'I saw a Lichtenstein that I recognised.'

'Good for you.' Frank tried to emphasise his lack of interest.

'It was called "Whaam"… With two "a"s… Not like the band.'

'I've no idea what that means, but I'm glad it has been such a culturally stimulating visit, George.'

George ambled on. He clearly intended to make Frank sweat for getting him up to London. 'There's a bar there, Frankie, from where you can view the Thames… More than one bar, actually. Lots of them, to go by the signs.'

'A bar overlooking the Thames? Astonishing.'

'St Paul's is slap bang in front of you, the other side of the river…It takes up a lot of space, you get an appreciation of it that you can't when you're close up or even from a far distance – Richmond, say - when you can see just the dome… It sits there like a colossus.'

'It's a bloody cathedral.'

'That's right. What's that old building near to it with a green copper-ish roof? Looks like something Florentine?'

'I've no idea.'

'And then there's that school - the City of London Boys'?'

'What are you on about?'

'How's that lady friend of yours? The Indian one?'

'Amita. Very well, thank you. Now, let's get a move on and find somewhere to sit. I'm freezing, I've had to wait ages for you.'

'I'm enjoying the stroll.' He wouldn't be rushed. 'And there's been some work on Blackfriars Bridge as well. They've extended the Station on to it! Someone in the bar told me that.'

'Fascinating.'

'Isn't it? It has echoes of the old London Bridge, before it was burnt down. I'm told there were plenty of businesses sited on the bridge in those days.'

'George, I don't recall.'

They were approaching the Golden Hind now, lying in dock.

'The river's at high tide. It looks very scary from up there in Tate Modern. You can get a proper sense of the river's power... Ominous... It made all those people crossing the Millennium Bridge look like twigs wanting to be swept away... Imagine if the Thames Barrier collapsed... Or if the jihadists blew it up.'

'Imagine.'

'Yes. What do you think of it anyway?'

'What do I think of what?'

Pause. 'The Millennium Bridge.'

'I don't think I've ever thought anything of it.'

'I wouldn't want to walk across it. At least, not now. Not having looked down on it from up there.'

They were walking past Southwark Cathedral.

'Lots of young people there in Tate Modern. Surprised me somewhat.'

'Young people are often surprising. It's something that has its ups and downs.'

'Maybe they just go there for the view. I'm surprised the Germans missed it.'

'Missed what?'

'St Paul's.'

'I wish they bloody hadn't.'

Borough Market was closed now but the Market Porter was open, open but chock-full. They continued down Borough High Street and found a quiet pub where George approved the bitter. He started to compare it with the beer at his local, in a Kent village.

'George!'

'OK. What is it you want to talk about?'

*****

Colin had sounded unnerved and rather anxious when Frank and he had finally come to speak, the more so as Frank grilled him. There were indeed men who had been using the flat, though he didn't know what for. He hadn't wanted to involve Mr Adami since he was paid to ensure things like this didn't happen. He was truly sorry, he had hoped to resolve the matter without anyone else's involvement. The first time Mr Rai raised it, Colin tried to get into the flat but was met with a shiny new lock on the door. He sat that afternoon out in Southern Fries, just on the off chance, and a white van pulled up late in the day. Two men got out, the driver a medium build guy with receding ginger hair. Colin found it difficult to estimate the age of balding people but, under pressure from Frank, hazarded a guess at mid to late thirties. While the other man – who was black - started offloading some boxes from the back of the van, Ginger went to open the front door to the flat. At that point, Colin made his way outside and challenged him, asking him what he was doing. Ginger looked back at him and - apparently puzzled – replied, what did Colin think, he was going into his flat, wasn't he? He jerked his head backwards towards the door behind him. Colin eyeballed him, saying that he didn't think so, that flat was unoccupied, and he should know, he was the managing agent. The other man just continued carrying boxes up the stairs, not paying him any attention. Ginger then had the cheek to say that Colin needed to stay more on top of his job since, as he could see, the flat was occupied now. More to the point, the man volunteered that the owner had been kind enough to lend it to him for free. He ignored Colin's challenge to name the owner but, in any event, Colin knew that that this was not the kind of fellow with whom Mr Adami would ever associate. Colin sat around thinking about it for another day or so and then took up position in Southern Fries again – it wasn't good for his waistline - until he saw Ginger tip up a further time and enter the flat. Colin rang the doorbell and, on Ginger's answering, told him he didn't want any trouble, he would pay him a couple of hundred quid in cash if he cleared off there and then – him and his mates. He showed him the cash in his pocket. Ginger, courteous to the last, said he greatly appreciated the offer but they rather liked the flat. They were, he repeated, there at the invitation of the owner. Ask him. Door shut. Colin had been unsure what to do next. He realised now that he should have called Mr Adami by then at the latest. Frank had told him he was disappointed, he had always felt confident before this in relying on Colin. Colin, he mused, might be a big man physically but he was not cut out to deal with a situation like this.

*****

'What do you think, George? What's your take?'

George raised his eyebrows, shrugged his shoulders. 'I don't know. There's not exactly much to go on.'

'"Guests of the owner?" "Ginger?"… You couldn't put some feelers out, George, could you, take some soundings? You're the best person to ask. You can see where I'm going.'

'I could give it a go.'

It was more than ten days later before the phone rang by way of reply.

'I was very taken with Tate Modern.'

'Yes, George, I'm sure it's a wonderful building.'

'Well, it wasn't the building so much, more the location…'

'Yes, yes, OK, OK. Do you have any news for me?'

'I do, as it happens… It's about your friend Nick.'

'What about him? He's dead.'

'Yes, that's part of the problem, it seems.'

'And what's the other part?'

'Ginger. You were spot on. It is the young laddo. Very impressive.'

'Bugger. I had hoped I was wrong.'

'Yes, I can see that. It appears your Nick still owes his dad some money.'

'What's that got to do with me? Why doesn't he go after the wife?'

'The old man's not called the Squire for nothing, Frankie. He's a gent. He wouldn't do that, except as a last resort. No, he seems he thinks that, you and Nick being such good mates, you might want to help out.'

'Mates! Hardly! And certainly not now he's dead. Help out how?'

'Well, by giving his lads some rent-free accommodation for starters. Seems that's why he sent laddo down there. Apparently it's convenient for transit. But the money's what he's really after.'

'That useless idiot, Nick!'

'Easy, Frankie.'

'How's it going to end?'

'Well, maybe he's just trying it on. Seeing if you'll 'fess up.

He's a fair man generally – if he decides you weren't involved, he might leave you alone.'

'Yes, but what should I do now?'

'Propitiate him, Frankie, that's the first step. Send him a present. That used to do the trick. Something he'll know you value highly.'

'I'll give it some thought.'

'Word is you've got a new boy working for you? Any good?'

'He has his points.'

They talked on.

*****

Harry and Arthur stood outside Mrs Tate's front door, laughing together over what had just happened. Harry claimed that Arthur had blown it from the start, zero-ing in on her health.

'It was so obvious you wanted her out of the way. You sounded like an undertaker sizing her up.'

'I was just being my usual courteous self.'

'You need to be more savvy, Arthur. Being nice and polite isn't always enough.'

'You make me sound like a right geek!' protested Arthur. 'Look!' He flexed his biceps for Harry's benefit. 'I bet you wish you had a body like mine.'

'You bet I do.' Harry ran the flat of his hand down Arthur's torso. 'Maybe if I worked on it,' he teased.

'Dream on.' Arthur punched him gently in the stomach. 'You're far too scrawny.'

'We all have our dreams,' said Harry, smiling. 'You may be a geek, but even geeks have their fans.'

'Well, old Mrs Tate's not one of them. Come to think of it, she might be the wolf out of *Little Red Riding Hood*, that one, dressed up as a little old lady. She could have gobbled you up.'

'I'm too scrawny, remember. She would be more interested in you. You're the one with all the muscle.'

Arthur laughed. 'And you're the savvy one, I suppose?'

'More than you. So what was all that about you needing to use the toilet? You'd only just been. It was weird.'

'It does rather suggest prostrate problems, doesn't it? No, I thought that, if we were going to get booted out, I might as well grab the opportunity to take a look upstairs. The bathroom was a ploy.'

'Cunning. And was there anything worth seeing?'

'It all looked in good nick.'

'I thought maybe your hands were still sticky.'

Arthur said next stop was the students', even if the trip was unannounced. Harry said they'd still be in bed, and so was all for knocking them up. He rang the bell.

'Hallo?'

'Hi there! We're from the landlords.' He thought he might as well brazen it out; and it worked, the door buzzed open.

At the top of the stairs, a long-haired guy wearing an Abercrombie & Fitch top stood inside the entrance to the flat. Mid-twenties. He greeted them with a puzzled look. 'Dude,' he called over his shoulder, 'are we expecting anybody from the landlord?'

Harry knew he could handle this better than Arthur. 'Didn't Colin call you? He said he'd sorted it, let you know we'd be round this morning.'

Whereas the Abercrombie guy looked quite friendly, his mate did not. Tall, gym fit, shaved head, trying hard to look gay. Probably not the real thing. He put his arm across the doorway blocking their way in. 'No, he never said anything about anybody coming round.'

'Well,' said Harry, continuing in his business-like manner, 'we're sorry if there's been a mix-up but, if we could just come in and take a look round...' He peered under the guy's arm and could see that the flat was actually quite tidy. There were some pot plants and even a pile of ironed clothes. Maybe they really were gay.

'Well,' the guy echoed, 'we're sorry if there's been a mix-up too.' The students looked at each other.

'The thing is, mate,' explained the Abercrombie guy, 'you don't really look the part. And this is our home, see, we're not going to allow just anyone off the street to come and take a look round'.

Harry said that he and Arthur had come a long way and had a busy schedule. The tall guy told him to fuck off back to school, lunch break would soon be over.

Back in Southern Fries, Arthur said it was quite funny, how the students had claimed Harry was still at school. Harry wasn't laughing. At all. Realising this too late, Arthur changed the subject and complained about the perennial problems he was having with his desktop back home. It was practically antique. A dialog box kept popping up alerting him to some problem he didn't understand, and the only way he could get rid of it was by re-booting. He bet Harry would know what was wrong. Harry didn't feel like being helpful, he told Arthur to contact his supplier.

Facing the window, Arthur became distracted by something out in the street. A white van had pulled up outside Mr Rai's. They could see a man swing round from the far side, keys in hand, cocky. Arthur was on his feet. By the time the man had reached for the lock, Arthur was tapping him on the shoulder. The man turned round on his heel and listened attentively. Then, when Arthur had finished, he gestured to the building behind him. Arthur shook his head and waved his finger at the man who, smiling politely, went inside and shut the door behind him.

Chapter 8

Harry and Frank were feeling mischievous. When Arthur turned up at Frank's at 7 pm as arranged, Harry opened the door in business mode, shirt sleeves rolled up, acting preoccupied and not in any mood to be distracted. He didn't look one bit like someone who might still be at school. Waving Arthur in without a look, he pointed to where the bike should be left so that it didn't get in the way. Inside the main room, he briefed him on how Frank and he were on an important conference call, negotiating the final points on a major acquisition. Things, he said, were very much in the balance and could go either way. He left no doubt that Arthur's arrival was a distraction. As instructed by Frank, he talked loudly in terms of net present values, tax gross ups, reps and warranties, and conditions precedent. Arthur frowned, nodding attentively and asked if there was anything he could do. Harry shook his head dismissively; Arthur would obviously be out of his depth. He said that Frank and he needed to be in the next room wrapping things up, it shouldn't take more than ten / fifteen minutes. Arthur was to wait where he was, Harry pointed him towards the kitchen where he could fix himself anything he wanted – there was beer, gin, whisky. Whatever.

On the other side of the door, in the office, Frank was squeezed into Harry's new chair, gasping, eyes screwed shut as he tried to stop himself bursting out laughing. When Harry slipped through the door, Frank nodded blindly to show he knew he was there, still struggling to keep his mouth shut.

Saliva was bubbling on the edges of his lips. Harry knelt down beside him and, whispering, asked if he had heard everything. Frank nodded. Had he been too loud? Frank shook his head. Had he been convincing? Frank nodded faster. He caught his breath.

'It went just as we expected! He's such a gullible idiot!' he spat, spraying Harry with pent up saliva and ending up in a fit of coughing. 'Despite thinking he's so clever.' He patted Harry on the back.

Harry agreed. 'Yeah. We totally had him.' He didn't see how himself, but he could see Frank was loving it.

They stayed there, looking at the door expectantly, Frank's chair jiggling under his weight. Harry wondered what was supposed to happen next,

'Go and see what he's doing,' commanded Frank, hushing Harry with his finger at the same time.

'How? I'm supposed to be on a con call.'

'Through the keyhole,' Frank waved, exasperated by the stupid question, 'through the keyhole'. Harry made a note to remember when Frank could be watching him from there – that was something he would milk. He crept forward and reported back on what he could see.

'He's sitting on the couch. Reading some papers, I think. Wait! He's taking a swig out of a glass. It could be water. No, I think it's gin and tonic! What an arsehole!' The door was just behind Arthur's left shoulder, so Harry's view of him was limited. He still had those uncool sideboards, they were trim but tapered out too widely at the bottom. Maybe they weren't uncool, maybe they just weren't Arthur. Uncool equals Arthur. Arthur's fair hair stopped an inch off his collar, revealing his muscular neck and the masculine curve of his shoulders through his striped Polo shirt. Harry stayed at the keyhole, watching him.

'Is he looking this way?' demanded Frank.

'No.'

'Make him!'

'How?' It was Harry's turn to be exasperated.

Frank cleared his throat and called out loftily, seeking to cast his voice into the next room. 'We hear what you say, gentlemen, but the fundamentals don't support that price. We stand by our final offer!' He dropped his voice. 'Did that get any reaction?'

Harry was on his knees, head down at keyhole level. 'I think he may have raised his head.'

After a moment, Frank carried on. 'What do you mean, you'd be taking a haircut? You can take a bath for all we care!' He paused again. 'Any luck this time?'

'He has got up. He's facing the bookcase!'

'Let me see! Let me see!' Frank shuffled up to the keyhole, also on all fours, his hand resting on the flat of Harry's back to steady himself and then sliding slowly down to feel its way over the spread of his buttocks and in between them where it stayed. Neither of them moved.

After a while, Harry told Frank that there was no point them both trying to look through the keyhole at the same time. Frank patted him on the bottom and shuffled back onto the chair.

'Time's running out, gentlemen,' he decreed.

Harry thought he should add something. 'We're going to wash our hair!' he shouted.

Frank looked at him, perplexed as ever. 'Eh? "Wash our hair"?'

'That's what you say, isn't it? You wash your hair?'

'People in business, Harry, never wash their hair.'

Harry looked back through the keyhole. Arthur had picked out a book and was browsing through it. It was now more than ten minutes since he had left him there.

'Give him a couple more,' murmured Frank.

Harry propped himself up against the wall, legs outstretched while Frank was hunched in the chair, his back to the desk. They didn't talk, they were cooling down after the excitement. There was a quiet knock on the door and the handle started turning. Harry leapt up to stop him coming in, Frank whirled awkwardly round in the chair to face the desk and picked up the phone. Harry's head met Arthur's coming round the door. It was Arthur's turn to whisper now.

'Hey, I just thought I'd pop my head round and see what was happening. Everything seems to have gone quiet.'

'We're pretty much finished. Done all we wanted. Out in a mo.'

Harry shut the door on him.

'That was fun,' said Frank.

'Yes, but we didn't really get one over him, did we, Frank? I mean, wasn't that the idea?'

'The point is, Harry, we enjoyed ourselves.' He patted his bottom one more time.

*****

Harry, Frank noted, had been wrong. Arthur had not helped himself to a gin and tonic. He would hardly have minded if he had, but he did begrudge his presence otherwise. It was now more than a fortnight since the meeting with George, and things were moving slowly. There was that gift to the Squire to see to, something Frank must value highly. In the meantime, Arthur was a distraction, even if he had been so easy to play thus far. His clumsy approach had antagonised Mrs Tate, losing him that dear lady's co-operation. The students had booted him out of their flat and wouldn't be allowing him back in. Frank wasn't actually much vexed at his

134

bumping into the laddo; it was just a little irksome - as was Arthur - but there might be some small value in hearing his version in addition to Harry's. He did, though, resent Arthur's ringing him up and saying that he wanted to 'talk business'. On top of which, wasn't it supposed to be part of Harry's job to keep him away? Harry was far too soft when it came to dealing with Arthur, far too indulgent.

'Arthur, my dear fellow, a delight to see you again! We should be meeting at Portofino, not here! Sampling the Genoese cuisine!'

'Frankie, or should that be Frank? Portofino sounds great. I'd be happy to join you there for a glass of that fine red wine – with *fritto misto*, of course. But how are things going? It sounded kind of racy in there.'

'Oh, it was nothing, nothing. Just a song and a dance.' Frank was bored with that game now and irritated at Arthur's tactlessness in alluding back to his own supposed *faux pas*. 'Harry, dear boy, drinks all round!'

While Harry was acting as cocktail waiter, Arthur pointed to Frank's library. Frank heard him complimenting his taste and range of interests. Frank's eyes glazed over, his mind closed down. Amita was the only person who ever looked at the books. His interest in culture was purely as a means to attaining financial ends, not as something in its own right.

And I see you're a fan of Gombrich too,' he picked out *The Story of Art*. 'A fine art historian.'

'Oh yes, a very fine one.'

'My mum's got that!' Harry was coming through from the kitchen carrying a tray of drinks.

'What's that, Harry?' Arthur showed a keen interest.

'Yeah, she studies art history.'

'Your mother is a remarkable woman, Harry.'

'Really?' Harry stopped.

'Leaving school without any qualifications to go and work on the family market stall selling jewellery, and then educating herself to degree level and becoming a teacher in an inner city school. There are not many people who can say that.'

Frank had never much bothered to discuss Harry's parentage with him, but he suspected this biography owed as much to the boy's imagination as it did to Arthur's lack of the same.

'And, in addition to making jewellery and being a maths teacher, she finds time to study art history?'

Harry nodded dumbly.

Frank thought he should step in. 'She is a veritable polymath,' he applauded. 'One of the finest women I have ever had cause to meet. And a devoted mother. She has invested so much of herself in her offspring.' Offspring? That could be singular or plural, couldn't it, leaving room for any brothers and sisters Frank didn't know of?

'She certainly sounds it. And, no offence, Harry, but isn't she at all regretful that you haven't followed her into further education?'

Harry mumbled something about grades.

'She recognises… as indeed does Harry's father…,' Frank remembered there was a father, '…that Harry's individual talents would not best benefit from a formal education. He needs to be out here employing his native wit and honing his business skills.'

Standing beside him, Harry's speechlessness was testimony to this primitive nature. Arthur was frowning, as if trying to make sense of it all. Had Frank missed anything? 'And as for her jewellery,' Frank threw in, 'it should be sold on Bond Street! Who would buy from anyone else? But, enough, young Harry here has been embarrassed enough, it is time to talk business. I take it you've come round to tell me Dahlia is now

136

in a position to sell?'

'We're getting there, Frank, and I couldn't have done it without Harry. But we've got a problem, which is why I've come round'

'Problems, Arthur, can be good news. They represent opportunities. All you have to do is solve them.'

'And that's what I'm going to do. As Harry will have told you, there are squatters in number 41.'

'Squatters? In number 41?

'Yes. I've met one of them, and he wasn't your stereotype anarchist squatter.'

'Thank heavens not!'

'He's not the sort of guy you'd want to mess with, Frank. He had the cheek to say he was there with the owners' consent. So the question is, what do we do next? Well, I've been looking into that and the answer is, we move fast. I've instructed solicitors this morning, they'll serve notice on the squatters tomorrow, and we will be able to get an eviction order within four weeks. That's what I came round to say.'

Instructed solicitors. Notice tomorrow. Squatters. Frank regarded Arthur standing there in front of him, British to the core in his faith in the institutions of the State, in fairness, justice and the rule of law. Presumably, he still believed in the police as keepers of the peace, on the side of the public. Arthur and his ilk had no understanding of this country, which they still thought of as belonging to them. They were the customers in Stefano's restaurant, with their big swanky kitchens but no kitchen knives. Arthur believed that he could turn up at number 41 with a couple of bailiffs – officers of the court – and watch laddo and his mates slope off, assuring him that they had tidied up the place before leaving. It wouldn't occur to him that those same bailiffs would spend their spare time working for laddo and his father, terrorising people out of their properties and into the night. He had no idea of the world he really lived in.

'Arthur, my dear chap. There will be no instructing solicitors, no serving of any notices.'

'Why not? They're all lined up and ready to go.'

'Because I am the owner of the property.'

Well, so is Dahlia.'

'Arthur, my dear man, go fuck Dahlia. I presume that's what she's hoping. I can't see why else she'd employ such an amateur to assist with her affairs.'

After five or six minutes, the time came for Arthur to leave.

*****

Harry saw Arthur out. He watched him mess with his bike in the hallway. It had been agreed that Frank would look further into the matter of the purported squatters, Arthur would leave it in his hands for now. He had been shaken by Frank's insults, but he hadn't totalled. He had accepted that he might not know all the facts and that being an osteopath didn't of itself qualify him to deal with these matters; but he had wholly rejected Frank's suggestions about Dahlia – which he knew had not been meant. He remained her representative and, as such, had a responsibility for her interests. Harry was starting to feel bad. So, as Arthur was carrying his bike backwards down the stairs, Harry asked if he was still having trouble with his desktop and offered to maybe come down to Brockley and take a look. Some time. Possibly.

Back inside, Frank asked if his mother really had started life as a market trader. Harry replied that there was some truth in what he had told Arthur, his mother did study art history and she probably would make a really good teacher. Arthur and he had had a pint up at the market. Harry wasn't used to alcohol, it made him say all sorts of things. As regards a father,

Harry did have one of those too – he was a solicitor, a bit of a twat but not in the same way as Arthur. Frank said they should toast lawyers as upholders of liberty and the rule of law. He told Harry not to socialise with Arthur.

'Why not?'

'Because I say not, Harry.'

'Don't tell me you're jealous, Frank.' Harry laughed.

Frank looked at him coldly.

*****

A few minutes later, Harry was lying back in his chair, chatting loudly to Frank in the kitchen, when Amita appeared. He hadn't known she had a key. In fact, he had thought he was the only one with a key apart from Frank. She messed with his hair as she passed by, saying hello Harry. He hadn't really got to know Amita and he felt a bit like a house pet being patted by a stranger - rather like Sarah's dog being pampered by Marianne - but he didn't mind her being there. She walked towards the kitchen where Frank was shaking ice into the glasses.

'Ohhhh, is that for me, darling? You're sooo considerate, and psychic too! But it's freeezing out there.' She shivered. 'Why do you put up with the weather in this country? It never knows what to do. Rain or shine. Rain or snow. Snow or shine.' She swung her head from side to side like a pendulum. 'It's not fair, how can one know what to wear?' She pulled a face.

She undid the belt wrapped tightly round her winter coat. Her waste was very slim for someone of her age (whatever that was). The coat was left folded over the back of one of the dining chairs. 'This gorgeous boy was leaving the building as I came in. He had a bicycle, very athletic. And he opened the gate for me. They're sooo polite, British men. And this one was hunky, very masculine, sooo sexy, I just wanted to squeeze his bottom. But he is too young for me,' she sighed. 'I'm just a wizened old witch nowadays.'

Frank didn't admit to knowing Arthur, and Harry wasn't going to say anything. Arthur seemed to appeal to the older woman, first Dahlia and now Amita. Who knew how old Jane was? Amita wasn't wizened though, and Frank was assuring her of that. The two of them were sitting side by side on the couch, rattling their glasses, lights dimmed down. He supposed that gin and tonic had been meant for him but he didn't mind, he was due out with a client later. She and Frank made quite a nice couple as they sat there, companions for each other as they grew old. It wasn't as if they had nothing in common. She clearly had an eye for the younger man and, as for Frank, well, so did he. They would probably be quite lonely otherwise. Frank didn't seem to have any real friends, just business contacts. Harry didn't know what brought Amita to London. Frank was asking her where they should eat that evening, and Harry watched as she leant over him to stroke his moustache, saying that food could wait till later. It was a bit of a tease and, Harry thought, a little inappropriate. Slowly, disturbingly, he came as he sat there to realise that she was starting to kiss him, open-mouthed, and that Frank was doing nothing to stop her. She was acting uninhibited, she didn't seem to care that anyone else was there. Then, turning round, her hands pressing on Frank's chest, she called out in a tone as low as the lights, 'Run along, Harry'.

*****

Still with time on his hands, Harry stopped off at a gay bar in Soho and ordered a Coke. It was cold outside, he had almost slipped on the black ice forming where the rain had fallen. Turning round, he leant back, elbows resting on the bar, pretending to be a cowboy in a Western saloon, holster hanging from his belt and crotch on display. It didn't cheer him up. Looking round, he couldn't see anyone else his age there. The place had a Sunday evening feeling to it. He picked up a magazine. Back at Frank's, he had collected his jacket, checked in the pocket for his IPod, and said bye. With a little wave. He was still a bit taken aback. He had thought that it was he and Frank who were in a relationship. OK, there wasn't any sex but that wasn't because Frank didn't want it – look at the way he'd been stroking his butt just before – it was because he wouldn't let him have it. He knew that Frank liked younger guys but he had thought his interest in him was something more special. In fact, he had been convinced right from that night at Portofino that he was more than an escort to Frank. But, now Amita had come along, where was he supposed to fit in? He was used to couples having rows in front of him, not sex.

He became aware of a guy standing alongside him, recommending the film whose review he was pretending to read and telling him how he looked just like one of the stars. He thanked the guy for the compliment and left the bar. Later, looking round his client's bedroom while his nipples were being sucked, he thought maybe he should go to the gym and start bulking up. He told the client he was really good and suggested he move further down. The client liked the idea and, as he did, Harry pondered on what had happened with Amita and Frank. After a bit, the time came for him to lie on his back, legs bent. The client told him he was really tight. Harry said it was a perfect fit. Frank and Amita. He gasped, as if involuntarily. Arthur and Jane. He gasped. The client pulled out, rolled him on to his side, and started again. On leaving, he texted Sophs to ask if he could stop over at hers that night. 'Of course. XXXX'. Sophs knew he was gay but not that he was an escort.

*****

Sophs had a flatshare in Bermondsey. Harry had met the flatmates but they weren't his type of people. Of course not, mocked Sophs, they're students. Anyway, they were out. She asked how life with Frank was going. He looked round the room and remarked that this was the life he was missing, was it, floor cushions, listening to Amy and watching Sophs smoke weed? She asked if Frank still fancied him. Harry acted surprised and said, of course, he was perfect rent boy material, wasn't he? But then he added, no, Frank had a lady friend. This was news to Sophs who was convinced Harry had said he was gay. Well, he replied, maybe he was bisexual – wasn't everyone a bit? Not Sophs. As far as she was concerned, the nearest she had come to a lesbian experience was a miserable and mistaken crush in Year 10. Harry wanted to know how her studies were going – and what about Sam? She was very firm; studies were fine and Sam was yesterday's news. That was OK by Harry. He asked if her flatmates would mind that the place smelt of weed; and she said, no, she had bought it off one of them. He wanted her to know that he hadn't talked to Sam, that he wouldn't, and that she had his support one hundred per cent. That prompted her to kiss the top of his head and say, bless, he was lovely but she didn't want to come between him and his best mate. Harry replied he felt like they'd stopped being best mates years ago. Sophs said she'd thought as much but hadn't wanted to say anything. Then she got up to stretch her legs. Her skirt was so short, it hardly covered her stockings. She asked what Frank's girlfriend was like. He answered that he thought she was the sort of person who was used to getting her own way. Sophs told him it was time he stopped looking so scruffy, he could make quite a dandy if he tried. She ran her

142

hands through his hair and said it should be shorter – a spiky crop with a side part would suit him. He said he liked it messy and she said, OK, textured, but definitely cropped with a side part. That was the look right now. Some skinny chinos would show his legs off nicely - he had nice thighs - and he should buy some espadrilles too. Harry said he didn't like canvas shoes, they didn't keep his feet warm enough. She conceded that he could wear boots instead, so long as they were DMs. Also, she had seen this guy in the street with this great check shirt, not like the usual ones. She asked if he had met anyone he liked recently. Harry started telling her about Arthur as they sat close together on the floor.

*****

Harry came down to the kitchen in his T-shirt and boxers. He knew that seeing people half-naked first thing made Steve feel queasy, but he had a question and wanted to catch his dad before he left for the office.

'Hey, Dad, how was your run?'

Steve was standing by the breakfast bar, downing spoonfuls of Granola. His focus was on getting going to the station and questions from Harry were a distraction.

'It's icy, well below freezing; but the gritters have been out overnight, so I just ran in their tracks.'

'Well, make sure you don't do yourself any injury.'

'Is there something you want?'

'As it happens, I have a legal question for you.'

'I thought you were the lawyer now.'

'There are these squatters in one of Frank's flats and I thought you might know how to get rid of them.'

'Send someone round with a wrecking ball and scare the shit out of them.'

'And that's what you'd advise a client, is it?'

'Haven't the faintest idea. Ask your mother, she's supposed to be the real estate lawyer.'

When he asked her, Marianne answered vaguely that the law had probably moved on since her day and that she hadn't been on the landlord and tenant side anyway. She rang him that afternoon though. She had bumped into a legal friend. The advice was pretty much the same as Arthur's. A court order would take no more than four weeks. Enforcement was another matter. 'But hey, Harry, I don't think you should be getting involved in this. There could be aggro. You should leave it to the professionals.'

'It's OK, Mum, I can handle it.'

At least now she would have some idea how serious his work was.

*****

It was past 9 pm later the same day and icy cold as Harry walked back up the hill to home. The Doc Martens had good grip, he could have slipped otherwise. Marianne had had the driveway gritted. Inside, she was watching a documentary about the siege of Leningrad, looking like she felt under siege herself. There had obviously been some sniping going on. Steve came in from the kitchen, plate in hand, and asked if he'd found out what he needed about squatting.

'Mum filled me in, thanks.'

'I told you she was a real estate lawyer. Best thing to do is send in the lads though. I bet that's what Frank has in mind, isn't it? One day, you'll go round and they'll have disappeared. Sometimes, that's the only thing to do with these toerags, take matters into your own hands.'

Marianne remarked that she was surprised to hear a solicitor speaking like that, leaving aside that she couldn't imagine Steve ever rolling his sleeves up and taking someone

144

on. And, anyway, he shouldn't be legitimising violence. She gestured towards the TV.

'"Legitimising violence." For fuck's sake! Where do you get these phrases? I can just see Sarah telling Bob not to legitimise violence as he blasts another hare with his 12 bore.'

'Am I to infer that you look up to Bob as a role model for masculinity?'

'Oh, don't start. I could have picked anyone.'

'But you didn't. Well, he does have all the attributes needed of a man, according to Sarah.'

'Yeah, yeah, they're blissfully married and live in a castle in Lalaland.'

Harry thought he'd better break it up. 'So, Dad, how's the election campaign going?'

'It's going very well, thank you, Harry. I appreciate your showing an interest.' He looked over at Marianne who had turned back towards the television.

'Got any more secret trips to the States in the pipeline?'

'There should be one coming up in the next week or so, as it happens.'

'You think Andy has any rabbits he's going to pull out of the hat?'

'I don't know about rabbits, but he does have a very attractive stage assistant.'

'What do you mean?'

'Well, his wife left him a few years ago. She wasn't exactly a good looker, but it earned him the sympathy vote all the same. Now, though, he has hooked up with this bimbo and moved her in with him. She's only twenty-nine years old.'

'Lucky Andy, I guess.' Harry wondered how he could steer the conversation away from whatever clash Steve was engineering with Marianne.

'And not only that, she's a bimbo with a brain. Works at

Goldman's.'

'And does this bimbo with a brain have a name?' Marianne sounded weary but obliged to get involved.

'She does. Sally.'

Marianne shifted in her seat to look round at him. 'And have you met Sally?'

'I have. Andy introduced me as the competition.'

'She doesn't know what she's missing.'

That didn't go down well. 'There is one consolation though.'

'And what's that?'

'I get all Andy's sympathy vote.'

'Why? Because Andy's got Sally?'

'No.' Steve sounded puzzled that she needed to ask. 'Because I've still got you.'

*****

Harry wasn't going to stop working round at Frank's just because of Amita. He found himself observing the two of them together. She would come round to the apartment with flowers to give it some colour. She complained that the place was poky. Frank replied that that was the way the British had liked their mansion blocks when it had been built, back in the 1930s. She said the British had no taste. They bickered like that. Amita seemed to have no problem with Harry being there. In fact, strangely, she wanted to see more of him, not less. She would take him shopping for clothes – out of his own money, of course, but with the benefit of her taste. She admired him as he tried on a suit at Paul Smith but disagreed with the assistant, insisting that pleated trousers would look much better on him than flat fronted ones. She got her way, the trousers went off for tailoring. She dusted down the lapels of the jacket and stood back to inspect him as if he were some kid trying on a school uniform. There were shirts at Liberty costing £100 each and this time it was Harry who tried doing the insisting, but in the end he found he couldn't disappoint her. To compensate, she took him downstairs for tea. It was to be her treat. They shared a pot of Orange Pekoe and she demanded he have the scones with strawberry jam and Cornish clotted cream, while she could only manage one salmon and cucumber finger sandwich supplemented by a glass of champagne. Not all the shopping was for his benefit. They browsed through the fabrics at Liberty, Amita tutting at the quality, talking of how all the best stuff was kept back in India but still pawing over every item. She needed new clothes to wear round town and would hold up a blouse against her frame, asking 'Harry, how would I look in this?' She was quite flat-chested – a friend had told her that she could never be seen in Rio unless she had a boob job first – but slender too and with flawless skin. Harry did not know how he was supposed to reply to these questions, so he just said 'It suits you' or 'You'd look really good in it' until Amita told him to stop paying her compliments and be more discerning. After that, he tried speaking his mind. Frank had said that escorts should be discerning. Harry wasn't sure if Amita's hair was thinning on top or whether it had always been like that. Her teeth jutted out. She practised Reiki and visited an aromatherapist.

Now that Amita was around, Harry decided Frank's and his relationship had moved on and wasn't sexual anymore – if it ever really had been. It was platonic and business-like - two entrepreneurs working together - and that was good. He observed a genuine tenderness between Frank and Amita. Frank was quite demure in her presence, not the rumbustious fellow Harry had been used to seeing. And he was attentive, he would plump cushions for her and, standing behind, slide the dining chair under her as she sat down. Harry watched how it was done. He didn't always have to run along in the evenings. Sometimes when he had finished up at Frank's, he would be invited to dinner with them at a restaurant, and Amita would recommend what he should have from the menu, introducing him to scallops and clams, complaining that the tuna wasn't sushi quality and that London was expensive, drab and sooo boring. Harry could tell from the way he looked at him that Frank was pleased with the way he behaved – like a proper escort. They never went to Portofino though, and Harry felt he shouldn't mention it. She took him to the ballet - Frank gave up his ticket. On one occasion, she made him drive her out of London so that they could tour round Windsor and, another time, Stratford upon Avon. While he quite liked being in demand, these trips distracted him from his work with Frank and took him out of circulation escort-wise. So, after some thought, he asked Frank if he would compensate him for looking after her; but the old guy's response was that none of this was at his initiative or for his benefit and that, as a businessman, Harry should deal with Amita direct if he wanted paying. Indeed, Frank thought Harry should be compensating him for his lack of availability. Although he pretended to be joking, Harry could see that Frank was irritated by the amount of his time Amita was taking up, but he hadn't raised it with her himself. Harry didn't mention it either. Amita said she would bring him back some treats next time she was over from KL, and were there any DVDs he wanted?

*****

Brockley, London SE4. Since Arthur would expect him to come that way, Harry had picked up the Overground from Shoreditch at Canada Water. He would be able to talk about the journey down, the kid screaming on the carriage floor and refusing to climb back into her buggy. Walking along Brockley

Road, he spotted a 'Freephone funeral parlour' followed by two further undertakers' within a couple of hundred metres, all of which did give the impression that Brockley was not a place where the living rested in peace; but then he saw the cemetery. There was a florist's on the other side of the road – 'flowers for all occasions'. He reached the end of Brockley Road, where it turned into Stondon Park and SE4 suddenly became SE23, and realised he must have missed a turn. He had been expecting something more in the way of a high street with Brockley written all over it, but it had never appeared. Now he sat on a bench facing St Hilda's, Crofton Park, its fierce brown stone and truncated tower intimidating to a non-believer like him, but there were signs welcoming locals to events. Yoga was on Monday evenings. He started re-treading his route. Somewhere between here and the station was the street where Arthur lived.

Once inside the flat, he was surprised that Arthur had not been able to resolve the IT problem himself. Maybe, just maybe, this was a pretext for something else. There was always a chance. After all, he had the sort of brain that could beat a supercomputer at chess. It took Harry just a few minutes to figure out what was wrong and sort it. He didn't pretend to over-complicate things or take the opportunity to big himself up. When he finished, Arthur offered him a beer, but he didn't want any alcohol just then. He sat down. He was going to ask about Jane.

'Jane's very well, thank you, Harry. Or at least she was at breakfast-time. She has gone to her parents for the weekend, up in Nottingham.'

'That's funny. My dad comes from Nottingham.'

'Really? And then he moved to Hackney. That is funny. Nottingham is quite attractive in parts. I could see myself living there.'

'Really? You don't plan on staying in London?'

'No, definitely not. That's one of the great things about being an osteopath, you can take the job with you pretty much wherever you want to go.'

'You don't want to be tied down?'

'Well, I'm not exactly bohemian, Harry. I just want an affordable house, preferably detached, with good schools nearby and plenty of open roads for cycling. All very boring and unimaginative, I know.'

'It doesn't sound boring at all. It suits you. Where my dad's from in Nottingham isn't particularly attractive though. It's probably not the same neighbourhood as Jane's parents'.'

'Probably not. They live on the proverbial Acacia Avenue. Built to keep the working classes out.'

Arthur opened a can of lager for himself. Harry watched his Adam's Apple yoyo up and down as he gulped. 'But you didn't go up to Nottingham with her this weekend?'

'No, I'm right here with you, Harry. I like to have a bit of space to myself. Besides, I don't really enjoy being with the in-laws.'

'Jane's parents? Why, what are they like?'

'They fuss over me too much, especially since Mum died. They seem to think there's a big void in here that needs filling.'

'It must be really hard for you.'

'You sound just as bad as they do, Harry. What about you and your mum, do you rock along just fine?'

'Oh, yeah, we're pretty close. I've never really thought of living anywhere far from London though. I went to Stratford last week – didn't like that too much. Not enough to live there, anyway.'

'You've lost me, Harry, what does Stratford have to do with anything? Apart from the Olympics.'

'No, not that Stratford. Stratford-upon-Avon.'

'Oh, home of the Bard. What took you up there?'

'I went with Amita. Frank's girlfriend.'

'Frank has a girlfriend? I didn't know that.'

'Yeah, she lives in KL half the year. She's got a house with servants there. And then she spends the rest of the year over here, in London. No servants, not unless you count me.'

'And she lives with Frank when she's over here?'

'No, she has her own place in Kensington. I haven't seen it, except from the outside.'

'So, is she pretty loaded, this Amita? Has she some high flying job?'

'I think she must have an independent source of income. I don't see her doing any work.'

'Lucky her. And what were the two of you doing up in Stratford-upon-Avon? Did you go to see a play?'

'No, although we did take a look at the theatre. Apparently, it has only recently opened. Amita wanted to do the whole tourist routine – photos of her with ye olde England backdrops, that sort of thing.'

'And your job was what? Cameraman? General escort?'

'Both, I guess.'

'Cool. I've never been to Stratford-upon-Avon. I'd like to, some time.'

'Well, maybe you and I could go up there together sometime.'

'Let's do it!' Then Arthur started to frown. 'But tell me, Harry, is working with Frank what you expected it to be? Do you get a lot out of it?' Those jade eyes could be quite searching.

'Well, I know he can be really rude and swear a lot but, most of the time, he's not too bad.'

'I don't think I'm his sort of person.'

'No, you're not. If it's any consolation, nor are many

people. He likes everybody to see things the way he does, and he gets stressed if they don't.'

'But you're different? You can say what you want?'

'Most of the time. Although he does try and control me too. I mean, I don't think he'd be too pleased if he knew I was down here with you right now. Just the two of us.'

'Why should he care?'

Good point. Harry didn't have an answer. 'I dunno. No reason, I suppose.'

'Are you going to tell him?'

'Probably not.'

'Why? Would it piss him off?'

'Maybe. I know I said he has a temper but don't get me wrong, Frank wouldn't hurt a fly. And I do like working with him.'

'You certainly do the legwork when it comes to Regent's Row.'

'Regent's Row is not the only thing I'm involved with. We've this JV with a French woman, Dominique; it's import-export, well, import anyway. My job is to test whether there's any market in the UK for these Limoges porcelain figures. Dominique supplied the first consignment, and Frank left me to find out.'

'Cool. And you think you'll offload them?'

'I already have! Frank gave me the names of some guys who retail that sort of thing – they're his contacts but they're not going to do me any favours. So I started by taking Dominique's base price, multiplying that by what should be a reasonable margin for us, and then trying to work out the minimum margin the retailer would need to make.'

'And how did you deduce that?'

'Well, my mum has a friend who runs an art gallery, so I rang her and asked what margins galleries typically make, then

152

used that as the basis.'

'Clever thinking. And did it work?'

'It did, yes! The first guy told me the price I was asking was way too high and that he'd never be able to pass that on to his customers; but I'd checked out these arcades off Piccadilly and reckoned I was offering a much better deal than theirs.'

'So, how did you convince him?'

'I didn't, I walked away. He was never going to buy. But I made a sale to the next one, and that gave me the confidence to go on.'

'That's very impressive.'

'Trust me, Arthur, I'm not the sort of guy who gives up easily, not if there's something I want. The irony is though, I think all that Limoges stuff is gross. I'd never buy it myself. There are figures of cute little kittens wearing bows and drinking milk, and there's even one called "faun with first tooth". That is so sentimental, isn't it? The colours are well garish, they almost make me want to throw. I bet you'd feel the same.'

'Well, I suppose someone must like it, otherwise they wouldn't buy it. And you made that happen.'

'Cheers, Arthur. I guess that means I'm responsible for spreading bad taste across the planet.'

Arthur went to the bathroom, leaving Harry alone. He got up and sat where Arthur had been, to feel his body heat. Looking round, he thought that, for rented accommodation, this flat was better quality than the students', but it was messier. The brown carpet needed vacuuming. There were untidy heaps of papers, and clothes that were probably waiting for the washing machine. Harry had had to squeeze past two bikes in the hallway to get into the flat. Looking round, he guessed the bedroom was at the back. Hearing Arthur coming back, Harry jumped up to return to his own seat and asked if Arthur really had thought he was an escort when they'd first met.

Arthur didn't reply straightaway. 'I'm told that too often I blurt things out without properly thinking them through first. It's not a very clever quality.'

'So that means you did think I was an escort?'

'Well, it was just something Dahlia said before we arrived.'

'Did she say Frank hires escorts to go to dinner with him? Something like that?'

'Something like that. Is it true?'

'Nah. At least, not that I've seen. Anyway, he's got Amita. But I bet you didn't know he thought you were some sort of master criminal?'

Arthur looked puzzled. 'I didn't, as it happens. Why did he think that?'

'He claimed you were part of a dastardly crime syndicate that was plotting to swindle Dahlia out of her assets.'

'Well, look around you, Harry. If I'm part of a crime syndicate, it's about time it disbanded since it's not been having much success. Did you believe him?'

'Of course, not.'

'I can be a bit of a twat, but I'm not a criminal. Anyway, to turn the question round, is Frank always honest?'

'Well, I don't think he's dishonest. He may bend the rules a bit but that happens all the time in business, doesn't it? Even in osteopathy, I guess.'

'Well, osteopathy certainly entails some manipulation, but I'm not sure that's quite the same thing.'

Harry noticed some gym kit and cycling gear scrunched beside the sofa. 'Are you really into sports, Arthur? The Olympics, that sort of thing?'

'I most certainly am, Harry. Why? Fancy a game of squash some time?'

'I fancy the idea, but I'm not really sporty enough. You'd beat me too easy. My dad goes running and my mum does Pilates, but that's about as far as it goes in my family. I'm not bad at dancing, but I don't suppose that's an Olympic sport.'

'I can't dance for toffee. It's something I've always wished I could do but, when we go clubbing, I'm better off sitting back with a beer and watching everyone else. Your mum must have difficulty squeezing everything into the hours of the day though. What with Pilates on top of everything else.'

Harry let that pass for the moment. 'Wouldn't you miss seeing all your friends if you went to live in Nottingham?'

'I don't suppose I've really thought about it in those terms, Harry. I have a close-knit set of friends and I hope I'll never lose touch with them, but you have to allow people to move on and do their own thing, haven't you? Anyway, there is always social media.'

'Yeah, we could hook up, you and me.'

'We certainly could.'

'You know I said my mum was a teacher?'

'Yes, Harry.'

'Well, she's not. She works for the NHS.'

'A medic, like me! Are you now going to tell me she didn't leave school without any qualifications and educate herself up to degree level?'

'She would make a very good teacher. Probably. And she does study art history.'

'NHS. Art history. Pilates. Mother of Harry. That sounds like enough to be getting on with.'

'We're not really that close.'

'No? I'm sorry to hear that.'

'We could be, but we don't really share things. Same goes for my dad and me. And they don't share anything at all with each other, not even the same bed.'

'Sadly, that seems to be the way it goes with some couples.'

'Do you and Jane ever…?'

'Well, we definitely row, but we've not yet made it to the separate beds phase. There wouldn't be room in this place.'

'I haven't told them I'm gay.'

'Oh? Why's that?'

'I dunno. I suppose I thought I'd wait for them to work it out for themselves. If that makes sense?'

'It does. Sometimes people don't know what's staring them in the face.'

'Did you know I was gay?'

'Well, I had an idea.'

'And that doesn't change anything between us, me telling you now?'

'Nothing whatsoever. So, is there anyone special?'

Harry laughed. 'Apparently not.' He stood up, sweeping his hair across his brow and looking at his watch. 'I reckon it's time I was going.'

'You don't have to go on my account, Harry. I enjoy having you round, shooting the breeze.'

'I think I do. I'm meeting up with someone up in Holloway and I don't want to be late.'

Arthur stood up too and stretched his arms above his head. 'Well, I suppose that means I should get on with some work now that the computer's fully functioning again. Thanks again for your help. The pressing question now,' he scrutinised the can in his hand, 'is should I open another beer?' He was totting up both sides of the argument. 'No, the decision is made, no more beer. Sadly, business and pleasure just don't mix.'

On the way back to Brockley station, Harry watched this black guy swing out of a bar with a bottle of Heineken, pouring from it onto the ground as he walked, getting rid of the froth. They nodded to each other.

*****

Harry was sitting in the kitchen, eating lasagne out of its plastic tub, when they burst in through the back door. Adele led the way past Marianne, who was picking the key out of the lock, followed by Cathy and Louise. Wet boots and trainers were kicked off – except of course Adele's, which left tracks all over the kitchen floor. The girls were returning from a boat party on the Thames. Not surprisingly for late February, it had been Arctic out there on the river, with a wind chill factor on a par with that in Novia Scotia (so Louise said, her sister lived there). Any of the four of them could have told the birthday girl's husband that this was going to be one not wholly welcome surprise party; but at least they had made the effort to go, unlike the various boys who had wimped out on their wives and stayed indoors, passively watching sport. Anyway, they all agreed, Ham House was always worth a visit. Adele said it was freezing indoors and ordered everyone, Harry included, to find every radiator in the house and turn it up to max. Steve was away for the weekend, and he wouldn't find out what they'd done until the next gas bill arrived. Harry stayed mulling over whether to finish the lasagne, which was cold in the middle. Marianne had the cafetiere off the shelf and was waving it around, offering coffee. Cathy and Louise were Surbiton mums too, Cathy was the mother of his friend Mark who was at college somewhere in Dorset. Mark's grades had been hardly better than his. Cathy asked if he was still thinking of going to college and Marianne butted in to reply that he hadn't made up his mind yet and was just hanging out for now. Seeing Adele smile at him knowingly, Harry shrugged at her. Louise had popped to the loo – she had pleaded she could not hold on much longer – and, on returning, said she'd had a nose round and spotted a bowl she'd not seen before. Marianne said it was from the Maghreb. Steve had accused her of being spendthrift, yet again. Groans all round.

'He should chill out,' said Louise, 'and not think of everything in terms of money. What do you reckon, Harry?'

'I reckon it would have been cheaper to fly to Tunis on Easyjet and buy it there.'

'Oh, he's just like his father,' said Marianne, dismissively.

'Don't tell him that,' replied Harry.

'Harry has a point, Maz.' Adele did like to think she looked out for him. 'You know what, I think he can be quite discerning. We should have taken him with us to Rome.'

The others wanted to hear more about the trip to Rome. Adele recounted how they had been staying close to the Spanish Steps which, once they had been climbed, allowed near-panoramic views of the city. The Tiber was surprisingly narrow, given its great place in history and literature. As ever, Marianne had been the proverbial mine of information, and her knowledge of Italian had been a godsend, not least when it came to restaurants. The food had been heavenly. Adele had pigged herself, she didn't care about her weight any longer; but Marianne could eat a horse and still not put on any pounds. When it had come to visiting places, Marianne had been focused on the Renaissance while Adele herself wanted to see more classical Roman remains. They had teamed up to visit the Sistine chapel but otherwise had tended to go their own ways during the daytime. Adele's own favourite was the Pantheon. Modern day Britain, she said, could do with a pantheon - there were too many religions out there bickering with each other and everyone else. She had sent her boys a photo of its front, asking if either of them could translate the words above the entrance without resorting to the Internet.

158

The answers had come back OK but not perfect. She couldn't eliminate that there hadn't been any skulduggery, after all she had Googled the answer herself.

Harry junked the remains of the lasagne into the waste bin, intending to slip away unnoticed.

'Bye, Harry,' Adele called out, winking at him.

'Bye, Harry,' joined in Cathy and Louise.

Upstairs was quieter. Steve would have resorted to the study in no time. Harry shut himself away in his bedroom. Steve was in the States, on his second trip there that year. Harry stood, elbows on window sill, looking out into the garden at the back. He knew that Steve had aspirations to build a swimming pool there on the right hand side but that these would never be fulfilled since he would never be able to face raising the subject with Marianne. Ironically, were he to do so, she would give the go-ahead without any conditions; but, for Steve, even that would represent a defeat since there would have been no argument to have won. Harry had texted Arthur earlier that week, apologising for piling all that family stuff onto him and explaining that he had been exaggerating as usual. Arthur had texted back, no worries, thanks for the help. Scrolling down, Harry came across the photo Adele had sent him from Rome. It was of the Pantheon, presumably the same one she had sent her sons but without the general knowledge test. M AGRIPPA L F COS TERTIUM FECIT. He fed the words into a search engine. MARCUS AGRIPPA SON OF LUCIUS IN HIS THIRD CONSULATE MADE THIS. There was a text from Frank sent earlier that day; it was blank, Harry could envisage the old guy looking at the screen perplexedly and hitting Send just to get out of there. Frank and he were due to revisit Dordogne Delights on Monday. He had wanted to meet Frank there – it was, after all, only fifteen minutes from home – but he couldn't explain that and so would have to take the train up to Fulham and then drive Frank down. Frank never drove himself anywhere, not now Harry was there to do it for him. Apparently, there were some packages that needed bringing back to Fulham.

Half an hour later, he opened the door. All sounded quiet; but, coming downstairs, he saw Adele still in the kitchen and heard Steve's name being mentioned.

'Hi, stranger,' called Adele. 'Decided to be sociable after all?' She was munching on some shortbread. Steve would have said something about how trousers didn't flatter someone her size, but only once she'd left the room.

'Talking about Dad, are you?'

'Not really. Your mum was telling me about Sarah's house in Burford and your stay there at Christmas.'

'So you are talking about Dad.'

'What makes you say that?'

'Because Christmas was all about him and that house. How he hated it. How their house is bigger than his house. How Bob has more money than he has.'

'It's true,' confirmed Marianne. 'He doesn't like Bob at all.'

'I can imagine someone like Steve having problems with Bob. He can be a bit in yer face, isn't that right? What do you make of him, Harry?'

'Harry can't stand him either. Which is a shame, because he has a heart of gold. He'll help anyone out if he can. Plus, he keeps Sarah very happy in the bedroom department, lucky cow. While I have to make my own entertainment.'

'Please,' said Harry, 'this is your son here.'

'Well, what am I supposed to do?'

'And the house, Harry?' asked Adele. 'What do you make of that?'

'It's called "The Barn".'

'What's so wrong with that?'

'Who would buy a barn, convert it into a seven bedroom mansion and call it "The Barn"?'

'Well, it's a bit unimaginative, I'll give you that.'

'Who cares what it's called?' protested Marianne. 'What matters is that it's lovely, especially inside. It's so spacious and they've gone to great trouble to make it look nice. You should see the kitchen, Adele.'

'Come on, Maz, what have you ever seen in a kitchen?'

'Yeah,' added Harry. 'And it may "look nice", but the place is totally characterless.'

'OK, you're probably both right. It is a bit impersonal.'

'I told you Harry was discerning.'

'I'm just standing up for my baby sister. I suppose it does feel like it has been designed to be rented out. It lacks colour. Do you know, Adele, there's one room where everything's white? The walls, the furnishings, the carpet, everything.'

'Not any more, it isn't.'

Adele asked Harry what he meant.

'Harry had an accident with the rug, that's what he means. Don't even go there, although it was quite funny. Actually, they do have this gorgeous log fire which really makes the place. Gives it a warm, lived-in feeling. I'd like one of those.'

When Harry warned that he hoped she wasn't being serious, Adele asked what he had against it.

'He didn't like being asked to help with bringing the logs in. It messed with his shirt.'

'Wouldn't it go against all your so-called environmental principles?' Harry challenged his mother. 'You'd be responsible for chopping down trees and damaging the ozone layer. It would be totally hypocritical.'

'He has a point, Maz. Although I think "hypocritical"

may be going a bit too far.'

'Hm, well I could pay for some extra trees to be planted somewhere. That's what all those rock stars do, isn't it? You know, I'm starting to warm to the idea.'

'Ha ha. Very funny.'

'Well, I'll leave you to fight it out between yourselves.' Adele squeezed Harry's knee under the table, then tested the cafetiere. 'This coffee's cold. Let me warm it up in the microwave.'

'Oh, it's not the same reheated. I'll make some.'

'You stay there. I'll do it. I know where everything is. You and Harry can chat.'

Harry and Marianne watched as Adele opened one cupboard, then another, searching for the coffee, banging the doors shut. She wasn't tall enough to see what was on the top shelves. 'Ah, there it is.' She clattered around, filling the kettle, leaving Marianne and Harry sat silently at the table. Marianne shuffled her cigarette packet around and Harry looked the other way.

'So, Harry,' called out Adele, 'talking of your dad – since that's what you think we were doing – how are things going with his plans to take over Grant Matcham Watchamacallit?'

'Pretty well, so he says. He's in Chicago, talking to the top team out there.'

'Chicago?' Marianne looked up. 'I thought he was in New York?'

'That's because you never listen. Chicago's where the head office is.'

'I do listen. It's just I don't always say what I'm thinking.'

'Why's that, Maz?'

'You know Steve. He's very competitive.'

'Do you not think he's right for the job?'

'It's not so much that. No, I'm sure he could do it. It's

162

more that it feels he's a bit of a one man band.'

'Really? What do you think, Harry?'

'I think he'd appreciate a bit of support from Mum.'

'I do try to support him.'

Adele brought the cafetiere over to the table along with a mug for Harry. She pressed down the plunger. 'And what about this new job of yours?' She pushed the mug towards him. 'How's all that going?'

'Well, thank you for asking; and, since you have, the latest thing we've got going is a scheme for importing goods from France. Culinary delights. We can supply you with foie gras, confit de canard, champagne and truffles, all at a fraction of the price you'd pay at Fortnum & Mason.'

'Well, that's a good thing because I get paid a fraction of the salary of someone who shops at Fortnum & Mason.'

'Don't do yourself down, Adele. You're just the sort of customer we're looking for. Plus, I can throw in some Limoges porcelain figurines to brighten up your mantelpiece.'

'I think my mantelpiece is cluttered enough as it is, mostly with bad stuff from school. What do you reckon to all this, Maz? Have you bought any French delicatessen from Harry?'

'I didn't know there was any on offer.'

Harry drummed his fingers against the table. 'That's because she never asks. She's all into what my friends are up to, but never me.'

'That's not fair. I don't see them, I see you all the time. Anyway, I didn't know you sold foie gras.'

'It's not just foie gras. There's loads of stuff. Didn't you hear what I just said?'

'Well, what would you like me to buy? The confit sounds nice.'

'See!' Harry gestured towards Marianne, Adele had heard it for herself. 'She's always fucking patronising me. She doesn't take what I'm doing seriously! Just because I'm not clever enough to go to college.'

Marianne grimaced. Adele tugged Harry's arm down onto the table. 'I'm sure that's not what she means. And I think getting British people to eat more French delicatessen is a very good idea. Don't you agree, Maz?'

Marianne looked at Harry across the table. 'I'm sorry if it seems like I don't pay you enough attention. It's just I don't want you to think I'm fussing.'

Harry didn't reply.

It was Adele who broke the silence. 'You know, Maz, Harry's really grown up, what with all this new work, hasn't he? And he's starting to fill out and look rather manly too. I bet they're queuing up.'

Marianne carried on looking at Harry. 'I'm proud you're showing such initiative, being your own man, not following the crowd.'

Just for a moment Harry thought he might choke. 'Thanks, Mum.'

'And I'm sure he'll find the right girl when he's ready,' added Adele. 'Just make sure you don't eat too much deli food. We don't want you getting podgy like me.'

*****

Looking in the mirror and weighing himself on the scales, Harry couldn't see any sign that he was getting podgy. He didn't know what he used to weigh but he did know his diet had got a lot richer since he'd hooked up with Frank. It wasn't down to foie gras at any rate, he hadn't eaten any and wasn't sure he wanted to. It was more likely due to spending too much time at Fabrizio's. He thought he got enough exercise with his clients to keep his weight down. He looked slim and trim enough in his Paul Smith suit even if - despite Frank's view of

164

the world – most punters weren't interested in what he was wearing or in dinner, theatre and other social occasions; they were interested in what he wasn't wearing. He pulled on his jeans and buckled up his white Lowlife belt. It was Monday morning, time to leave the house and go fetch Frank. They were off to visit Dominique and Dordogne Delights.

*****

Dominique greeted them each with a kiss, then closed the office door behind them. Well, she announced, the Limoges trial had been a success, most of which was down to Harry. Failure would have meant the time had finally come to draw stumps. Sales had been constant over the weeks since they had last met, which Dominique pointed out actually represented an uplift since that period was traditionally the post Christmas hangover. Frank remarked that it remained unclear whether the average goose liver connoisseur was also partial to Limoges porcelain. He asked Harry for his opinion. Harry said he thought it had legs.

'Well then,' declared Frank, 'we shall go with it. You know, Dominique, Harry is the finest assistant I've ever had. I can't imagine what I would do without him.'

'Make him a proper partner!'

'Yay!' Harry cheered Dominique on.

'Sometimes these things are out of one's control. Now,' Frank checked his watch, 'it's almost midday. Time for us to try some of this foie gras ourselves.'

Dominique edged through the doorway with a trayful of plates, glasses and food that she was protecting from accidental bumps. The receptionist – Chantelle – held the door back for her while strangling the neck of a wine bottle with her spare hand. The foie gras was a muddy block that Dominique, with close attention, cut into four precise quarters. She seemed short-sighted, the way she bent so far over it. Each quarter was placed on a separate side plate with a slice of French bread, some salad leaves that she said were rocket, and a dash of unexplained brown sauce. She handed the plates out one by one while Chantelle poured a sandy coloured wine into small squat glasses. When Harry said he couldn't drink and drive, Frank held up his hand like a traffic policeman might and said that Montbazillac was a dessert wine, hardly alcoholic, and that there was no risk at all of putting him over the limit. Harry took just a sip, it was sweet and viscous. No-one spoke at first, the other three sank into a religious-like contemplation; while, to him, although he wouldn't admit it publicly, the foie gras tasted no different from the liver sausage his Gran had used to put on his plate. Foie gras and Limoges figurines, he could sell them but not to himself.

'No man of taste and discernment, Harry, could forego the offer of such a delectable creation!'

Dominique nodded in agreement, the pate squeezed from the bread onto her fingers. Where she came from, she explained to him, they had foie gras with every meal – just like the British with chips. Dominique was trim, eating foie gras certainly hadn't put any weight on her.

Frank was taking two top range hampers back with him to Fulham, Harry did the carrying. Frank started talking of how he knew he asked a lot of Harry but he would try and make amends. Passing over Putney Bridge, he remarked fondly how he had always meant to take a trip down the river to Greenwich. Past Tate Modern. Harry thought the wine must have got to him. This burbling continued until they reached the apartment, where Amita was waiting. He presented her with Harry, holding out a hamper.

'For me? A present? Nooh! Oh, Hari, Hari, put it on the table.'

Harry did as he was told and went off to fetch the second one. On his return, Amita was laying out the contents of the hamper on the table as if they were body parts. She sniffed the specimen cassoulet through the glass jar and prodded the cured ham to check it was dead. The champagne should go in the fridge. Noticing the second hamper, Amita asked like a birthday girl if that was for her too. No, Frank replied solemnly, that one was for business, not pleasure. He patted Harry's back.

Chapter 9

It was 6 pm that same evening and Harry was sat alone in the back of a cab, belted up with the second hamper on the seat next to him and a backpack between his feet. The air in the cab was stuffy. Outside, it was quite warm with spring not too far round the corner. Monday evening, a rush hour of sorts, the cabbie called out that he couldn't avoid going through the centre of town, there were no rat runs nowadays, not since the authorities had sealed them all off. At Piccadilly Circus they turned north up Regent Street, it was going to be a longish journey by cab standards. Frank had spent most of the afternoon watching an old World War Two film about Malta, whisky to hand. Outside on the street, he had hailed a cab and stood by as Harry loaded it up, before closing the door on him without a word. Past Camden Town Tube, the street lights shone blearily.

Now it was dark, the market was empty. There were no stalls, just numbers painted in white on the road identifying the location of each pitch. Frank had given Harry cash for the fare. He placed the hamper on the side of the road with the smaller but denser backpack on top. Most of the shops had closed; those staying open were mainly takeaways, like Southern Fries in front of him. He wondered if the upmarket deli down the road was still open, did the middle class pioneers feel free to wander up this street unguarded at night or were they happier bolted up inside the four bedroom houses they'd cleaned up? Tomorrow's Shoreditch, they'd be calculating. Southern Fries was still doing some business, there was a group of teenagers in there, killing time with a plate of chips. The mobile phone shop next door was shut, completely blacked out; but, upstairs, old Mrs Tate looked like she was home, that was a doorbell he would not be ringing. Tate Ancient. The students could have been in too, there was the hint of a table lamp behind the three-quarter closed blinds. Studying. There was no doubt about number 41 though, the lights up there were full on behind scanty curtains but the white van parked outside Mr Rai's prevented Harry from seeing if the newsagent's was still open. He bent down, heaved the hamper and backpack up in one go, steadied himself, then crossed the road to ring the doorbell.

The door buzzed open. There was no light on in the hallway. He felt along the wall inside the door, focusing on keeping the backpack nicely balanced on top of the hamper, and found a timer switch. Kicking the door shut behind him, he started moving up the stairs, hesitantly. Halfway up, the timer clicked off. He was standing in the dark. After a moment, the door above him opened, lighting up the stairway, and a face appeared, looking down at him. 'Jeez! You can't carry all that by yourself!' A man bounded the short distance down the stairs, two at a time, and took the backpack off him, turning to run back up. Harry followed at a slower pace, and entered the flat holding the hamper out in front of him.

'Hey, you shouldn't have tried to do that all in one go. You could have done yourself an injury!'

The guy giving him this advice was black, Afro-Caribbean, fit. Unexpectedly shy, Harry's eyes dropped down. Dark matt boots – brand unknown – brown tapering trousers, beltless, a black Fred Perry top, this guy was quite stylish and he was looking at Harry friendlily enough, buzzing a bit, unwilling to stand still. The backpack swung in his hand. He was waiting for Harry to say something. Frank had told him to just be his usual self. He glanced round the room, seeing what else was there, who else. Now he had seen inside all three flats. This one was also furnished, which he hadn't been expecting. The ceiling light had no shade. Some boxes in the back were stacked up like kids' building blocks. And then there were the three men. To the left of the black guy, a pallid white man was stretched out in a cane chair, studying him chillily. He didn't have the energy or good looks of his mate. Side-parted fair hair, an off-white T shirt over a lean but muscular frame, thick black tattoos of some script climbed like spiders up his forearms and onto his biceps. Further round the room, sat by the window on a chair tilted back against the wall, was the redhead he had seen with Arthur, now looking at him unimpressed. What had the guy been expecting? Someone older maybe. Three men spread round a room, they had been waiting for him and now he was supposed to speak.

'Hi, I'm Harry.'

'Hey, Harry, I'm Rob.' The black guy moved towards him. 'Let me take that.' He took the hamper gently off Harry and stepped back, evidently surprised it wasn't heavier.

'I know the hamper's not heavy,' said Harry, trying to sound like he was on the same level as the other guy, and not at all defensive. 'It's just it's a bit awkward, being wide. Especially with the other stuff on top. You know.'

'I know. You've done OK, Harry. A hamper, is it? Sounds a treat. Look, take a seat,' There was a sofa, towards which Rob nodded. 'Take the weight off your feet.'

Frank, Harry repeated to himself, had told him to relax and just be himself. He made his way over to the sofa and sat down, conscious that he was the object of the three men's attention.

'What's in the backpack, Harry?' Rob looked at him

expectantly as he crouched down to unzip it, not taking his eyes off him but still as friendly as ever. Harry reckoned he was all right. 'What have we here, guys?' He was fumbling around. 'Cans? Six? Twelve?' He peered inside. 'Looks like it's beer, guys. Yup, Stella.' He turned round to the other two and tapped his chin. 'Now what is it they say about people who drink Stella, guys? It escapes me.'

'It's for wife-beaters,' said the tattooed man.

'Wife-beaters? Oh, that's it, yeah. People who beat up their wives. You keep any Stella back home, Grovesie?'

'No, it's not allowed. Has to be Argentinian sauvignon blanc, that's what she says.'

'My girl's the same. Well, there are no wives here, so what's it all for?'

'Looks to me,' the redhead spoke for the first time, 'like whoever sent this is expecting us to have a party.'

'Boss?' queried Rob.

'Have a beer, of course! Crack it open.'

'Good idea, boss! I'm always up for a party.'

Rob pulled out the cans and flicked them open. One for the redhead, one for Grovesie, whose fingers Harry noted were studded with rings, and one for... 'Here, Harry. This one's for you!'

'I think maybe I should go now.' Alcohol did funny things to him.

'No, Harry stay! You can't go, you've gotta stay for the party. It wouldn't be a party without you, Harry.' Harry didn't want to offend him, he took the can out of Rob's outstretched hand. One would be OK. Rob banged their cans together, beer spilled over Harry's fingers. 'Probably not your usual tipple, but cheers all the same. Anyway, you haven't told us, what's this all about? What's a young guy like you doing here right now with a free crate of beer?'

'It's from Frankie Adami.'

'From Frankie? Frankie Adami? You hear that, boss? Frankie Adami has sent us Harry here for a party, along with a crate of Stella.'

'Frankie Adami? Well, I never.' The redhead raised his can to Rob. 'The old man used to talk about him. Very old school, he used to say, very hospitable. Anything he had, he'd offer to share. "What's mine is yours", that sort of thing.'

'Well, he's certainly been generous this time.'

Grovesie didn't look like he wanted to party, he just studied his can. Harry thought he was probably in his late twenties; but he wasn't sure about Rob, who was standing right in front of him, his crotch almost in his face.

'So, Harry,' Rob fell down into the sofa beside him, 'how do you know Frankie? I've never met the man but he's one of those legends from the past you hear about. And never a bad word neither, people only ever have complimentary things to say about him. So,' he nudged him, 'what's it with you and him – are you family, related, something like that?'

Harry had never heard Frank talked about so admiringly, except by the man himself. He hadn't realised he had such a reputation. 'No, nothing like that. We work together. In fact, I'm his business partner.'

'Really, Harry? Wow, that's pretty big. I'm impressed.' The sofa was quite cramped for the two of them, especially with Rob jigging up and down like this. 'So yous two pretty close then?'

'Yeah. I'm involved in all the big decision making.'

'Cool. So, like, what do you do, Harry?'

'Well, I'm in charge of the IT…'

'Well, Frankie's an old geezer, isn't he? He probably hadn't even heard of Windows before he teamed up with you. Good looking boy like you.' Rob laughed, nudging him again,

172

then swallowed a mouthful of beer and wiped his mouth.

'He's not that old.' Harry laughed along with him, wiping his own mouth. Rob put his arm round the back of the sofa, brushing Harry's shoulders.

''Course not. And what else are you up to? What else is Frankie into?'

'Export – import, that kind of thing. You'll appreciate I can't say a lot about it.'

'Of course not, Harry, it's confidential. That's between him and you. So, what do you do apart from the IT? I mean, your role has got to be big, hasn't it? Being Frankie's partner.'

The Stella was making Harry feel more at ease; and Rob was making him welcome, even if the others weren't joining in yet. 'Well, I handle the real estate portfolio. That and the French side of the business.'

'The French side? Really, Harry? I bet you speak the language like a native, an educated guy like you. And real estate too? So, is this portfolio a big one?'

'Pretty big.'

'And where is it? Like Mayfair, that sort of place?'

It's mostly up West. But, of course, there's this as well.' Harry waved his hand around, lord of the manor-like.

'This place? This little flat? That's amazing. I didn't know that. Hey, Grovesie, did you hear that? Harry runs this place.'

'Really? That's amazing.' Grovesie's can was resting on his stomach. He didn't sound as impressed as Harry would have liked.

'Grovesie used to do some work for Frankie, a few years back. Isn't that right, Grovesie?'

'Yeah, just menial stuff. Couriering, that sort of thing.'

'Don't knock yourself, Grovesie, don't knock yourself. But it wasn't the level of stuff Harry's doing? Nothing so high tech?'

'No, nothing high tech like what Harry's doing.'

'Grovesie has some stories about Frankie, Harry.'

Harry felt he should explain more about the real estate. 'It's not just this flat. It's the whole building, the newsagent's below as well as the next two along.'

'Wow! You're the man, Harry, you're the main man. Anyway, enough of that.' He pulled back from Harry to observe him. 'Where were we?' He looked around. 'We've seen the Stella, done that. Oh yes, the hamper! So what's in the hamper then? Is that part of the party, Harry? Is it lots of picnicky type stuff?'

'Well, not exactly.'

'Can we open it and see, Harry?' He jumped up and went behind Harry. Harry could hear him in the kitchen, rattling some drawers.

'Well, I guess that's up to you guys. My job was just to bring it up here and hand it over.'

'You're doing yourself down, Harry,' Rob called out, 'you're the heart of the party.' He returned with a Swiss knife and stood alongside Harry, his hand swinging. 'What do you reckon, boss? Shall we open it up? See what's inside?'

'Only if you're careful. We don't want any unnecessary mess.'

'OK, boss.'

Rob took the knife and carefully slivered off the hamper's packaging before teasing open the lid. The knife slipped into his back pocket as he laughed, pulling out the hamper's contents one by one, showing them off to the others who stayed leaning back in their chairs, not so interested. 'Hey guys, hey guys! Look, this is very fancy gear! "Pate de foie gras." Now what's that about?'

'Well,' remarked Grovesie, 'it's certainly not meant for people like us. Not wife-beaters.' He shifted in his chair, scratching his crotch uncomfortably.

'You're right, it's way too sophisticated,' agreed Rob, sadly. 'Shame. I like a treat. Can't we keep any of it? Boss?'

'No, put it all back, just as you found it.'

'Oh, OK. So…' Rob turned back to Harry, looking and sounding disappointed, 'so, if we're not supposed to have the hamper, what else have you got for us, Harry?'

Harry thought he might be able to help. 'Well, if you're after a treat, I'm sure I can come up with something. That hamper's top of the range but, if you want something a bit cheaper, just say the word. I'm your man.'

Rob looked in the direction of the redhead. 'Thanks, Harry, that's really sweet of you, but I think we're done with hampers.'

The redhead was the next to speak. 'The thing is,' he addressed Rob, 'I'm confused. I mean, what's it all for? Why has Frankie Adami sent us all these presents?'

'Yeah, Harry,' Rob sat down, cuddling up to him again, 'I'm confused too. I mean it's all very generous but, like the boss said, why would Frankie send us all these lovely presents?'

'Well…' Harry didn't really have an answer, his job was just to hand the stuff over. Grovesie eased himself out of his chair, loped lazily over to the Stellas, and picked one out which he cracked open and handed to Harry before returning to his seat. 'I guess it's an act of friendship.' Harry leant forward to put his half-drunk can down on the ground and swigged from the new one.

'Interesting. That would make sense, Harry.' Rob put his finger to his chin again. 'It's not an act of war, for sure. But why would Frankie Adami want to do that? I just don't get it.'

'Well, maybe he just wanted you to have something. Like your boss says, he's a generous guy.'

Grovesie got up again and stretched his arms towards the ceiling. Yawning, he ambled over and stood at the bottom of the stairs.

'Yeah,' conceded Rob, 'I guess that's it. Still, it's a bit of a mystery.' Rob leaned away again so as to look him up and down. 'And what's your part in this mystery, Harry? Where do you fit in?'

'Well, I told you. I work with Frankie.'

'Yes, I know, but why did Frankie send you up here tonight, a good looking guy like you? Why's that?'

'Because he knows I won't let him down?'

'I think you're right.' Rob looked him up and down again. 'Hey, I like your gear, Harry. Nice top!' He started stroking Harry's shirt, playing with the buttons and undoing them. 'Black's always best. Hey, and your pecs are really well-developed! You work out much, Harry?'

'A fair bit.'

'It shows. I don't go down the gym nearly as much as I should. Just don't find the time. Lazy.' He slipped his hand through the shirt, unbuttoning it as he went, his fingers stretching down to Harry's stomach. 'Tut tut, Harry, you need to work a bit harder on those abs.' His hand pushed down, testing the muscles. 'And smart pants too – you're joking me, you're joking me, I got a pair just like them!' Harry put his hand on top of Rob's to make him stop. 'And look, now your hand's on my hand.' His fingers tapped against Harry's skin. 'Hey, Harry, this is nice, isn't it?' Harry didn't reply, he just kept his hand on Rob's. Rob looked up. 'Hey, Harry, I've got an idea. Why don't we take a trip upstairs? After all, you're in charge of this place, aren't you, and you've only seen downstairs?' He picked up Harry's hand and pushed it down hard onto his own crotch, rubbing it slowly up and down. 'Like that, Harry, do you? Like that? Want some more?'

Harry couldn't think of anything to say. The Stella was confusing him. He was feeling Rob up, Grovesie was standing by the stairs, tapping his feet, the redhead was watching him impassively, and Frank was back at his apartment waiting for him to call.

'Boss?'

The redhead switched from looking at Harry. 'You do whatever you want.'

'Oh.' Rob pushed Harry away. He sounded let down. 'I was expecting more of a team effort. I'm not sure I'm in the mood now. Laters maybe.' Grovesie shook his head impatiently and sat back down.

The redhead spoke again. 'Ask him if anyone had been complaining about us.'

'Yeah, Harry, has anyone been complaining about us?'

'Well,' Harry's throat was dry, he gulped down some beer. 'Mr Rai thought you might be squatters.'

'Squatters? Us? Mr Rai – is that the charming Asian man downstairs? He's always so polite. You pop in there from time to time, don't you, boss?'

'From time to time.'

'But Frankie doesn't think we're squatters, does he, Harry?'

'No, of course not.'

'So, does he want us out of here or something?'

'Well, Mrs Mounis wants to sell the place.'

'Mrs Moo…?'

'Mrs Mounis? She owns half of it.'

'Half of this? There's another owner? So why does this Mrs Moo want to sell?'

'Apparently, she needs the cash.' Harry was feeling more relaxed now. 'Her husband died and he didn't leave her as much as she thought, so now she wants to sell the properties.'

'The properties? So there's more than one, it's not just our little flat? The next two along, you say? Is that the takeaway and the… the one with those Muslim guys?'

'Yeah, the mobile phone shop. Yeah, those and the flats above them. That's Mrs Tate above the mobiles, she's a sitting tenant, won't budge. And then there are the two students next door to here. They're complete tossers, really unco-operative. They wouldn't even let Arthur and me through the front door.'

'That wasn't very nice. So she – Mrs Mounis – is short of cash because her hubbie pegged it owing money. That right? I bet she'd make a tidy sum selling these properties, wouldn't she?'

'That's right. Especially if they were sold with vacant possession. Then they could be redeveloped. That's what Arthur says, anyway.'

'And Arthur's who again?'

'Arthur's a friend of Mrs Mounis', he's handling the sale for her. He likes to do everything by the book. He said Mrs Mounis should get a court order to evict you if you were squatters.'

'He sounds a very decent sort of guy.'

'Oh, he is. Dead honest. He's not bad really.'

'And Arthur works with you and Frankie, right?'

'Sort of.'

'Interesting. Good man, Harry, good man.'

Harry had run out of things to say, and he was almost out of beer. The redhead, addressing Rob, said that he thought it was time Harry went home. Rob complained that they still hadn't had the tour upstairs; but, when the redhead shook his head irritably, he slapped Harry lightly round the back of the head. 'Another time.' They stood up and, while Harry was making it to the door, Rob rooted round inside the backpack and tossed him an unopened can.

'Here you go, Harry. But don't drink it on the Tube, Harry, that's not allowed.'

Grovesie opened the door for him.

Out on the street, Harry rang Frank.

'Hey, Frank.'

'Harry, is that you?' He sounded surprised. 'Are you OK?'

'Sure, I'm fine. Those guys were cool. Nothing I couldn't handle.'

Chapter 10

This is the first time Harry can remember anyone coming to dinner. A partner from Steve's target law firm flew in from the States and, when he mentioned he had never seen inside a typical English family home, Steve invited him to dinner at his own. Marianne told Adele it was sixty / forty the man would be running for the door before the end of the first course. Adele couldn't make it that evening, she was too preoccupied checking up on her elder boy's GCSE revision; so, short of anyone else to ask, Steve recruited Harry with the unnecessary promise of a ride in 'the Maz'. No-one usually ate in the dining room, but now Anna has vacuumed the blue velvet carpet and polished the walnut table. The French windows at the back of the room open out onto the garden, from where Marianne has picked some early daffodils that are glowing in a cut glass vase. The radiators are full on. Steve is in charge of the cooking.

But upstairs in Harry's bedroom, the dinner party can wait for now. The house music is playing back to him just how good he's feeling and Harry is getting ready to celebrate. The night before, he'd met up with Frank straight from those guys in Regent's Row. They'd drunk champagne in that St James's wine bar, under the eye of the German waiter. Harry had taken Frank loudly through every detail. The Redhead was the boss man. Rob had sort of tried it on but Harry had knocked him back. Did Frank remember Grovesie and had he had those weird tattoos back then? Frank waved him on. They'd sliced open the hamper and tried to get him drunk but Harry had stayed his usual cool self. As Frank had told him. Frank put his arms round Harry and kissed him on the lips. The Maltese way, Harry supposed. Harry had waited for him to stop but in the end had had to pull back with a laugh. Anyway, things are back to normal. And in the bedroom, the music's getting louder and Harry's going to dance. In fact, he's going to strip to video – who knows it might go viral? Even Arthur might get to see this, one way or another.

For the show, he has selected a green top, Lowlife belt, and sagging jeans bunched over his Converse trainers. He toys with a baseball cap but his hair's looking good, cropped the way Sophs has suggested. He has shaved specially for the occasion. The beat is waiting, it wants him to get started. The audience is out there, so let the camera roll. He has not rehearsed. Begin with a sway of those sexy hips, then lift your left hand slowly up to stroke your chest as the music takes control. That last button's undone, lift your top teasingly to show the guys some six pack. Yeah. Now stretch out your right arm, clench that fist and raise it in the air in celebration. Hold it there. Keep your feet steady on the ground but roll those shoulders provocatively, then shake yourself down! One hand presses against your stomach, the other that outer thigh. Looks good on the monitor, but will they believe you'll go all the way? (Check the door.) Now, move your left hand nonchalantly into the trouser pocket. The beat quickens, this is trickier, so turn around and let them see some butt. Shake it fast as a tease! Back and face the camera and swing that right hand round - give it all a stir. Run those hands down those thighs, but seesaw your arms to remind them you're dancing and sway those hips some more. This is where the beat really takes off. OK, there's the top, thrown to one side, you're showing your torso, first the front, then the side, what will happen next…?

Thirty minutes later, it was all change. The dress code for

the evening had shifted to Paul Smith, the suit with the pleated trousers that Amita had selected, an open shirt. No tie, Frank would disapprove of that. Marianne was sporting light blue slacks that showed off her slender figure and, on top, an ivory blouse with silver chain and pendant. Those slacks would chime well with the dining room carpet, in a two tone way. Harry had kept his own chain on and was also featuring a yellow wristband and a blackened ring with an inlaid silver skull. He was planning on having another tattoo to go with the rose, but he wouldn't be going for tarantula tracks like Grovesie's. Something to do with Arthur perhaps. A Knight of the Round Table. Mother and son were sitting together in the living room, listening out for the arrival of Steve and their guest. There was the sound of a key in the lock.

*****

Unlike Steve in his GMR standard issue suit or Harry in his Paul Smith, Mike Berger was dressed smart casual. A thick jacket kept out any chill, although this looked like a guy toughened by North American winters. While he was easing the jacket off their guest's shoulders, Steve told Marianne that he had just been showing Mike the Maserati.

'That's a fine piece of engineering your husband has there, Marianne.'

Marianne said she thought that every time she saw it. Mike went on to apologise if they were a little late; at his suggestion they had dropped in at the local pub way up the hill for half a pint of bitter.

'The Dog and Duck,' interjected Steve.

'And was there anyone in there we know?'

Marianne took Mike on a tour of the house, Steve was off to his swanky kitchen. There was no active role for Harry at the moment; his job was to sit there on the sofa, waiting for the others to return. Like champagne on ice. When they had all re-congregated, Mike commended Steve on his and Marianne's taste in interior design. Harry asked if he had seen the wet room, then shut up. The conversation moved into the dining room. The first course was a cheese soufflé, which Steve styled as one of his signature dishes. Mike savoured it. Steve wanted to talk about business but Mike insisted on being more inclusive. Marianne and he shared an interest in twentieth century American art, particularly Rothko. Mike didn't look like he spent much time in an office. Harry reckoned he must be at least fifty-five, but he was in good shape physically.

'So, Harry, are you still at School?'

Harry was bewildered. It didn't look like Mike was having a laugh. He didn't think he looked particularly young for his age, even if he could pass himself off as being nineteen. He thought of how American models on the Internet tended to be more beefy and mature than their European counterparts. Before he could answer though, Steve and Marianne charged in to explain to Mike in their different ways how school in England meant just that and didn't extend to university as in the States (Steve's point), that Harry probably didn't realise that (Marianne's), he was having a gap year (Marianne again) and, after that, he was going to college (Steve). Or school. Mike looked over at him with what appeared to be private amusement.

Harry didn't contradict anything his parents had said but he did start explaining how he was currently learning the nuts and bolts of business, such as the ins and outs of cost benefit analyses and what on-costs were. He got as far as adding that he was doing some legal work on the side before Steve broke in to ask if Harry could help carry some dishes to the kitchen. The conversation turned to Marianne's career.

The main course was a Tagine of Lamb, which Steve

described as cooked the authentic Moroccan way. The choice came as a surprise to Marianne. She asked Mike if he had ever been to Morocco and described how they enjoyed slaughtering lambs there, how you could walk through a village on a feast day and see blood running down the gutter. 'I hope Steve hasn't done something similar in our kitchen.'

Steve joked that he was quite prepared to organise a slaughter if one was called for.

Mike looked round the table, nodding approvingly. 'Steve, Marianne. The food here is quite good.' He took a mouthful of the lamb, chewed it at some length, and swallowed. 'Harry.' He nodded again.

Marianne said it had nothing to do with her.

When it came to coffee, the conversation turned to how Mike had a place in Vermont to which he and his wife retired for long weekends. It was remote, he said, surrounded by two hundred acres of its own. No-one could find you there.

'We have a hideaway in the Cotswolds,' said Steve, which was of interest around the table. 'About an hour and a half's drive away. Marianne's sister lives nearby, so it's a great opportunity for us all to get together. Her husband and I are good buddies. They're very picturesque, the Cotswolds, Mike, very popular with Americans, I believe. You should go there.' Not, thought Harry, before Steve had found his imaginary place and bought it.

Coffee concluded, Steve asked Mike if he had a full schedule for the rest of his stay in London.

'Well, I could have a full schedule if I wanted. But I thought I might take some time out tomorrow to see the sights. Take a trip round London.'

Marianne suggested the National Gallery, the Courtauld, Somerset House, and even the London Eye. Steve said there were some great open deck bus tours.

'All fine suggestions, no doubt, thank you. But I wondered if Harry here,' he looked across at him again, 'could be prevailed upon to escort me. A young pair of eyes to guide an old man. I appreciate you're probably tied up at work and I know it would be a great imposition, but I thought I'd venture to ask.'

Marianne said that she could check her own schedule, she was sure Harry was too busy. Steve said he was certain he could arrange a professional tour guide. Harry was pleased to accept.

*****

It was a breezy March afternoon by the Thames. Wrapped-up gaggles of tourists were standing on London Bridge, looking uncertainly down the bridge towards the Tower. Coming out of the railway station, Harry noticed the signs pointing across the road to Borough market, advertising hot meat baguettes, homemade pork pies, even ostrich sausages. And, for those hungry for calories, chocolate brownies. He wasn't hungry, he had found some muesli before he left home. Steve had banged on the bedroom door before going to work and shouted that the future of Grant Matcham Rose rested on his shoulders but that it wasn't too late to cry off sick. Marianne was also working. She told him he should get by if he just pretended to a vague interest in history and culture. If she had the time, she would start at the Courtauld and then take Mike up St James's Park to look at the monstrosity that was Buckingham Palace before paying a visit to the Queen's Gallery. It was supposed to be a work day for Harry too. When he rang Frank to let him know he wouldn't be turning up, he was told he was unreliable, untrustworthy, always letting him down at the last moment. He demanded Harry give up being an escort. Frank could be a bit of a control freak but Harry wasn't bothered since it just showed how the old guy depended on him. So he didn't answer back and explain that this had nothing to do with escorting. After a while, Frank calmed down to say that, since Amita was on a trip to Italy, he was planning to go to Portofino that evening where Harry could join him. Unfortunately, Harry had to reply, he might be booked up all day. That hadn't helped smooth matters.

Mike had said that his office was on the right hand side of King William Street, just north of the river. The sign behind the reception desk indicated that there were six floors with one company occupying the first five and another squeezed in at the top. Mike's was the one on the sixth – Brown O'Keefe Rabinowitz & Styler. The guys behind the desk looked like this was the job they did when they weren't working as bouncers. The reception area was very spartan, just a couple of couches to one side. The bouncers told him to go and sit over there.

When Mike walked out of the lift, it looked like he was wearing the same smart casual outfit he had had on the previous evening. It might be casual but it was still a uniform, pressed to perfection. He waved towards Harry and then came to sit down beside him, tugging on his trouser legs so they rode up and didn't stretch over his knees.

'So, Harry, have you given much thought to where we might go this afternoon?'

Harry had given it some thought. He'd recalled Frank talking of taking a trip down the Thames to Greenwich and the Thames Barrier. He had also mentioned Tate Modern which had the advantage of being next to the Globe Theatre, a sucker for any tourist with its Olde Shakespeare aura. Otherwise, there was shopping; Harry didn't know if London was a match for New York or Chicago, but Amita swore that John Lewis had the best fabrics of any department store in the world (outside of the Indian sub-continent). He laid out the various

186

options before Mike.

'Each of those sounds worthy of a trip in its own right, Harry. However, and I hope you'll forgive me for this, I've been doing my own research this morning and I was envisioning something a little less lively.' He pulled out a guidebook and opened it at a page flagged with a Post-it. 'A cemetery.'

Outside the building, they crossed the road and Mike, with a gentlemanly wave, hailed a cab. Seated inside, Harry asked if he always dressed for the office like that.

'Unless I have some important meeting requiring the affectation of gravitas, yes. Then I'll wear a suit. Maybe we Americans are not as buttoned up as some of you Brits.' He glanced over at Harry, now wearing his new check shirt and some skinny black chinos.

'I'm strictly casual, Mike.'

The cab made its way north past Monument Tube. Harry asked Mike if he always travelled round London by cab.

'Most of the time, it's the most convenient means for me. But I do travel on the Underground as well. You know, Harry, back in my office, there are fellow Americans who won't travel on the Tube without taking antiseptic wipes. They're afraid of catching something. What do you think to that?'

Harry laughed out loud, remarking that he could make a fortune scaring tourists about the health hazards of London and then selling them protective potions. Mike's laugh was softer.

'Ever been to the States, Harry?'

'No.'

'You never know, you might make a fortune there too.'

Shortly afterwards, the cab pulled up. They were at Bunhill Fields, a cemetery just north of the City. By Old Street. EC1.

'This is your heritage, Harry.'

'I expect I should know all about it, Mike, but I'm afraid I haven't a clue.'

According to the notice board at the entrance, 123,000 people had been buried there by the time it was closed in 1854; and yet it couldn't have been more than three or four hectares in size. Harry could see through the trees and over the tombstones pretty much to the other side.

'Don't you think it's spooky, Harry?'

On entry into Bunhill Fields, the atmosphere became tranquil, the sound of traffic subsided. Not that it was some magical forest. A narrow path appeared to lead straight through the cemetery, bordered on either side by a five feet high iron fence. Harry could have climbed over that. Tombstones rose up silently all around, their surfaces eroded by the climate so that the details of the lives they had recorded had been erased. According to Mike, there would be documentary records elsewhere. Dank moss covered both the gravestones and more grandiose memorials. Mike read aloud from the guide book, reciting names of famous people buried there. There were two Cromwells – R and H – were they related to Oliver? This was the burial ground of Dissenters, Protestants who for one reason or another had been opposed to the established church in England. There was a steady flow of people along the pathway, a woman in a denim jacket behind a 4x4 pushchair, a slight Asian in a veil. The ground undulated, the grass was scattered with leaves and twigs, even small branches. Perhaps the explanation was that there had been a storm recently but, to Harry, this mess seemed wrong in a place where dead people lay. He knew from Steve that those trees were oaks and limes, but he couldn't name the others. Crocuses and daffodils appeared in the distance. The path opened up in the middle of the grounds and Mike pointed out the figure of a small man lying on top of a monument.

This is John Bunyan
Author of the Pilgrims Progress
OB^T 31ST AUG^T 1668
AE^T 60

Almost like Text. Over on the other side was a more ordinary memorial to William Blake - 'Poet – Painter', that sounded like Rock Star – and his wife Catherine. And next to that a needle-style monument to Daniel Defoe rose up, recorded as being 'the result of an appeal in the Christian World newspaper to the boys and girls of England for funds to place a suitable memorial upon the grave of Daniel De-foe, it represents the united contributions of seventeen hundred people. SEP^T 1870.' Harry asked if De-foe was French. Mike, his tour guide for the moment, gave him a potted history of Bunyan, Blake, Defoe, Dissenters, the Pilgrim Fathers and the establishment of the American colonies, and the War of Independence from the British Crown. A tramp lay seemingly comatose on a bench further along, his legs hanging clown-like over the bench's arms showing off a new pair of trainers, his head pressed unsupported onto the boards at the back. Eventually, it started to spit rain, so they moved off and out of Bunhill Fields onto City Road, red buses crossing either way in front of them. Then they turned left and there was Old Street, Harry's home turf.

The next place Mike wanted to visit was Covent Garden. When Harry said that he would find it very touristy compared to Bunhill Fields, Mike replied that he was a tourist with eclectic tastes. Covent Garden, Soho, Piccadilly, Savile Row, by 6 pm Harry was starting to feel knackered even if Mike showed no such signs. Then Mike said he was peckish, not having eaten since midday. At last, Harry saw an opportunity to take the lead. There was, he said, an excellent Italian restaurant just a few streets away.

He thought Mike would like Portofino. It might not be a smart as Frank liked to pretend, but it did have an authentic feel. Harry wasn't sure if Stefano would recognise him but he decided to hail him by name anyhow, just like Frank did. Stefano responded.

'Welcome back, sir, welcome back. It is always such a privilege.'

If he didn't recognise him, then he was very convincing. Harry reckoned it was in their mutual interests to pretend to know each other, Stefano's because it showed everyone that he had loyal customers and didn't rely just on passing trade, and his because it would serve to impress Mike. He told Stefano how much he enjoyed coming back to Portofino and asked for a table looking out onto the street. That way, he wouldn't be missed. They didn't have to wait long before the *focaccia* and olive oil arrived, together with a glass of Prosecco for each of them.

'Compliments of the house,' the waiter told him, respectfully. Harry wondered if he would have got the full works without Mike and, instead, had been larging it up with one of his mates. As Frank had done, he led the way in pouring oil into the saucer and dabbing bread in it. He asked if they had similar Italians back in the States.

'There's no shortage of Italian restaurants back home, Harry, but it's the proprietor that gives each one its own character. Like your Stefano.'

They shared the bread. The menus arrived. Harry recommended the *tomaselle* but said that the restaurant had a particular reputation for *fritto misto*. He explained that he knew the restaurant from his work, he often bumped into business

190

contacts there.

'Are you something of a networker, Harry?'

They ordered, each having *fritto misto* and Mike suggesting they supplement it with a glass of the house white wine. Over the starter of a shared plate of salami and ham, Mike asked if he ever missed not having any siblings. Harry thought about it and joked that he reckoned his parents inflicting one child on the world was enough. Mike related how he himself was an only surviving child, his younger brother had died of an AIDS-related illness a while back, in the 1980s. They had both been in their twenties at the time. AIDS had cut its proverbial swathe through many in his brother's circle, leaving gaps that still felt inexplicable to that very day. The shock that had roared through their lives had been all the greater for his parents since they had not known their son was gay. Mike wanted to know if Harry's generation still regarded AIDS as a threat; and he replied that, no, there were enough pills around nowadays to keep an HIV condition under control.

Harry could see Mike took him seriously; so, when Frank walked in as expected, he knew he could introduce the two of them, showing them both the circles in which he moved and, in the process, doing his bit for Steve's bid for GMR. That was the plan. However, when he raised his glass, Frank made no response, unless that was a flicker of shock before he turned to talk to Stefano who discreetly proffered the way to a table in the back room. Frank waved the idea away and sat himself down at a table some way behind at right angles to Mike and the yellow wall. Looking flushed, he ordered a bottle of wine. Dolcetto, Harry guessed.

Harry was confused and wondered whether he had misread Frank's expression. Maybe he hadn't spotted him. Mike was talking about how he was staying at a hotel near Kensington Palace. Harry raised his hand again to attract

Frank's attention, but still felt he was being ignored. A waiter came over and asked if there anything he wanted, so he ordered a glass of red wine, telling Mike how well it went with the fish. Mike told the waiter he was fine as he was with the white. Frank was scrutinising the menu.

The conversation had stumbled. Apologising, Harry asked Mike to repeat what he had been saying about his hotel. Echoing the waiter, Mike asked if something was the matter. He replied, no, it was just that there was a business contact of his the other side of the room. He focused on what Mike was saying. His last time in London, he told Harry, his wife and he had stayed at that same hotel. His wife had wanted to go walking in Kensington Gardens and they had seen a signpost to the Princess Diana Memorial. Intrigued, particularly given that his wife had been a fan of Diana's, they had followed the signpost until they came to another one, and then another one, each sending them on a wild goose chase that never actually got them to the Memorial. Harry told him they hadn't missed much, the Memorial was just a playground for kids.

Frank's starter arrived at the same time as their mains, and Mike asked Harry what his aspirations were career-wise. At this point, Harry decided to ignore Frank. He had no intention, he told Mike, of going to college – or school. His ambition was to be an entrepreneur, self-employed; that way, he would not be accountable to, or dependent on, anyone else. Mike remarked softly that he would be dependent on any staff working for him. Harry accepted that – it was just he wanted to be his own boss.

There was one moment when he thought he saw Frank look at him askance under cover of addressing a waiter. Mike kept the conversation politely ticking over. Harry had lost interest in his *fritto misto*, it tasted like straw. When they'd both finished their food, Mike said he was going in search of the

192

bathroom.

Harry picked up his wine glass and, smiling uncertainly, wandered over to Frank's table. 'Hey, Frank, didn't you see me over there? I've just been drinking red wine with my fish. What would Arthur say?'

Frank looked up, flushed. 'You knew I was dining here this evening.' He stabbed at his food.

'Yes.'

'You said you couldn't come.'

'Well, plans change. I'm here now,' said Harry defensively.

'You thought it would be fun, did you, to come and rub my nose in it?'

'No. Rub your nose in what?'

'You thought it would be fun, did you, to bring one of your clients here - where you knew I'd be dining - and make me watch you flirt with him before you go off and find a hotel room where you can whore yourself?'

'No. Anyway, Mike's not a client. And I wasn't flirting.'

'It was plain to see.'

'He's a business contact.'

'A "business contact".' Frank scoffed.

'Yes, actually. He's a really nice guy. I was going to introduce you.'

'You don't have any business contacts,' Frank spat. 'Except through me.'

'I know, but...'

'Why would you?' Frank looked up loftily. 'You've no head for business. None at all.'

Harry stepped back. 'That's crap. You know it is. I mean, what about that Limoges?'

Frank carried on eating. 'I made a mistake, I should never have kept you on. It was misguided goodness of heart. You're a drain on resources, you cost me money.'

'No, I'm not. I don't.'

'The only "business contacts" you'll ever have are those who pay you for sex. Like that man. That's the height of your ambition, is it, business as an escort?'

'There's nothing wrong with being an escort.'

'And very well suited to it you are too. You're emotionally stunted. Clueless that anyone might have genuine feelings for you.'

'I thought you and I meant something to each other.'

'So did I!' Frank's voice cracked as he rose. 'So did I! I took you in from nowhere and invested everything in you. I should have realised what a fool I was, how you must have been laughing at me behind my back. How could I expect anything else from a rent boy, whose whole purpose in life is to fake emotion? To mock those who truly love?' He dropped his napkin onto the table and called out across the room to Mike, who was watching from the door to the Gents. 'You have him, sir.' Then he left the restaurant.

*****

Harry logged on, not sure if he wanted to be seen as an escort or to go incognito; but it didn't matter, Jake was on line. His one Friend. 'hey kid hows it goin?' 'hey young lad well gd thx' 'been chattn with any ppl here?' 'sum well freaky guyz lol. so RUDE!!' 'there prob lookn for some chicken – lickn their lips.' 'gross haha' 'met ne1 fit tho?' 'just u young lad:)' 'still got ur v plates?' '☹ fml' Harry asked what he did when he wasn't trawling this site for filth. 'revising :-(my mums stressn at me thinks I cba.' 'Don't you want to go to college?' 'give a fuck' You could always become an escort. Loads of cash and you don't even need to get out of bed. Jake laughed, he wanted to know what life as an escort was like. Harry said that he'd been with a rich American that day. 'good in bed???' 'dunno we dint do nething' '????' 'he was str8 he dint know I was an escort' 'mental lol' 'he was well nice tho' 'how old?' '55?' 'u like older guyz?' Harry replied, not particularly, but there was this old Maltese guy he'd like to see raped. 'hes well lucky!!!' Jake then asked if he still looked like he did on his profile and Harry replied that his hair was shorter now and sorta messy nd a bit spikey. 'so ur well more fit and hot than in ur profile' 'lol' 'but u still like yunger guyz?' '18-25 ☺' Jake wrote back, haha, so Harry still wouldn't have him? 'still lookn at gettn bummd?' Jake wrote that he wanted to make love. It was Harry's turn to laugh, 'how gay is that??' 'ffs' Harry told him he was very persistent. 'if I send u a face pic will u meet up?' It depended what Jake looked like. 'u wont be disappointed' 'If I like you, I'll give you a discount.'

Jake's facepic pinged into his inbox.

Chapter 11

It was now almost a week since that scene at Portofino and Harry still felt he was right to be angry. If Frank really was in love with him, why hadn't he said so before and what was he doing with Amita? What had that kiss with her been about? And then smooching him in the wine bar! The signals were all wrong. Anyway, that was Frank's problem, his mess to sort out. Harry was more bothered about Frank's saying he had no head for business. They both knew that wasn't true. Frank claimed he never said anything he didn't mean, but he had never said Harry couldn't cut it as an entrepreneur. OK, sometimes he didn't turn up to work because there was something else on or he just couldn't be arsed – and, fair enough, Frank ranted at him about that – but, when he was there, he was one hundred per cent. He had worked really hard. He had made them money from that Limoges. And more. He had managed Frank's real estate. He had kept track of Arthur, exactly as Frank had directed. And Frank had used him as his go-between with those guys at number 41, which must mean he was reliable. He had not been a sidekick. Frank was talking crap if now he was saying he'd been acting out of goodness of heart. Frank never did or said anything except out of self-interest, even if he was now saying that he loved him. It all went to show that business and pleasure don't mix. There were plenty of other Franks out there to learn from, ones who didn't look like fossils from the twentieth century, ones who didn't need to do deals tucked away at the back of a restaurant with a bottle of cheap wine. Anyway, what would have been so wrong with Harry's taking a client to Portofino? The first time he had gone there, it had been as Frank's escort. First, Frank complained he was no good as an escort, now he was saying he was no good at anything else. Let's have some consistency here! Come to that, why did Frank let himself fall in love with someone he told everyone else was an emotional zombie? Harry wasn't sure how much Mike had picked up; but he did know he had phoned Steve the next day, thanking him for dinner and for the use of his son who, he said, made an excellent tour guide as well as thought-provoking company at dinner. Luckily, Steve hadn't thought to read anything into that, he just acted relieved. But he had noticed Harry's downbeat mood and had cross-examined him and found out he'd lost his job. Then he had said something unhelpful about Frank being dodgy and it being no great shakes. Marianne was more positive; she assured him the experience would have taught him a lot and help inform what he decided to do next. But that hadn't stopped Steve.

Who cared? None of this could distract him from how he felt about losing touch with Arthur. Not realising there could be any problem, he had texted him that he wasn't with Frank anymore but that it would still be great to meet up. Arthur, though, had read this as one of those 'Keep in touch!' messages that don't mean what they say and had replied, thanking him and wishing him all the best. There was no way to follow up on that. Arthur. He might be very clever intellectually but he had about as much emotional intelligence as a bowl of jelly. Harry got up, pulled the curtains shut and went back to bed.

*****

Frank was sitting in the chair that Harry had bought for the office, its feet unsteady on their castors. The room was cramped and hot, it smelt of sweat, the window needed opening but was stuck shut. Frank was annoyed, annoyed with Arthur. When the boy had been around, he had used him to fend Arthur off. Since the moment he was gone, however, Arthur - ever diligent in his duties to Dahlia – hadn't stopped trying to contact him direct. When his texts were ignored and emails provoked no response, he took to ringing Frank, first leaving messages and then calling doggedly until Frank could not avoid answering. Frank tried telling him that everything was being put on a proper footing and that a lease would be granted shortly. Arthur wanted to see the lease. Frank said it was with the solicitors. Arthur wanted to know who the tenants were. Frank countered that he thought it was a company incorporated somewhere offshore. Arthur was concerned that the squatters had been in the flat since at least the previous December, it was half way through March now and there were rent arrears to collect. Colin, said Frank, would see to that in due course. The truth of course, which Arthur could not know, was that these boys were never going to sign any papers, let alone pay any arrears. They were going to remain there, a constant headache, until they had got whatever they wanted.

On the plus side, Frank's gifts to the Squire and his boys had gone down well. His sending Harry had been much appreciated and Frank was to note the boy had been returned intact. The Squire had enjoyed the hamper. Now discussions were going on, not face to face but brokered by George who had the advantages of prestige and affability. George would give no offence and take none in dealing with the young laddo's father. The Squire, he relayed, recalled how Frank had a genius with numbers that he was sure could be used to help them out of this tiresome situation. So, Frank had sat down at his desk and worked up a few options that George had shared with the Squire. The Squire said they had the makings of a plan. Arthur, however, was not part of the plan and, not knowing anything of it, had now rang up Colin to tell him that he was going up to Regent's Row the next day. Arthur was always getting in the way. He had got in the way with Dahlia, he had got in the way with Harry, and now he was getting in the way of the plan. Frank picked up the phone and rang George.

*****

Rob had watched from behind the curtain as Arthur chained his bicycle to the lamp post outside Southern Fries and stood back to survey number 41. A minute or so later, he had gone inside the newsagent's before leaving for a trip round the market. He had a backpack on, the lock to secure the bike came out of that. He wore heavy boots and a thick Scandinavian-style sweater that matched his fair hair. In fact, he looked rather Nordic in appearance; perhaps his ancestors had come off the boats with the Vikings. It was half past one in the afternoon. He had browsed through the market, lingering at the fish counter in particular. Eventually, empty-handed, he had turned back and was now sitting inside Southern Fries with a cardboard cup of Fanta Orange. There were four tables occupied – there was Arthur's, there were a couple of girls with oversized helpings and three boys sniggering behind their backs; and then there was Grovesie, keeping an eye on the Daily Express while continuing to report back by text. Arthur picked up his backpack, put the cup in the bin provided, and left.

At last, the doorbell rang. Rob couldn't be bothered with all that talk over the intercom, he just buzzed the door open, then popped his head out of the door to look down the stairs.

'Hi there! Come on up!'

Once he had tramped his way upstairs, Arthur introduced

himself, apologising for turning up unannounced, and said he was there on behalf of the landlords. Rob shook him by the hand , 'Rob, man, Rob' - complaining that the intercom did not work as well as it should.

'I mean, that could be anyone coming up those stairs! The police, burglars, anyone!'

Arthur dragged off his sweater, shoving it into his rucksack and, reaching for a bottle inside, started gulping water down. He said it was warmer outside than it looked.

'You shouldn't be doing that, man, I'd have got you a glass from the tap!' Not really caring, Rob went to the window and looked out. 'It's hot out there, is it? I dunno. I've been stuck in here waiting all day.'

Next, he asked what all this was about landlords, and Arthur replied that he had just come to check that there were no problems with the lease.

'The lease?'

'Yes. You know, the lease you've agreed with the landlords' solicitors?'

Rob didn't reply, he thought he would just look blank and wait for Arthur to try again.

'You don't know anything about a lease?'

He shook his head.

'Oh dear.' Arthur looked like he was finding this heavy going. 'The thing is, do you think you have the consent of the owners to be here?'

'Oh yes, most definitely! We've got permission.'

'Great. At least, hopefully great. May I ask exactly whose permission?'

'Why, Mr Adami's, of course! Frankie Adami's! You don't think there's any way we'd be living up here without it, do you? That would make us squatters, right? There's no way we'd do that. It's against the law. Right?' Facing Arthur, Rob reckoned

200

he was the shorter of the two by some four or five inches.

'Well, Rob, it would be great if we could make that crystal clear. What would help is… do you have any documentary evidence that you're entitled to be here?'

He thought about it. 'Documentary evidence?'

'Yes. Anything in writing. A letter perhaps?'

'Oh, that sort of documentary evidence!' He pretended to think about it some more. 'No. We don't have any of that.'

Arthur pushed on. 'Well, at least we know where we stand. What needs to happen now is for you guys to enter into a lease, formalising the position.'

Rob was having to do a lot of thinking. He brightened up, he had a solution. 'But we don't need no formalisation, man!' His voice could get quite high-pitched when he was enthusiastic, which might be quite cute but was also, he sometimes felt, a little too girly. 'We're old friends of Frankie's. Way back. We don't need to go through all that lawyer thing – entering a lease. We're completely trustworthy, honest.'

'Yes, I'm sure you are, Rob, but other people might not see it quite that way. If Frankie were to sell, say. Or if you fell out.'

'Oh no, that would never happen, mate, we would never fall out. That bond's unbreakable. Like in *The Magnificent Seven*, know what I mean?'

Arthur might have known, but he had become focused on something else. 'Forgive me, sorry, just how many of you are there?'

'Oh, there's a whole gang of us. Why? Do you want to meet the rest?'

'Er, is anyone else here at the moment?'

'At the moment? No, I don't think so. At least, I've been here all morning and I haven't heard anything.' Rob put his hand on Arthur's shoulder. Physical was always good. 'Look, if it'll help put your mind at rest, let me show you round. Give you a tour. That way you can see that we're respectable people, model tenants.'

He led the way upstairs. There was a bathroom on the mezzanine floor, poky and not somewhere you would want to hang out. He remarked how, if you were lying in the bath and turned your head right, it would be bang up against the toilet bowl. If you closed your eyes, you would probably be able to smell it. The shower was a rubber hose. Upstairs were two bedrooms, the smaller one at the back looking out onto the Sainsbury's car park in the middle distance, the front one facing the market.

'Where are the beds?'

'The beds? Oh, we're still in the process of moving in. Did you see that water ingress at the back? That'll need fixing.' He leant on the window ledge, looking down at the market, talking to Arthur behind him. 'I love looking down there. You see all sorts in the market, different types like you and me, kids, grannies.' He turned away from the window to face Arthur. 'And what about you, Arthur, where are you from? Are you from round these parts? You don't mind me asking, do you? I'm the inquisitive type, me, always asking questions.'

'I don't mind at all, Rob. But no, I'm not from round here, I live south of the Thames. In Brockley.'

'Brockley? That's south-east London, innit? You would never find me down there, man. It's all guns and knives. Like Croydon.' He shook his head at the thought of it. 'Mind you, you'd be all right, wouldn't you? You look like the sort of guy who can take care of himself.' He squared up to him. 'I bet no-one ever chances their luck with you.'

'I'm not really the fighting type, me, more of a man of peace.'

''Course. No, I meant like when you were at school, that

202

sort of thing. Nowadays, it's all sport, isn't it?' Rob got excited again. 'What's your team? What's your team? I bet it's Palace, innit?'

Arthur said he was afraid not, he was an Arsenal supporter for his sins.

'Oh.' Rob was disappointed, 'A Gunner. I'm Spurs myself. Opposite side of the fence... Anyway, what's this about Frankie selling? Is Frankie planning on selling this place?'

'Well, not just Frankie. There are two owners. There's Frankie and then there's Mrs Mounis.'

'Mrs Moo?'

'...Nis. Mrs Mounis. Yes, she wants to sell.'

'Really? This little flat?'

'Well, it's part of a larger transaction but I don't imagine that's of any interest to you.'

'Quite right, it's none of my business. I'm just being nosy. Asking questions.'

Arthur looked at his watch. 'Well, anyway, Rob, thanks for the tour. It's been great getting the opportunity to meet you and clear everything up. So, can I take it everything's OK with the lease now? There's no obstacle to signing it?'

'You've worn me down, man! You've worn me down!' Rob raised his hands in an act of surrender. 'I'll sign whatever you want.'

'I really appreciate that, thanks. I'll get a draft sent ASAP.' Arthur turned to go back down the stairs to the main room. 'And we can sort out the rent at the same time.'

'The rent, of course, man, the rent,' Rob repeated absently, following him.

Downstairs, Arthur slipped his backpack on and held out his hand. 'Thanks again, Rob. It's been a pleasure meeting you.'

'Likewise, Arthur, likewise,' he murmured, limply

accepting the hand. 'Really good to get this sorted. You know, I never realised there was a problem in the first place.' He opened the door so that Arthur could leave, then had a thought. 'Wait up! Wait up! I'm coming down too. I need to go to the supermarket. Get some supplies in for the boys.' He reached for his jacket from a hook behind the door, putting it on as they left the building.

Outside, someone had vandalised Arthur's bike. The two of them crouched down to inspect it. The wheel was buckled.

'I can't believe it! This is such a nice area as well! Oh, mate, I really feel for you.'

Arthur was perplexed. 'How did that happen?' He looked round for witnesses or onlookers, but none was apparent.

'I know how!' suggested Rob, 'It'll be one of them lorries that pick up the rubbish, that'll be it. They never look where they're going. You should definitely complain to the Council.'

Arthur unbolted the bike and said he'd take it back on the Tube.

'Good idea! That way, someone can take a look at it. There's no way you can ride that now.' They started walking down the street. 'Hey, tell you what, there's a short cut through Sainsbury's car park to the Tube. It'll save you five minutes, maybe more.'

'Thanks Rob, that's really thoughtful.'

'No problem. Just pleased to be of service.'

They took a detour off to the left where there was a break in the shop row. Arthur was following, wheeling his bike as best he could. Down at the end, they turned right onto a pathway.

'This way, Arthur,' waved Rob over his shoulder.

Ten metres further down, he turned round, saying, 'Look behind you'. Arthur did as he was told, to see Grovesie step out and weigh in with a heavy punch to his stomach. The bike clattered to one side. Shocked and winded, bent double with his arms clutching his abdomen, Arthur looked up at his attacker. Grovesie was there waiting, fists clenched, rings glinting, ready for more. He pulled Arthur up and head butted him on the bridge of his nose. Arthur gasped, his hands flicking up from his stomach to shield his face. Blood started spewing through his fingers. His eyes, tightly shut, were streaming. He doubled up again. When Grovesie then kneed him in the chin, there was a crack of lower jaw on upper jaw, of teeth on teeth. Rob was impressed. Grovesie was always good at this, very good. Arthur collapsed, writhing on the ground like a poisoned animal. Something that had swallowed bleach perhaps.

'Pick him up! Pick him up!'

Grovesie hauled Arthur up by his shoulders. His head was huddled down towards his chin in an attempt at self-protection, his eyes still screwed shut as though he was pretending he wasn't there, his nose already swollen and blood spreading over the lower part of his face like a crimson beard. Maybe one or two fewer teeth than before.

'Put him up against the wall! Up against the wall!'

Grovesie ripped Arthur's backpack off him with a force that should have dislocated his shoulder with any luck. He pinned him up against the rough surface of the red brick wall behind them and gave him a few seconds to regain his senses. There was no-one else around, no-one to come and help him, no-one to run off and get help. Grovesie feinted an uppercut to his head with his right fist, causing him to jerk away in fear, and then made a second feint with his left. 'What? Are you scared? You're not frightened, are you?' One more for fun, and then a knee to the balls. Arthur's mouth gasped in response. Grovesie turned him round and, holding him in a half nelson, rubbed the right side of his face against the brick surface, slowly at first but then speeding up. It was like looking at a cheese grater. Rob had to turn away. Arthur started to scream.

'Shut him up! Shut him up!'

Grovesie released the half nelson and pressed the palm of his hand against Arthur's mouth, pushing his whole weight against him. He had got to be three inches taller than Arthur, who was hunched up anyway. Grovesie moved his right hand up to start squeezing his eyeballs. Rob waited.

'Don't blind him! Don't blind him!'

Grovesie pulled Arthur round and punched him in the stomach, one time after another. Arthur looked like he was about to pass out.

'Ease up! Ease up! Make sure he's able to take everything in.'

Grovesie let him go and Arthur slumped to the ground, in foetal position. Grovesie stepped back and looked at Rob, who ran in with a series of enthusiastic kicks to Arthur's ribs and stomach. After five or six, he stopped and then stamped on his legs. Arthur looked up at him from the ground. Now he did pass out. It was time to go.

*****

Nothing was happening, there was nowhere to go. His room was messed up and Anna couldn't get in to clean it because he was always there during the day. He was Facebooked up with nothing left to say. He had retrieved his guitar from Steve's room, but not so as to play it. There was a pile of clothes at the foot of the bed but he was quite happy to stay in his boxers and T-shirt whether he was in bed, on the bed, at his desk, or on a trip down to the kitchen. Even in the shower. No, he took them off in the shower. He couldn't be arsed with the wet room though. He couldn't be arsed period. Sophs told him not even to think about contacting Frank, but he had no intention of doing that anyway. That was the past. She did though suggest he get in touch with Arthur. That wasn't going to happen either, he wasn't going to let himself get hurt for no reason. So, it was back to the Internet. There was everything you could want there, especially if you had a credit card. Straight porn could be quite interesting, not least because some of these webcam guys were useless - they should never have allowed themselves to get posted. He scored them out of five. There was a site where bereaved people shared their memories of loved ones and he set himself up as a fifteen year old whose Gran had just died or 'passed over'; but, after a while, the whole thing got too much like daytime TV. It was a séance waiting to happen. Grant Matcham Rose's website contained a facepic of Steve, his profile described him as 'one of the leading mid-market corporate lawyers with recent expertise in private equity and CDSs. Whatever CDSs were. Or private equity. There were testimonials too. 'Steve gives down to earth advice which is of practical use to the client rather than legal mumbo jumbo.' 'Steve has a first class legal mind which he applies with a surgeon's precision.' Written by the man himself perhaps. He scored the profile three out of five. There was no sign of Marianne online except, of course, on Facebook and her page was no go territory so far as he was concerned. Most of the time. Under Music she had listed Bob Dylan, The Beatles and Debussy. (Steve was in charge of music in the house – The Jam, The Undertones, The Specials. The Jam, The Undertones, The Specials.) Under Books: 'The Portrait of a Lady', 'An Apology for the Life of Mrs Shamela Andrews' and 'The End of the Affair'. There was a story in there somewhere. And Movies – 'This is England', 'La Dolce Vita', 'Anything by Louis Malle.' 173 friends – don't come all at once; though, to be fair, she did mix with a lot of people, not just Harry's friends. So, excluding Facebook (which didn't count), two out of the three of them had profiles online. With facepics. He was bored of escorting, he had shown he was good at that. He didn't need any more cash at the moment, so he'd withdrawn his services. He kept in touch with Jake though. Jake was funny, especially now he knew who he was. Steve, when he wasn't obsessing about his own career, got annoyed and called him a loser, telling him to go out and find himself a real job. Harry shouted back that it had been a real job, a good one, and that he'd choose Frank over Steve any day. Marianne told Steve he was being too hard.

Come the evening, he left the house. Most of his mates were back from college, so it was down to the bars in Kingston every night. He made a twat of himself at first, showing how much cash he had compared with the debt-ridden students, but no-one said anything about it except by insisting on getting their own rounds in. That was a loyalty he probably didn't deserve. One night, when he was off his head clubbing, he tried getting it on with this cool looking girl who'd had her eye on him since he'd arrived; but, after a few minutes with his hands up her top feeling her subcutaneous fat, she had walked away. Again, none of his mates made any comment. They all knew he was gay but they also knew it was none of their business. They were cool about it. That was a night when Rather Not Say about drugs really meant what it was supposed to say. Sophs looked after him and they found a corner where they could talk for the rest of the night.

Not long after, Amita rang. He saw her name come up on his phone and it took him a split second to decide not to answer. She had probably called by accident. He had been meaning to delete her number – along with Frank's – from his Contacts. Then it flashed up, he had a new voice message. What could Amita want with him? Where did she need driving now? Was there a parcel that needed picking up from a friend's? Hadn't she realised that he and Frank had split up? She had, after all, been in Italy at the time. He was not going to play it back. He stayed on his bed.

The message was short. 'Harry, darling, ring me back. It's very, very important.' If it was so important, then she would phone him again; but, after ten minutes, she had not. When he rang, she answered with relief that she had been so worried he would not return her call even though whether or not to do so was, of course, his prerogative. She needed to see him, it was very, very important. When he asked what was so important, she said that it was something that could not be discussed over the phone, you never knew who might be listening in. You only had to read the papers. He said he was tied up with his new work, it wouldn't be easy to meet. She said she would take a cab to Old Street that evening. Amita probably imagined that all parts of London were like South Ken. He asked if there wasn't anything she could tell him in advance. She arranged for them to meet the next day at Liberty, for afternoon tea.

There was no use his pretending that this could have nothing to do with Frank and that nothing might have happened to him. Amita was hardly likely to come to him with problems of her own. Maybe he was very ill – the drinking, the no exercise – or maybe something worse. Maybe he had left a message for her to pass on. Whatever it was, why not discuss it on the phone? Maybe he and Amita were getting married.

The next afternoon he put on his skinny black chinos and a gingham shirt - clothes he judged appropriate for tea at Liberty. Amita was not in the tea room but she had booked a table. He sat down and ordered a glass of tap water. Ten minutes later, she arrived, overladen with impulse purchases.

'Oh, Harry darling, there you are. You'll be able to help with these bags.' She kissed him on the forehead, then looked at the menu and demanded of the waitress, where was the Orange Pekoe tea? The waitress, obviously new to the job, said they didn't serve Orange Peacock tea. Choosing to ignore this show of ignorance, Amita said that she always had Orange Pekoe when she came to Liberty. The waitress pointed to the list of teas on the menu and said that that was all they had. It would have to be Lapsang Souchong then. Just as the previous time, she ordered scones for him with strawberry jam and clotted cream. She observed that he was looking very thin. There was a Victoria sponge cake as well, a slice of which she put on her plate but did not eat. And, this time, they each had a glass of champagne. She asked what he had been doing and he answered, working for this new Internet start-up company; he reckoned it was going to be massive, he had bought some shares in it. She nodded, good, good, she wasn't listening. She said he should have some more cream with his scone. She wanted to talk about her trip to Italy. She had friends – Gina and Dario – who had invited her to stay at their villa north of Rome. Just for a short break. She had flown into Rome, to Fuimicino, from where they had fetched her. The weather had been pleasant, much better than in London – she shivered – but not warm enough to spend too much time outside. They had an outdoor swimming pool which Amita would not set foot in, but Dario braved a few lengths every morning before breakfast. He was very manly. Like all Italian men, he had a hairy chest. Anyway, Gina and Dario had been sooo hospitable, they had insisted on her staying for a full fortnight. She had been no trouble; she would have tucked herself away in a corner with a book, but Gina did so like to chat. She pushed the Victoria sponge towards him. And then she had returned to London. Her mood dropped to sombre and Harry felt some tingling in his stomach. She had come back to find Frank in pieces. It had taken time to coax out of him what was the matter, what had happened, because he never wanted to upset her, he was always very protective. But she had found out in the end, and then she had wasted no time in phoning.

'It's you, Harry. He feels so responsible. He knows what he said was unfair and untrue. He can't believe he could have been so cruel.'

She stopped and inspected him. He didn't know what to make of it or what he was supposed to say.

'He wants to make it up to you, Harry. I don't think you realise how important you are to him. Before you arrived, he was lonely. He has me, of course, but I have my own life and I can't afford to be in London all year round. He needs something else. And I don't know anything about his work, it's another world to me.'

She stopped again and looked at him, expectantly. He still didn't know how he was supposed to respond. She started once more.

'You've made him very, very happy and now he has gone and ruined it. He doesn't know if you'll ever let him make amends. Will you, Harry, will you just let him say he's sorry? You don't have to forgive him – I know I wouldn't in your shoes – but will you just listen to his apology?'

He found something to say. 'Well, I don't know.'

'Good. He's waiting for you now. In hope. Just in case you're prepared to show him the magnanimity of which he knows you're capable.'

While she was dealing with the bill, she asked him to gather up her bags.

The cab took a tortuous route to avoid construction works around Centre Point and ended up somewhere the other side of Covent Garden, Holborn way. Amita pointed at a pub. 'In there.' He looked at her uncertainly. Were they going into the pub now? 'Not me,' she answered impatiently. 'You. He's in there.' He clambered over the bags to get out street side, banging his head on the cab's roof as he did so; and, turning to close the door, he saw her shoo him away as she might do a

211

pigeon. The cab pulled out. From the pavement, it looked a bit of an old man's pub, but it probably packed out at the weekend. Stepping inside, he could see there was plenty of open space, not that many tables and not, it seemed, any Frank. He went further in, uncertain whether to ask at the bar for a drink or if they'd seen someone of Frank's description; and then he saw him, at a table hidden round the side behind a pillar, sitting on a banquette immersed in his newspaper with a large glass of red wine to one side. He looked up at Harry's approach, slowly pretending to show muted surprise.

'Hah, Harry, what are you doing here?'

'Nothing much.'

'Excellent.' He returned to his paper.

Harry put his knee resolutely on the stool opposite. 'What are YOU doing here?'

Frank folded the paper up, ostensibly irritated at being disturbed. 'I wanted a bit of peace and quiet, and I assumed I'd find it in here. It used to be a fine public house; but now, like everywhere else, it has been stripped out and "modernised" so as to drive out the old decent custom and bring in incontinent binge-drinking youth.'

'Seems pretty quiet to me.'

'For the moment.'

'So you weren't waiting to see me?'

'No.'

'Amita says you're completely distraught at losing me.'

'I'm sure she didn't say that. You will have misunderstood her.'

'I suppose that's because I'm an emotionally zombie and not capable of having genuine feelings for anyone.'

'I would never call you an emotional zombie. A little scared of opening up perhaps.'

'You did actually. At Portofino.'

212

'Ah, Portofino! One of my favourite places in London. One of its best kept secrets.'

'So no-one but you is allowed to go there, is that it? I don't think Stefano would be very happy with that. I mean, even you don't eat and drink THAT much.'

'Of course not. Anyone's entitled to dine there. It's just that it would be preferable if the people who do patronise it did so in order to enjoy the fine food and wine on offer, and not as a pretext for something else.'

'He wasn't a punter.'

'If that's what you say.'

'As I said, I brought him there to meet you. Anyway, I've given up escorting for now.'

Frank nodded, tight-lipped. 'That's probably for the best.'

'Why? I thought being a rent boy was all I was good for?'

'I never said that.'

'Yes, you did.'

'It's just that you're probably not cut out for it.'

'What are you saying now? That I'm no good at it?'

'What I mean is, you're probably intended for better things.'

'Like what?'

Frank shrugged. 'How should I know? That's a matter for you. Just something a bit more productive and self-improving than being an escort.'

'It's good money.'

'It's something for nothing.'

'So you really claim you aren't distraught at losing me?'

'I am not.' Frank was po-faced. 'But, now that you're here, you may stay for a drink.'

'Do you really think I'm crap at business?'

'You still have a lot to learn.'

It was nearly six o'clock. 'OK, I'll stay for one.' He looked towards the bar.

'Here.' Frank knocked back his wine and held out a ten pound note. 'And get me another glass of Merlot while you're up there. Please.'

When he returned from the bar, Harry placed the wine and his Diet Coke on the table, then came round and sat on the banquette beside Frank. They watched punters coming in for a quick after-work drink. Frank remarked how he was looking less scruffy than usual and patted him on the knee, asking what he'd been up to. He ditched the story about the start-up company and said, getting wasted with his mates most of the time. He relayed how Steve, total arsehole that he was, had been getting on his case, telling him to find some work and saying that the job with Frank had been a dead end. He had even suggested that Frank was a crook. Frank bristled and said that, if he ever met Harry's father, he would take the opportunity to put him right. Harry laughed, saying he'd enjoy seeing that, and asked how work was going. Dordogne Delights, it appeared, was still struggling along but Dominique was confident that they would turn the corner. Frank always tipped his head back when he drank, as if trying to avoid the wine sticking to his moustache. Harry asked how things were going at Regent's Row. Frank grunted non-committally. Eventually, Harry asked how Arthur was.

'Arthur,' Frank pronounced, 'has moved on. So now I'm having to manage everything by myself.'

'Moved on,' echoed Harry, dazed like Frank had smacked him round the head. 'What a loser.'

The pub was filling up with suits but there was, as Harry noted to Frank, no sign of any teenage binge-drinkers yet. Then, from their discreet position behind the pillar, he spotted a familiar bald head. He pointed it out to Frank saying, that dickhead's my dad. Frank's right hand slipped under the table and up the inside of his thigh until it found his crotch, which it covered cup-like. Swelling, Harry let it stay there. Steve was with a group of people, three men and a woman. He was trying to attract the barman's attention. Harry couldn't hear what they were saying until they moved further down the bar towards the pillar, pushed there by the tide of customers. One of the group was a lot younger than the rest, with the enthusiastic doggy-like manner of a junior lawyer. Not yet a fully grown mastiff. The others appeared to be clients of Steve's, this pub wasn't far from his office. The woman was German, she pronounced her Vs and her Ws the wrong way round, she was talking about a 'Vord Wersion' document. She was the top dog. The men were British, Harry picked up that they were due on a train up to Leicester but had some time to kill in the meantime. Steve was talking of how Matthew – presumably the puppy - knew all the local pubs. He joked that he clearly didn't have enough work to do. That was Steve's line in humour. It was pints all round, bitter for the Midlanders and lager for the rest. Steve took a sip. Frank remarked that he saw a family resemblance and asked some sketchy questions about Harry's home life. A table became vacant which Steve directed Matthew to grab while he settled up at the bar. The clients followed Matthew. Frank leapt up and, coming deftly round the pillar, blocked Steve off. Harry looked on, wondering what he had in mind.

'It's Steve, isn't it?' He addressed him grandly.

'That's right.' Steve looked at him quizzically.

When Frank pressed his hand firmly into Steve's, Harry choked. 'Gerry. We met last year. At David's and Sarah's.'

Steve detached his hand from Frank's, looking at it distastefully before glancing over his shoulder towards his clients. 'I don't think so. I don't know any David and Sarah.'

'Of course you don't, old boy! I was there with my wife

Diane. Remember?' Harry had seen this before, Frank posturing as some upper class grandee who 'knew people'. Now he was frowning, as if trying to recollect something. 'And your wife was called... Let me see if I can recall...Yes! Marianne!'

Steve, trying to make his way to his clients, was stalled. 'My wife and I go to any number of parties, it's sometimes difficult to keep count.' Harry pissed himself. Steve was trying for an easy exit. He wasn't interested in getting to the bottom of this, he wanted to be with his clients.

'I bet you do. From what I recall, you both thoroughly enjoyed yourselves.' Harry still didn't know where Frank was going with this. Nor, it was clear, did Steve.

'I'm sorry?'

'You don't remember?' Frank was going to prompt him. 'We swapped.'

'I beg your pardon?'

'We swapped wives. Remember now? Or, being even-handed, they swapped husbands.'

Steve snapped back. 'Like most men, I may sometimes complain about my wife, but I would never swap her for another woman and certainly not at some swingers' party. You're obviously confusing me with someone else.' He picked up his glass, ready to leave.

'Yes, Marianne. A little taller than you, possibly? Slim. Glasses. Bit of a feminist.' That was the line Harry had fed him. Admittedly, it covered fifty per cent of Marianne's friends, but the evidence was building up and it was getting more difficult for Steve to make a quick exit. 'Likes art history.'

'Perhaps my wife was at your party. I most certainly wasn't.'

'Come on. Diane said you were a bit of an Action Man yourself.' Action Man, thought Harry, that was a nice back-handed compliment. Macho. Dummy.

'I'm very pleased to hear it.'

'She has a bit of a thing for bald men. And as for Marianne? She was insatiable. I've rarely met someone so ravenous for sex.' Frank was imaginative, perhaps too much so.

'You're really claiming you slept with my wife?' Steve looked him up and down incredulously.

'What else? Look, the main reason I came over, old boy, is that I know Diane would be delighted to hear we've bumped into each other. She was rather miffed that we forgot to exchange details the last time.' It was Oscar material, it certainly did for Steve, who started jabbing his finger at Frank. He had forgotten about his clients for now.

'Look, you fat git. If you think I'm going to give some stranger my contact details just so that he can fuck with my wife, you've got another thing coming.'

'Well, you were quite happy about it last time.'

Steve started getting angrier. His clients were looking over, bemused, wondering what their host was up to. From the way the young puppy was trying to distract them, it seemed they were able to hear. The rate of jabbing speeded up. 'I can assure you, Gerry or whoever you are, that, if any man is going to fuck my wife, then that man is going to be me! And certainly not you!' He pushed Frank hard with his shoulder so that he could get round him. 'Now bugger off out of here!'

Frank glanced at Harry, concealed behind the pillar, and pulled himself up in a show of dignity. 'Well, if that's your position, so be it. What a shame. Anyway, if you change your mind, David and Sarah have our details.' He strode towards the door, showing to all how aggrieved he was, and exited. The show was over. Steve sat down with his clients, his back to the bar. Harry slipped past him and burst out of the door laughing onto the pavement where Frank was waiting.

'That was so good, Frank. He is so crap when it comes to anything to do with sex.'

That night, Harry gave himself to Frank and enjoyed his lips on Frank's lips and his body heat against Frank's. Maybe this was love, it was definitely union. And Frank was not the selfish old man that Harry pretended him to be, he was the man who knew everything about him and shared it. And it was true that all this happened on her sheets but Harry knew that it wasn't infidelity on Frank's part and that Amita had sanctioned it, and that the following night she would be lying there in that bed beside him.

Chapter 12

Harry was sat at the kitchen table, slumped over his IPad and a half-eaten stripey bowl of cereal. It was two-thirty in the afternoon, time for a late breakfast. He had lost interest in the game he'd been playing and was looking for something else. Marianne had just switched on the washing machine, which was emitting a high value, low volume hum. Five minutes earlier, he had had the room to himself. Now sitting opposite him, she was jotting down a list on recycled notepaper that looked like parchment. At the other end, perched on a work surface in red socks, was Steve. He was fidgeting, wanting to chat.

'It's still too much of a coincidence, isn't it? Don't you think? Maz?'

'What is?'

'That guy in the pub. Him claiming to know you, and all that.'

'It certainly sounds like someone's idea of a fantasy.'

'What did you say he looked like, Dad?' Harry had heard this before, but he still thought he could have some fun here - more than from gaming, although he kept his eyes on the screen as he wanted to look detached.

'Well...' Steve began. His heels started drumming against the cupboard below him; it would have been even more irritating if he had been wearing shoes rather than just red socks. 'He was fat and the wrong side of sixty. Borderline obese, I'd say. I don't imagine he pays much attention to healthy eating.'

Steve was bang on the money there.

'And a bit of a drinker too.' The drumming stopped. Harry looked up. 'Capillaries burst all over his face.' Steve sniffed.

Spot on again. 'And what was he wearing?'

Steve pulled a face as he thought. 'Well, he was quite well dressed as it happens. Nothing you or I would wear but, for a sixty year old... you know, baggy green cords, Viyella shirt and a tweed jacket, that sort of thing. He had a tie too. Bit of a toff, maybe.' Bit of a toff. Frank would love hearing that. Recognition at last. 'I suppose he could be some sort of country gent.'

'I bet that's where all the swinging happens. Out there in the country.'

'You reckon?'

'That's what I've heard. Maybe he knows Bob.'

'Did you hear that, Maz? Harry's saying he thinks Bob and Sarah might be swingers.'

'Well, since some strange man appears to be claiming out of the blue that he has had sex with me, why not throw in my sister too?' Marianne was more interested in her list.

'But there was something phoney about him. Maybe it was his hair. It just didn't seem natural for a man that age. I bet it was dyed.'

Steve looked puzzled when Harry laughed out loud. Frank would love being thought of as a country gent but he wouldn't appreciate Steve's comment about his hair. He was very proud of having so little grey and always insisted it was natural. Harry would enjoy sharing that with him. But this was getting boring, it was time to move on.

'Sounds to me, Dad, like you've got mixed up with some sort of dodgy business.'

'Dodgy business?'

'Yeah. Don't you think it sounds kind of sinister? I mean all that weird stuff about Mum. There has to be an explanation. So why would he target you? Think about it. You're a top lawyer. You're running a campaign to take control of your firm. Your name's up there in lights.'

'And?'

'And maybe someone out there's not happy about it.'

'Well, that's just tough.'

Steve was on a roll. Everything was telling him he was on track to win. Mike had signalled from across the Atlantic that Brown O'Keefe Rabinowitz & Styler were ready to embrace Grant Matcham Rose, that way creating a legal giant with a rather long name. They hadn't gone public though; Steve had floated the idea as part of his campaign but he hadn't admitted he had a firm in mind, let alone that the deal was in the bag.

'True. But suppose whoever it is has decided the best way to get you is by besmirching your reputation. So they hire this guy to accuse you in public of being a swinger.'

'Well, he wasn't very successful, was he? No-one heard.'

Harry thought back to Steve jabbing at Frank and swearing in front of everyone. 'What, you don't think any of your clients picked anything up?'

'My clients? No. They wouldn't believe it anyway.' That was a hint of uncertainty. Harry would carry on needling.

'Wouldn't you like them to think you're a man with a way with the ladies?'

'They can think what they like. Anyway, it must be fun living inside your head but, in the real world, none of that stuff happens.' Steve slid off the work surface and shuffled over to the fridge. As he poked around inside, its yellow light shone coldly out.

'You're probably right, I've been watching too many

films. But what about Andy?'

'Andy? What about him?'

'Well, he's got a lot riding on this too. Maybe it's Andy who's decided to play dirty.'

'Andy wouldn't do that.' Steve left the fridge door ajar. 'He and I are old friends. Isn't that right, Maz?'

Result. He'd rattled him. That was a definite wobble, Steve needing Marianne to back him up.

'I hope so.' Marianne didn't look up, she was finishing off her list but she was paying more attention.

'Dad?'

'Yes?' There was a hiss at the end of that.

'What will happen if Andy does win?'

Steve was munching on a stalk of celery. 'Well, he'll get to be managing partner, not me.'

'Yeah, but would that be the end of it? Would there be room for the two of you in the new GMR or would Andy want to get rid of you?'

'Get rid of me?'

'Yeah, you know, steal your clients and push you out of the firm. These things happen. You could end up losing everything. The house. The Maserati.'

Steve shook his head as he rinsed his fingers under the tap. 'You're being silly. It's not going to happen.'

'Fair enough. I'm probably being over-imaginative again. Let's hope so. One last scenario. Are you sure these guys in the US – Mike and the rest – are on side?'

'Yep.'

So there's no chance that you might announce the merger and they then pull out.'

'No chance.'

'But suppose they did… that wouldn't do much good for GMR, would it?'

222

'I guess not.' Steve was rooting around in the fridge for something else to snack.

'It would be a bit like a crash on the stock market, wouldn't it? Like when a company announces that it's going to merge and the deal falls through. Its share price craters. It would be the same with GMR. No-one would thank you for that, would they?'

Steve slammed the fridge door shut. 'One, GMR's not a listed company. Two, that's not going to happen. And three, I didn't realise that, when you started work again, it was as some hot shot investment analyst in the City. I thought it was just doing dubious deals with some toe-rags down in Fulham.'

Harry didn't care, Steve was always rubbishing his job. That was why he'd been winding him up. And he had had a result.

Marianne folded her list in two and stood up, looking ready to leave the room. 'Well,' she said, 'let's hope it doesn't come to that, you losing your job. We don't want us both ending up out of work.'

Steve's wasn't the only story in Surbiton. Marianne had expressed concern that the 'change process' she was running at the hospital was drawing to a close, meaning there were no more jobs to cut except those of the job cutters themselves. It was, she had remarked, just as she had predicted when comparing it to the French Reign of Terror, where revolutionary judges eventually fell victim to their own guillotine.

'It's not going to happen.' Steve was categorical but Harry knew he wasn't really being supportive, he was just holding on to his view that Marianne's was a job for life, subsidised by taxpayers like himself.

'Hm, I hope not. If we did both go down, that would leave Harry as the only breadwinner.'

Marianne sounded serious but Steve split his sides laughing. When he'd gathered himself together, he gasped that – if that happened – then at least they'd get back some of that money they had wasted on him over the years. Harry wasn't going to rise and Marianne hadn't joined in.

'When did you say the result will be announced?' she asked.

'Wednesday, 5 pm.'

'And is there going to be a big do?'

'There'll be a drinks party in the partners' dining room. I suppose it could be quite a big event.'

'Speeches?'

'Probably just a toast from Godfrey. Anything else will happen beforehand, just for the partners.'

'Ah, so this drinks party is not just an internal GMR affair? Family are allowed?'

'I guess so, yes.'

'Well, in that case, I think I might come along.'

'Oh, OK.' Steve looked so pleased, he was almost wagging his tail. 'What about you, Harry? Like to tag along?'

'Thanks, but I've something else on, that day.' No way.

'Shame. You might learn something about what business is really like.'

'You mean, like how to be a loser?'

Marianne intervened. 'Harry, will you come along for my sake? I'll be on my own otherwise, and those partners' wives are like a shoal of piranhas in high heels. I could really do with having you alongside me.'

Harry said he'd think about it.

Steve wasn't listening, he'd moved on. 'You know, Maz, we could always sell this place. Maybe now's the time to move. Go upmarket.'

'Upmarket? What have you in mind?'

'Well, you used to say you'd like to live in Putney.'

'I think that's a bit young mums for me now.'

'How about further out then? In the country?'

'Oh, is that what you'd like?'

'We could buy a place like Sarah's and Bob's.'

'What? And pretend to be the local gentry?'

'I don't see why Bob should have it all to himself. There's enough of the Cotswolds to go round.'

'Well, we could see what's on the market; but you have to win first. We don't want to take on more than we can afford.'

'What about you, Harry?' asked Steve. 'Any ideas where you would like to live?'

Harry asked if he had ever heard of Brockley.

*****

It was Tuesday afternoon. They had driven up to Finchley in north-west London. Getting out of the Mercedes, Harry observed that Lady Dahlia's house looked quite big for someone to be living in by themselves. Inside, it was heavily furnished. There was a grandfather clock in the hallway, where the only natural light came through the stained glass in the porch door. Every surface in the living room was covered. There were lace mats on occasional tables. There was a chest of drawers with polished brass handles on top of which stood a gathering of family photographs, keeping Lady Dahlia close to Nick and their children. Nick appeared tall, reedy, clean-shaven and fair, not like someone of Greek extraction at all. There were pictures of the two of them on holiday, arm in arm and sunglasses in hand, a Mediterranean expanse behind them. Anika was the tour guide, she'd sent a photo of herself in the Outback - not Uluru – shades on and smiling. Her brother Alex and her playing in the garden as small children, a young guy was helping Alex down the slide into a paddling pool while

Anika looked on from the side. Alex in his graduation robes. Anika with perhaps her fiancé. Nick, in a chair, looking older and tireder. The young guy looked a bit like Arthur, but obviously that wouldn't work time wise. Turkish rugs layered the floor. There was a freestanding corner cupboard displaying china, and a standard lamp stood behind the main chair, facing the television. It reminded Harry of his grandparents' home back in Nottingham. Steve's and Marianne's generation had swept away the last of this sort of clutter.

Lady Dahlia had left them while she finished preparing the tea. She would not accept any offer of help. The trolley she wheeled in had a plate of chocolate biscuits and ginger nuts on top and a teapot, cups and saucers below. She handed Harry a cup which he rattled on its saucer, trying to stop the teaspoon from sliding between the two. He declined any biscuits, while Frank accepted with a critical glance in his direction. He changed his mind and said he'd like a ginger nut. Smirking as Frank looked on, he took a cracking bite.

Dressed in charcoal with a maroon cardigan, her grey-black hair pulled back to display gold earrings, Lady Dahlia raised her cup into the air, holding its delicate handle between her sturdier thumb and index finger, and announced that it looked like they had a deal worth celebrating. 'Although,' she added, archly, 'you've been rather reticent about the whole thing, Frankie. Normally you're quite forthright when it comes to matters of business. So, go on, is it a good price? Or could we have done better?'

Frank placed his cup on its saucer and sniffed in contemplation. 'Every deal involves compromise, Dahlia; it's the degree of compromise that matters. Your advisors say this offer is top of the market. They even say it's bullish when one thinks of the risks entailed.' He stopped, took a further sip of his tea and then returned cup to saucer with teaspoon neatly to

226

one side, apparently having nothing further to add.

'And am I to infer from what you've just said that you disagree, that you think my advisors are wrong? After all, haven't you implicitly signed up to their advice by agreeing to the sale?'

'I have indeed, I have indeed. My own gut feeling, speaking as an old school entrepreneur, is that we let the buyers off rather lightly when it came to these risks, that they're not as great as they forecast, and that we should not therefore have discounted the asking price so much in order to cater for their purported concerns. But, as I said, I'm old school, I'm out of touch, these advisors of yours will no doubt have a much better feel for the market than I have. That's why I need Harry here to help me, a young head much better attuned to the modern world than mine is.' He stroked Harry's forearm.

'Well, I presume you took up all these concerns of yours when you met them, Frankie? I can't imagine you keeping your thoughts to yourself.'

'You're correct. I did. And I don't mean to sound at all unappreciative. It is a good price in itself. Far more than I myself could have afforded.'

'I'm pleased to hear you say that. Anyway, does anyone know quite who these developers are? All I've heard is that they're based somewhere in the Channel Islands. Are we sure they're good for the money?'

'Well, they've put down a ten per cent deposit, which does suggest they mean business. Apart from that, I believe they are a Guernsey company. What does it matter? The solicitors have done their due diligence, they say everything is in good order and I'm content to rely on that.'

Harry took another bite at his ginger nut. He too had asked who the developers were and, while he had not been surprised at the answer, other parts of the deal had made him stop and think. Frank was keen to share everything with him now that they really were, as he put it, partners. The buyers were the guys in the flat or, more precisely, the redhead's dad. Frank referred to the redhead as the laddo and he wouldn't reveal the Squire's real name either. The Squire had been intrigued to find out that the Regent's Row properties were for sale, something it turned out he had first heard via Harry. He had recognised that a sale would be complicated by his lads still being in possession of the flat at number 41 but there was still the matter of the money Nick owed him, a topic that got Frank spitting as it had – had had – nothing to do with him. Since, however, the Squire did not feel it appropriate to take up this matter directly with Lady Dahlia herself – not that Frank had ever suggested he might – it was unavoidable that the debt should be paid out of the sale proceeds of the properties. And since both the Squire and Frank had been put to so much trouble by this problem that Nick had created, it was also only fair that each of them should take a further cut from the sale price as compensation. Frank was vague about what these cuts amounted to, individually or in aggregate, but Harry had worked out that they came to a total of about twenty per cent of the value of the properties, maybe more. Twenty per cent of the real value, that was, meaning what Frank and the Squire's people assessed to be the true market value. Frank assured Harry that it would not be appropriate to explain any of this to Lady Dahlia; leaving aside that the debt to the Squire rendered her financial position worse than she already envisaged, it would distress her to know that Nick had died owing money. In fact, it could defame his memory in eternity, thus making it all the more important to shield her from such a revelation. Moreover, Lady Dahlia would never have considered that Nick's business dealings might not always have come within the compass of Her Majesty's Revenue; she would no more want to know about Nick's transactions with the Squire than the Squire would want her to know about him. All in all, the case for not involving her was unanswerable; while, equally, payment that was due should be made.

Harry got that. But his next question had been, how did Frank and the Squire expect Lady Dahlia to accept twenty per cent (or so) less than the real value of the Regent's Row properties? Did they plan to come up with a fake valuation or was the idea to pay off Lady Dahlia's financial advisors? Frank was affronted that Harry should think he might ever be disposed to defraud or suborn anyone; and, regardless of that, Lady Dahlia's advisors were first rate, best in the City, unimpeachable. No, the challenge had been to persuade them that the properties were worth eighty (or so) per cent of what Frank and his co-sponsor reckoned; and there was nothing dishonest or underhand about that. It was no more than business. In fact, Frank's first act had been to enhance the value of number 41 by producing a lease evidencing that the flat upstairs was properly occupied and not the subject of any squat. The lease was for a term of five years and had been entered into the previous September. Dahlia's valuers had expressed some surprise that it had not been for the more conventional term of six months favoured by landlords; but Colin, supported by Frank, had explained that it had proved a difficult property to let in the past owing to structural deficiencies and that, as a result, the owners had jumped at the opportunity to let it to someone who wanted it for longer. Colin had been promised the opportunity of work from the redeveloped properties, but he knew he was on probation for now. The valuers had scratched their heads but replied, no matter, the tenant could be paid off with a small sum to reflect his inconvenience in having to relocate; but this, of course, had led to Colin and Frank having to explain that an intelligent tenant would want to extract a share of the redevelopment value if he were to move out, not what Frank called some nugatory amount tied to inconvenience. So, the valuation came down. All agreed that the students at number 43 wouldn't be a problem, they could be got rid of tomorrow. Mrs Tate in number 45, however, was a sitting tenant, having lived in that flat for over forty years; and, she being a trenchant old lady, Frank had taken the valuers there so that they could hear for themselves how she would only leave feet first. The valuers' actuarial calculation was that that could be up to ten years away, whether through death or by her simply being too infirm to climb the stairs by herself. Frank had pointed out that the staircase was wide enough to cater for a handrail. But Harry knew that Frank had returned without the valuers to ask Mrs Tate if she had had any second thoughts and that, after some prompting by him, it transpired that she did. She had to agree with the concerns Frank raised. She wasn't as well as she had been, particularly since the fall when she'd broken her wrist; she wouldn't have coped then without her daughter's support – and she couldn't always rely on her, what with being so far away. She would be all on her own. The area had changed, it had lost its sense of community, people just didn't look out for one another anymore. She admitted to feeling less and less confident about going outside after dark and it would only get worse as she grew older. On top of all of which, she wasn't racist or prejudiced but she did fret about those Muslim boys downstairs; they were always very polite, but she worried about the place being raided by the police or the whole building just blowing up under her. So, Frank had kindly arranged for her to move out to Essex into sheltered accommodation near her daughter, a move planned for post completion of the sale. This, Frank emphasised to Harry, was a side deal that had nothing to do with Dahlia or her advisors.

That left the businesses downstairs. Colin had advised the valuers that Mr Rai had fifteen years left on his lease and that the owners of Southern Fries had no incentive to up sticks and move their deep fat fryers somewhere else, while Frank added that he didn't recommend dealing with the guys in the mobile phones shop. Reluctantly, the valuers had come to accept all of these constraints. Frank and the Squire, however, saw things differently. They told Mr Rai he was a peaceful gentleman, not the type to get involved in disputes, not someone who would want to stand in the way of a redevelopment that was for the benefit of the wider community. And Mr Rai agreed. Then, so far as Southern Fries was concerned, the turnover in the current premises was evidently lousy but there was a much better site available further down Regent's Row in the heart of the market. Colin knew the landlord. As for the mobile phones shop, well, such businesses were as transient as their name implied. Lastly, there had been concerns over planning and development value. The market was in a conservation area, so there was no certainty that the Council would grant planning permission of sufficient scope to yield an adequate return. In fact, there was talk of the Council actually preferring a more ambitious development a few streets away, thus making the market redundant. Rumours along these lines emanated from local councillors with whom the Squire's people had had words.

Stretched out on the bed, his arms behind his head Harry had asked what the Squire would do with the properties. Would he convert them into a bar? Another deli? Frank had sighed as he rolled over and said it would no doubt be something that turned over a lot of cash.

All this Harry had heard earlier that afternoon, before the drive up to Lady Dahlia's. In the car, he had wondered what Arthur would have made of all this. Now he watched Lady

Dahlia stirring her tea with her spoon, a habit perhaps harking back to when people still took sugar.

'And, in the end, we managed to do it all without Arthur. Poor soul.'

'Indeed,' acknowledged Frank, echoing for a moment her regretful tone. 'But now, to get back to brass tacks, the completion monies.' Harry was stuck chewing on his ginger biscuit; he wanted to ask what she meant but, by the time he had swallowed, the chance had slipped by as the subject of money trumped all others. Back in the pub, Frank had said that Arthur had 'moved on'. Harry had wondered at the time what that meant but hadn't dared ask. He had assumed getting back with Frank would mean picking up with Arthur too but 'moved on' sounded like he had lost interest. So, rather than pick away at his own vulnerability, Harry had concluded that there was no pretext for texting Arthur. He had tried to forget about him. He had assumed Arthur had made the decision himself; but now, from what Lady Dahlia was saying, Harry might have got that wrong.

The discussion of money tailed off, Lady Dahlia was talking of how she had never actually visited Regent's Row but had been hearing that the area was quite up and coming nowadays and not the no go zone it once had been. Frank was dismissive, he said that that reputation had always been rather overdone, it had served the media's purpose to overplay the level of crime then just as it now suited them to trumpet its regeneration.

'Which makes it all the more ironic, doesn't it?'

'What does?'

'What happened to poor Arthur.'

Harry jumped in. 'What happened to Arthur?'

'Oh, he got caught up in a bit of trouble, the poor chap.' Frank was pretending to care. Harry didn't like that.

'Beaten up, darling, he was beaten up,' explained Dahlia.

'How?'

'How? Oh, I'm not sure you'd want to know the details.'

'Yes, I do. Is he OK? When did it happen?'

'Well, it was some weeks ago now, round the back of that market apparently. When I visited him in hospital, he was very poorly. His head was all bandaged, his jaw wired up, he could only take liquids. And his leg was in plaster too, poor boy. Battered and bruised all over. I'm afraid they'd been particularly vicious.'

'But is he going to be OK?'

'I'm sure he will, darling, yes. He's back home now where Jane can look after him. Although I don't think he'll be working again, not for quite a while.'

'Do they know who did it?'

'Who knows? Quite possibly, but you can't depend on the police nowadays, can you? Arthur's no memory of what happened, none at all.'

'And it was right by the market? Is that what you said?'

'So I understand. But you should phone him, Harry, give him a call. I'm sure he'd appreciate it.'

Frank added nothing to Lady Dahlia's account. Driving back to Fulham, Harry bit his lip. In the rear view mirror, he could see Frank sitting moodily in the back.

'When you told me,' Harry talked into the mirror, 'back at that pub, that he'd "moved on", is that what you meant? That he'd been beaten up? Is that what you normally mean when you say someone has "moved on"?'

'It wasn't the right time to tell you. We needed to get ourselves straightened out first, you and I.'

'Why didn't you tell me later?'

'I knew it would upset you. I never found the right moment. I didn't want you to be hurt.'

'You never liked him, did you? So go on, then. Tell me. What happened?'

'Harry, Arthur's the type of person who blunders into things without thinking. He gets in the way. I appreciate you're distressed just now, Harry, but it's no surprise he ended up getting into trouble. People like him do. It's nobody's fault but their own. You'll grow to understand.'

Back in Surbiton that evening, Harry rang Arthur. He said he'd been to Dahlia's that afternoon and that she had told him about the beating up. He said he would have rung earlier if he had known. He asked if there was anything he could do to help. Arthur replied in characteristic Arthur-speak that he appreciated Harry's calling, it was a pleasure to hear from him as always, that he didn't quite recognise himself when he looked in the mirror, his chin was possibly a little shorter now which was an improvement, and that he was confined to Brockley for the time being, which was also a good thing since he'd become rather inattentive where it came to his studies. Harry wanted to know if he could come and visit; to which Arthur replied, maybe when he was in a fitter condition. Harry spent the rest of the night trying to squeeze as much meaning as he could out of that conversation.

*****

The next evening was the occasion for the announcement of the new managing partner. When Harry and Marianne turned up, formal business was still under way. 'They always overrun, these things,' commented Marianne. They were shown upstairs to the partners' dining room, the venue for the party. Harry didn't remember having been there before, but she told him he'd been brought along when Steve had been made a partner.

'And how old was I then?'

'Oh, you must have been five or six. It was much stuffier then - this room - things were much more hierarchical. They didn't have anything like these long tables and benches, everyone had their own chair, ranked by size. The senior partner had the biggest, with a long ladder back he could recline into, while the most junior had what were practically stools. It was all rather *Goldilocks and the Three Bears.*'

Waiters sauntered round, offering a choice of orange juice or champagne.

'The music,' Marianne confided, pointing upwards, 'is Saint Saens' *Carnival of the Animals*. I imagine whoever chose it for this evening was having a private joke.'

'So, go on then, what do you think of the art?'

'Those pictures? A bit bland, don't you think? An attempt at lightness, perhaps. But look at those poppies and grassland, the picture has no centre. And those daffodils in that vase, they look like they could do with some water. Very after Van Gogh, not. Mind you, in the old days, the walls were full of portraits of grand old men in wing collars, staring down intimidatingly.'

'Dead lawyers?'

'I always assumed so.'

'The ghosts of Mr Grant, Mr Matcham and Mr Rose.'

Marianne laughed. 'It was certainly very creepy.'

A few other wives had arrived, but not yet any husbands. In fact, Harry realised, he was the only guy in the room apart from the waiters. So, for the moment, the room was flush with oestrogen. Friends greeted each other, showing off their latest fashions, sharing how their second homes in Cornwall had been flooded, just like the locals'. They'd all been in it together. He could not see Marianne ever wanting to be part of this tribe, or being invited. Ever egalitarian, the contacts maintained were a couple of secretaries from when she'd worked there. She would meet them for a drink once in a while, making sure each time that Steve knew to his irritation what she was up to. He wondered if those contacts would survive Steve becoming managing partner; maybe the old girls would be less keen on meeting Marianne then.

'Oh, Harry, look! There's Hilary!'

As with the secretaries, Harry had heard of Hilary but never met her. Marianne waved her hand vigorously, like a fan. The woman whose attention she caught waved back. She was standing on her own, looking very tense, as if she was in the middle of a field of static electricity. She buzzed over and remarked that she had always liked Saint Saens. Marianne and she started chatting.

Hilary's name had come up when Marianne and Steve were arguing about the status of women at Grant Matcham Rose. She had been a contemporary of Marianne's there. Apparently, being very competent and knowing how to play the partners, she might well have made the grade herself; but she too had been going out with a fellow lawyer and, when they had both come up for partnership, she had appreciated how it would injure his pride if she was seen to surpass him. So, she had stayed at home and they had had a family, three boys about whom she was now updating Marianne.

'And Tom has discovered a talent for acting. At Christmas, we went to see him in *Oliver!*. As Fagin! At twelve years old! He was smaller than some of the urchins, bless him!'

'I was Nancy once,' revealed Marianne. 'Rather long in the tooth for a whore. I must have been at least thirty.'

'I am sure there are some very serviceable whores over the age of thirty, Maz. And I've no doubt you were very good in the part.'

'Bill Sykes was certainly quite dishy. And what about your middle one? What's he doing?'

'Olly? He's in his third year up at Oxford. Christ Church.

236

Just got a new partner. Says it's quite serious.' She pulled a face, excitedly. 'And what about you, Harry? What are you up to?'

'Harry's taking time out,' offered Marianne, 'while he makes up his mind what to do.'

'That's very wise,' said Hilary, addressing him. 'People nowadays allow themselves to get pressurised at too early an age into making life-defining decisions.'

Harry thought Hilary probably made quite a good mum. 'She's covering up for me,' he said, jerking his thumb lightly towards Marianne. 'I'm a lazy bum really.'

'And what's wrong with that? Enjoy it while you can. So, do have you any love interest at the moment, a good looking young man like you?'

Marianne took over as usual. 'Oh, there's this girl – they really suit each other but somehow they never seem to get it together.'

'Oh, it was like that with Olly. There were always girls around but they were never, you know, girlfriends.'

'It's the same with this one.' Marianne prodded his back.

'And then he told us he was gay...'

Marianne stopped prodding.

'Suddenly, it all made sense. The parents are always the last to know.'

Boom. Suddenly it all made sense. Harry thought he would step away and study the prints on the wall.

A man sidled up alongside him and addressed a picture. 'Hello. Who are you?'

Harry answered that he was Steve's son.

'Oh, that explains it. I thought you were a bit young to be married to one of the girls. Mind you, you could have been someone's toy boy.'

Harry had clocked that there was no-one else his age

237

there. The man was a partner's husband, fifty or so, apparently lost and looking for someone to hang on to.

'So, Harry.' Name check completed. 'Are you going to be a lawyer too?'

'No.'

'Still studying?'

'Yes. Oxford.'

'Oh, right! Which college?'

'Christ Church.'

'Reading?'

'PPE.'

Those were his only lies. The two of them chatted until a third man joined them, after which Harry wandered back towards Marianne and Hilary. Marianne caught his hand without looking and squeezed it, keeping hold.

'Do you think GPH will turn up?' asked Hilary, glancing round the room in anticipation.

'Oh, I'm sure he will,' replied Marianne. 'He'll want to make a toast.'

'Should we call him Sir?'

'He probably wouldn't notice if we did.'

Hilary giggled. A third woman joined them, someone who obviously knew Hilary. Brittlely confident, bangles on arms, hair straight out of a salon, she didn't bother to introduce herself to Marianne before addressing Hilary.

'I always knew it was going to be Andy. Didn't you?' She stood there, poised on her heels, pretending that what she had said was common knowledge but knowing that this was her big scoop.

'I beg your pardon?' It was obvious to Harry that Hilary was uncomfortable, but that that was of no concern to the other woman.

'He's the one with the charisma, people look up to him,

238

and he's held in such high regard outside the firm. The clients love him. It could never have been the other one.'

Hilary didn't know where to put herself, but Marianne stepped in. 'Forgive me if I'm playing catch up, but are you saying that Andy has been elected the new managing partner?'

'Yes. I made Neil promise to text me as soon as it was announced. You heard it here first.' And with that she moved on, eager to be the first to break the news rather than allow her own gossip to get ahead of her. They waited until she had broken in on someone else's conversation.

'Oh, I am sorry, Maz. How do you think Steve will take it?'

'Probably not very well.'

Partners were starting to trickle into the room, chatting among themselves excitedly. Harry thought the men looked like schoolboys who had just got away with being very naughty. Trays were swept clean of glasses. Husbands and wives co-mingled. Andy strode in to a patter of applause from some of the younger wives.

'Crawlers,' pronounced Marianne, still holding tightly on to Harry's hand.

Andy looked conceited, cocky. That, Harry thought, was probably what the clients bought into – a man that cocky must be doing something right. They were too dumb to realise that what he was doing right was getting his hands inside their wallets. Steve would never have been able to compete with someone like that, someone so comfortable in his pot-bellied skin with his place in the world. Steve – clever, chippy, highly motivated – had had to fight every inch of his career, and Harry respected him for that. A woman standing by the door gave Andy a small hug and he rested his chin lightly on her shoulder, cheek to cheek.

'That must be the "bimbo",' whispered Harry.

'Sally,' Marianne whispered back. 'Yes, you're probably right. Although if she's a bimbo, then bimbo has become a derogatory word for a lissom, clearly sophisticated woman with not a whisper of blonde hair.'

It was true. She looked graceful and was elegantly dressed. 'He probably didn't mean it.'

Now, there was Steve. The arm round his shoulder was GPH's – Godfrey Howe, as he was known to the world beyond Grant Matcham Rose and, reportedly, his wife.

'Marianne, my dear, we've had a cracking debate into which both Steve and Andy have invested heart and soul; but now the people – and, just as important, the clients – have spoken and it's time for us all to move on. Steve understands that, I know. For my part, I must now look forward to a life of Mediterranean cruises and ballroom dancing.'

'And a few non-exec directorships, no doubt, Godfrey.'

'If I'm lucky. If I'm lucky. Champagne!' He summoned a waiter. Steve was forced to take a glass and look round in an attempt at brightness. Andy came over, leaving Sally in control of a conversation elsewhere. He kissed Marianne as if she was one of his closest friends, then started praising Steve to her, listing his qualities, his vision, his ambition for the firm, his single-mindedness, his 'willingness to go it alone', his refusal to be held back, his disregard for outdated custom and practice. Five minutes later, Marianne told Steve and Harry it was time to leave.

She pointed out a pizzeria some distance from the office, midway to Waterloo. Steve hadn't had anything to say as they'd been walking along, except to acknowledge that he could do with something to eat. Harry asked the waiter for a table at the back, away from the other diners. While they studied the menu, Marianne asked what the margin of Andy's victory had been. It turned out that it hadn't been the landslide

Harry had first assumed, but Steve was convinced that the people who had voted for him had been driven mainly by fear of what might happen to them under Andy. Much worse than that had been the character trashing he had received in the last few hours before the vote, something that must have happened with Andy's connivance. First came murmurs of his poor handling of clients, reports of a bad temper. Then there had been some chat – Steve didn't know who had started it - about him going behind everyone else's back and talking pre-emptively to an American law firm about a merger. It had even been reported that he'd divulged the contents of GMR's books, an act everybody else would regard as treason. Names of US firms had been speculated on but there was no consensus on which one it was. A 'friend' of his - a 'friend' who'd ended up voting for Andy – had suggested he make a rapid rebuttal. But he couldn't, not least because it was true, albeit distorted. All he could say was that it was exaggeration and how he had never disguised his pro-American sympathies. The announcement of the merger had been designed to be the icing on the cake of his acceptance speech but there was no chance of anyone voting for him seriously when his integrity had been so impugned. These attacks had been on his very professionalism as a lawyer. It had all been calculated. If the news had broken even a couple of days earlier, he would have been able to liaise with Brown O'Keefe; they could have co-ordinated their positions and it could have been communicated that these had just been some informal discussions between friends. At least, that had been his first thought. As it happened, Brown O'Keefe were the icing on someone else's cake. Andy announced in his own acceptance speech that he would be taking GMR into talks with the US law firm about finding an accommodation between the two businesses; but he empathised that he would do nothing without the full backing of the partnership. 'Fine man, Mike Berger, fine man,' he commented to Steve under cover of widespread applause. Marianne and Harry listened as it all came out awkwardly over the pizza. When the time came to leave, Harry left cash on the table.

It was 8 pm before they got a train back to Surbiton. The rush hour was over but, what with people nearby, there was nothing they could say. Harry was conscious that the story wasn't all told. Steve stuck his head in a copy of the Evening Standard that someone had dumped on the seat. On arrival at Surbiton, they walked up the hill and, in the dark, Steve shared with them that he had not been as clever as he had thought financially and had made a couple of wrong decisions investment-wise. Coming into the house, Harry sensed it was time to leave Steve and Marianne by themselves. In his room, he sat at his desk, dwelling on what had just happened and nursing his thoughts about Arthur. After a while, there was a tap on the door and Marianne entered.

'This room used to be so tidy.'

'Where's Dad?'

'He said he was going to bed.'

She sat on the bed and told him that Steve would have to leave Grant Matcham Rose pretty much immediately. He was hurting a lot, he had been badly treated, his position was untenable. On top of which, there were these financial matters that needed to be got to the bottom of. All this was complicated by her own job being in the balance. The next few days would not be easy, she said, and she was glad they had Harry there to rely on. When she asked if he was OK, he nodded. She ruffled his hair and left. He plugged himself into his tunes. He didn't pick up the sound of the Audi outside, starting up and pulling away.

Chapter 13

Sunday, four days later, and no-one had heard from him. At first, Harry had found himself shocked at the way Steve's career had crashed, and how he'd pretty much foretold it. Guilt made him wonder if he was to blame. He'd laughed when Frank set Steve up as a swinger in front of his clients. He played the scene in the pub back to himself, followed by his going back with Frank for sex that night. And since then. He might not always like Steve but he did love his dad. Perhaps he'd decided to go up to Nottingham; Marianne had rung her father-in-law for a chat, but there was no sign he'd heard from him. If he had, he would have told her, he 'wouldn't be doing with any nonsense'. She had also called Steve's secretary that Friday afternoon, Harry stood by her side as she did. She asked Mary to let her know if Steve popped up. Mary would have understood. They all got on well with Mary. Then there was Sarah, she had to speak to Sarah; but when she rang, she got Bob. Bob had assured her that he'd seen this happen before and that, although it was always a bit messy, people pulled through by and large. He was there if he was needed. Off the phone, Marianne made light of the situation, joking that Steve couldn't have gone far since the Maserati was still in the garage. Harry had checked, it was still there. She also made light of the fact that she had lost her own job. She had known she was At Risk but she hadn't expected to be axed so soon. They had called her in on Friday morning – the executioners – and passed their grim judgment, thanking her for her years of service as they did so. She was still having to serve out her notice though. Her line was that change was good, especially for Steve who had been bound to GMR for far too long. You never knew, she said, now the spell had been broken, he might turn out to be a well-adjusted, chilled-out dude who everyone wanted to hang out with. Like Harry. Harry told her they needed to find out want had happened financially. So, that Sunday, the time of the week when Steve usually liked to occupy himself with paperwork, they went into his bedroom. Nothing appeared out of place, his bathrobe still hung from the back of the door, his shoes were still lined up on parade. A suitcase had gone, but not – so far as either of them could tell – any suit. Jeans, chinos, tops were missing, it went to show which clothes he liked best. He had taken the clippers he used to shave his head, they agreed it would have been a bad sign if those had been left behind. On the bedside table, there was a biography of an Eighties rock band, the bookmark revealing photos of its members on stage at Glastonbury. Harry joked how Steve still needed to go on about the one time he'd been to Glastonbury. Inside the chest of drawers were neatly presented collections of socks and boxer shorts – signs, as Marianne put it, of how anally tidy he was. Harry said that was gross, even if true. Two drawers down, things were different. Tucked away in a corner but still out of place, there was a pile of unopened envelopes, perhaps twenty-five in total, all of them face down. Harry turned them over and, sitting on the floor, began to open them. They related to money, chronicling falls in value to demands for payment.

Forty-five minutes later, he had worked out they were about to be homeless. There wasn't much else to do. Harry had his own business to deal with, his own demands for payment. He was due at Frank's later. He left Marianne there with the letters.

*****

He didn't pay attention to Frank's instructions because he already knew what he had to do. He didn't need a shot of brandy. He didn't acknowledge the old man's attempted hug before he left. This time he hailed his own cab. The journey that the first time had seemed protracted was now over before he had finished thinking. The market was empty, the street lights absorbed by the black of the tarmac; it was half past seven at night. Harry rang the doorbell for a second or two longer than was needed. This time he made it to the top of the stairs before the timer clicked off.

'Hey, Harry, how you been?' Rob let him through the door, shaking him by the hand, friendly as ever. The redhead – the laddo – was standing in the kitchen doorway, suave in a black polo top. There was no sign of Grovesie.

Harry didn't reply. Instead, he looked straight at the laddo, who acknowledged his nod with a grimace of a smile.

As before, Rob was the garrulous one. 'It's good to see you, mate, good to see you. Take a seat, take a seat.' He tried to usher him that way.

'No, thanks, I'll stand if it's all the same.' He kept looking at the laddo, he didn't want to engage with Rob.

'Cool. Standing's cool.' Rob opted to sit down himself though, slouching, stretching out his legs. 'So what brings you here, my man?'

'He knows what brings me here.' He pointed at the laddo with his finger, then raised it to the ceiling. That looked a bit too much like a pretend shooting. 'You do.' It would be obvious from his swallowing that he was nervous but he kept his eyes trained on the laddo, his target.

'I do what?' replied the laddo.

'You know why I'm here.'

'You're just a posh teenage brat.'

'Maybe. You still know why I'm here.'

'Why's that then?'

'You've got something for me.'

'No, I haven't.'

'You have. I'm not stupid.'

The laddo went and sat on the table by the window, showing his irritation in the way he swung his legs, his ankle boots twitching. Harry was giving off that he was unconcerned.

'Harry! Harry!' Rob intervened from the sofa. 'Don't be like this, man, don't let's fall out. Otherwise he might give you something you really don't want.'

'He's got a package for me.'

'A package? What sort of package? Is it a hamper, Harry? I like hampers.'

Harry hadn't meant to talk directly to Rob. 'I'm not talking to you, I'm talking to him.' He pointed at the laddo again, but quickly this time, just a stabbing motion.

Rob didn't reply. Harry was in a tricky position, he couldn't stay focused on the laddo and still keep an eye on Rob. The doorway was close to his right, but he wasn't going there just yet.

'Why would I,' the laddo emphasised the last word, 'want to give you a package?'

'Because that's part of the deal.'

'What deal?'

'The deal. You pay me cash now, and the sale goes through tomorrow. First instalment today, second tomorrow. Ring your dad if you don't believe me.'

The laddo gritted his teeth. 'Why am I having to deal with a brat like you? It should be Frankie here. Not one of his pretty boys.'

'Well, you've got to deal with me.' Harry had insisted on being the one who made the trip. Frank had had no say and the Squire had cleared it.

From the corner of his eye, he could see Rob, who had been shifting restlessly, sit slowly up. The laddo pulled himself off the table.

'Harry? What sort of a name is that?'

'It's my name.'

'Who calls their kid Harry?'

'My parents, I guess.'

'Do you love your mummy and daddy, Harry?'

'Of course.'

'I bet they'd be really upset if anything happened to you. Wouldn't they?'

'I don't know. I suppose so.'

'Sit down, Harry.'

'I don't want to sit down.'

'Don't irritate me. I told you to sit down.'

'I'm OK where I am, thanks.'

'Sit the fuck down! On the ground! Now!'

Harry dropped to the floor, pretending not to be scared. He hunched up. Rob was leaning forward now, his elbows pressed against his knees, studying him without any of that bonhomie. The laddo walked behind him. There was no noise except for the distant rumble of a jet and the hum of the fridge. Harry didn't like it being so quiet.

'So,' he asked, looking straight ahead, 'what are you going to do with this place when it's yours? I suppose you're going to kick everyone out on to the street?'

Rob replied. 'We have a plan, Harry, we have a plan. Those students won't know what's hit them, Harry. You said you didn't like them. We listen to you, Harry, we listen to what you say.'

Harry pictured the two students trying to rationalise with a dumb Grovesie on their doorstep. The idea gave him a slight thrill. The laddo interrupted that thought.

'Lie on your back!'

'What?'

'I said, lie on your back!' The laddo ordered him sharply.

'Why?' Harry pleaded. He regretted that slight thrill.

'Just fucking do it!'

Harry lay flat on his back. No more arguing.

'Shut your eyes!'

He shut them.

'Now spread eagle!'

Back home in the study, there was this Leonardo drawing of a naked man stretched out and viewed from above. *Vitruvian Man*, Marianne called it. Harry felt like a twenty-first century version of that, there to be inspected and anatomised, a cartwheel of head, hands and feet, clothed but naked, eyes shut, palms outstretched, vulnerable but untouched. He was feeling almost dreamy as the laddo's boot thwacked into his side, into soft tissue just below his ribcage, blowing out – what? A kidney? At least he hadn't gone for his ribs, or his crotch, at least not yet. Was this what it felt like to be Arthur? Where would it end up? The pain radiated out to his stomach and refluxed up into his throat. He wanted to be sick. He rolled himself over and curled loosely up, eyes closed. He counted the seconds, the acrylic carpet itching against his cheek, then started counting again until he felt compelled to turn over and look upwards. There was the laddo, standing above him, his boot caressing Harry's side, ready to kick him again. But then he returned to sit on the table, legs still swinging. He must have changed his mind

'There you are, Harry.'

'What?'

He jerked his head. 'Beside you. Frankie's cash.'

Harry shook his head. There next to him was a small

black canvas bag.

'Cheers. Thanks a lot.' Although trying to sound defiant and sarcastic, Harry knew he meant it as he eased himself up onto his knees.

'You really could do with the shit kicking out of you, but I've more important things right now. Next time.'

Blocking out anything else, Harry unzipped the badge and looked inside. 'I have to count this.'

'Don't piss me off any more, Harry. I said, I have things to do.'

'I still have to count it.' One hundred bundles of one hundred notes of £10 each, each wrapped in an elastic band. He started counting out the notes of a randomly selected bundle. The laddo went upstairs to the bathroom and there was the sound of a toilet seat dropping down. Harry finished the first bundle and started running his thumb quickly down some of the others, just a cursory check that everything looked as it should do. That was what he had been told to do. No funny business. He zipped the bag and stood up abruptly to leave.

'Harry's about to go, boss!' called Rob.

The toilet flushed and the laddo came down the stairs, wiping his hands on the seat of his trousers.

'Happy now, Harry?' he enquired.

'Yep.'

'Well, off you go.'

At the door, Harry turned round. 'Is this where I walk out and get halfway down the street before some knobhead jumps me from behind, beats me up and runs off with the cash?'

'Could be, Harry,' said Rob, still leaning forward. 'Could be. If that's what you want.'

Tucking the bag under his arm, Harry found his way down the stairs and let himself out onto the street. It was starting to rain. He zipped up his coat and counted thirty steps down the street, then stopped. If anything else was going to happen, it might as well be there and then. There was no-one else around. Nothing happened. He doubled back and, as he'd planned, went into Southern Fries. It was nearly eight. The staff were getting ready to shut up shop. He pulled out his phone and made the call.

'Frank?'

'Harry! Are you all right?'

'Everything's fine.'

'They gave you the money, no trouble?'

'Nothing I couldn't handle. I'm going to keep it, Frank.'

'What?'

'I'm keeping the cash, Frank. I'm not coming back.'

'What?' Frank sounded confused, his plans off course.

'I'm taking it all.'

'Come back, Harry. Amita's not here. We can talk.'

'I'm never coming back.'

'How about we split the money fifty-fifty?'

'Never.'

'Come back, Harry. Keep it all.'

'You can't buy me.'

'Just come back.'

'Bye, Frank.'

At that, Harry pressed Disconnect, then scrolled up his Contacts list so he could make one more call. The staff were trying to shoo him out.

'Arthur, it's me. I'm coming to see you right now.'

*****

Tube - London Bridge – Brockley - close to 9 pm. On opening the door, Arthur looked up into the sky, holding his hand out, palm side up.

'Is it still raining?'

'Not really. It was earlier. More of a drizzle now.'

Arthur stepped back into the hallway. 'Anyway, hi there, Harry. Come on inside. Welcome back to Brockley.' He sounded tired.

'Hi.' Six months before, Harry had never heard of Brockley. He walked past Arthur, black bag in hand. There was only one bike in the corridor to get past this time. He made to push at the door to Arthur's flat, then hesitated and turned round. 'Is this OK?'

'Go right ahead, Harry. My home is your home.' That was more than tired, that was worn out. Clutching the canvas bag, Harry made his way in.

Inside, the only source of light was the TV, broadcasting some no doubt highbrow programme now on hold. There was a single opened bottle of Bud on the floor by the sofa but no glass in sight. Arthur was fiddling with the dimmer switch, turning the light slowly up. Harry hadn't noticed it before but he was showing signs of baldness, there was an outcrop of hair above his brow that was gradually getting isolated. Baldness was OK. His eyebrows were still bushy. Harry couldn't pick out his eyes in the dim light but he could remember what they looked like. His nose seemed thicker at the bridge, Harry imagined it had been broken. His face looked like it had come in for some treatment, there was a gauze dressing covering his right cheek bone. No sideboards any more. His lips were fine, they looked untouched; and his chin was still a little too long. Maybe his eyes were a bit puffy. His eyes had always been his best feature, even if it did turn out he was really muscular and well-defined underneath. He was leaning on a stick that allowed him to take the weight off his right foot, lifted a couple of inches off the floor. Those white socks would be part of his sports kit.

'You're not looking too bad.'

'Thank you, Harry. The doctors will no doubt appreciate the second opinion. Unfortunately, though, most of the damage is under cover and can't be seen.'

'What sort of damage?'

'A few broken ribs, a punctured lung, a burst spleen, that sort of thing. Mostly offal-related.'

'And your leg?'

'Femur broken but duly on the mend, thank you.'

'And what's that?' Harry pointed at the dressing.

'That's a dressing, Harry. The wound underneath is still quite raw, so it needs protecting from infection. I don't want to be catching necrotising fasciitis.'

'Necro what?'

'Necrotising fasciitis. Flesh-eating disease.'

'Oh. Could that happen?'

'I suppose there's a remote probability but the chances are not. I may need to have some plastic surgery to my face in due course, though.'

'You should get them to sort out your chin at the same time.'

'Good idea. I'll make sure I mention it next time I'm at the hospital.'

'Are you having a lot of treatment?'

'Not as much as I was. Mostly physiotherapy. Which is practically heresy for an osteopath. We're not supposed to believe in physiotherapy.'

Harry wasn't sure if Arthur was joking. There was something else though. 'Is Jane here?'

'Jane? No. She got fed up with me and has gone off for a few days. She says she needs a break from looking after a whiny, self-centred invalid.'

'Oh.'

'I know. There's a dark side to me that no-one else sees. Anyway,' he started limping across the room, sort of like a war veteran, 'I'm being inhospitable. You've come all this way from wherever you've just come - an hour or so's journey away - so I should offer you refreshment of some kind. A beer? Or are you still not drinking alcohol? Coffee? We've only instant, I'm afraid.'

'Beer, please.'

'There's some Budwar, will that suffice?'

'Budwar's cool.' Harry watched Arthur wheel round towards the kitchen. 'No, wait! You sit down, I'll get it.'

'Cheers. It's in the fridge.' Arthur dropped onto the sofa.

On the kitchen table, there was a plate showing signs of a pasta tomato sauce. On the side was a microwaveable tub, enough for one helping, with a label identifying its contents as Bolognaise and stating the date it had been put in the freezer. Harry supposed Jane had written that. He himself would have cleared up as soon as he had finished eating, Steve's DNA had that hold over him. He returned to the main room.

'I've been to Dahlia's house.'

'I know. You told me over the phone.'

Harry sat down opposite Arthur, pulling the bag alongside him. 'She's very concerned about you.'

'I know that too. She shouldn't be. I'm beneath contempt.'

'No, you're not! What makes you say that?'

'I completely let her down.'

'How? By getting beaten up?'

'I let her down by claiming I didn't know who had done it.'

'You know? She said you couldn't remember anything.'

'That's because that's what I told her. The truth is, I was too scared to admit I know who it was. The last thing I want to do is to have to point the finger in public at those guys. It wouldn't end there.'

Harry didn't disagree. He could envisage Rob and Grovesie lined up at an identity parade, training their eyes on Arthur through whatever darkened screen he was standing behind, telling him that they had his address, they knew who Jane was. 'What good would it have done telling her?'

'Well, I could have forewarned her that she was getting mixed up with a load of scumbag crooks who were out to rip her off.'

'I don't think it would have helped.'

'Yes, I conned myself into thinking that. I rationalised that, by telling her, I might actually make things worse since it could end up putting her at risk of physical harm.'

'No, I mean I don't think that anything you could have done would have changed things.'

'Thanks. I think. So why did they beat me up?'

'Because you were there?'

While Arthur was trying to figure that out, Harry slipped the bag between his feet.

Arthur was frowning. 'So, has the sale gone through?'

'Tomorrow. The whole thing completes tomorrow.'

'I imagine Frank's coming out OK from all this.'

'I've split with him. I decided to split as soon as I heard.'

'Heard? Heard what?'

'About you getting beaten up.'

Arthur's jaw dropped. 'Are you saying Frank was involved?'

'Yes. He definitely knew about it anyway. I couldn't stay, knowing that he'd been involved. Not feeling the way I do about you, could I?'

'The bastard.'

'You never stood a chance with those guys. I mean, they

254

are hard.'

'You almost sound like you've met them.'

'I have.'

'What?'

'Frank used me as the go-between, between him and the Mr Big up there.'

'Blimey.' Arthur looked shocked, maybe even a bit impressed. 'He must rate you really highly. Or not at all. Pardon me asking but did you and he ever…?'

'No. No way.'

'So they've taken Dahlia to the cleaners.' Arthur looked over towards the window

'Yes.'

'Conmen. Low lives.'

'Well, I guess that, the way they look at things, it is just business. They suckered the people advising Dahlia. Frank's good at things like that.'

'And you're saying I'd have seen through all this?'

'No disrespect, Arthur, but I'm not saying that at all. I know you're very intelligent, but you're training to be an osteopath. These guys know what they are doing.'

'And they still had to beat me up.' He scratched his nose. 'You seem to have all the inside information, Harry.'

'I've worked out most of it. I wasn't involved, though! You do know that?'

'I believe you, Harry. So, anyway, you're saying Frank made a killing?'

'He has taken a slice, yes.'

'Is it a lot?'

'Well,' Harry pushed the bag forward with his feet, 'this is some of it.'

'What?' Arthur had been straining to reach his Budwar, but now he pulled up sharply.

'Half of it's in here. In cash.'

'You mean…' Arthur's surprise turned to incredulity. 'You're telling me there's a bag of swag between your legs?'

'Yup.' Harry unzipped it and picked out one of the bundles which he tossed over onto the sofa beside Arthur. 'One hundred thousand pounds in total.'

'Fucking hell.' Arthur was open-mouthed. He left the money where it was. 'Where did you get hold of that?'

'I collected it. This evening. From those guys.'

'Those guys? They actually gave you £100,000 in cash?'

'Well, they didn't exactly give it to me. It's meant for Frank. It's part of the deal. They pay Frank 200K, that's his share of what they've conned Dahlia out of. He gets fifty per cent today and fifty per cent when the sale goes through tomorrow.'

'But what's it doing here? In my flat?'

'I think you should have it. As compensation for what happened.'

'Jesus, Harry, you must be mad.' Arthur shrank painfully back, his eyes flashing alarm. 'Those goons are probably after you right now. Take it back and you might just get off OK. But there's no way – I'm telling you, no way – I'm touching that money.'

'No, you've got it all wrong.' Harry swept the bundle off the sofa. 'They don't care what happens to it now. As far as they're concerned, I'm Frank's authorised representative. They've given me half his share, now it's up to Frank to deliver. End of.'

'Well, you're being very cool about this, Harry, but what about Frank? He's not going to miss that he's £100,000 down, is he? He's not going to let you get away with this.'

'He already has.'

'What?'

'I rang him and told him. I said that everything was over between him and me, and that I was keeping the cash.'

'And what was his reaction?'

'He said that I could have it all if I went back.'

'And you believe him?'

'Yes.'

'You don't think he'll come after you?'

'Nope.'

'And you didn't tell him you were coming here?'

'For fuck's sake, Arthur!'

'God, he must think a lot of you.' He swigged from the bottle but held the mouthful before swallowing. 'And you're absolutely sure you and he never slept together?'

'I only have sex with people I really care about, Arthur.'

Arthur shrugged. 'Well, Harry, I admire your balls.'

'Will you take the money then? Now you know it's clean?'

'I wouldn't exactly call it clean. And I think that Dahlia has a greater claim to it than I have.'

'Well, give it to Dahlia then'

'I think that might raise more questions than it answers.'

'So, what should I do with it?'

'I don't know. Give it to charity? Just take it away'

Harry shrugged, picked up the bundle of notes, and packed it neatly into the bag which he then zipped and slipped back under his chair. 'Arthur?'

'Yes, Harry?'

'Is there a single fibre in your body that isn't straight? You know, heterosexual?'

'Well, I've had pretty much every part examined over the last few weeks and no-one's mentioned anything otherwise.'

'So, you'd never consider sleeping with another guy?'

'It's not going to happen, Harry.'

'Not even if I gave you £100,000 cash.'

'Not even if you gave me £100,000 cash.'

'How about £10,000 then?'

'Not even £10,000.'

'Hey!' Harry jumped up out of his seat and bounced onto the sofa next to him. 'How about I just look after you then? Until Jane gets back?'

'Thanks, Harry, but I think you need to be looking after yourself. Anyway, two guys sharing a place together, it's always very messy.' Rain could be heard through the curtains, beating against the windows. It had started again. 'I can offer you a bed for the night though. Here.' He pointed down at the sofa. 'It's late for you to be setting off back to Old Street. And it's pissing down.'

By the time Harry woke early the next morning, the rain had stopped. He could hear Arthur snoring in the bedroom. He sat on the edge of the sofa and looked round. He stripped off his top and picked a rugby shirt from off a pile of unwashed clothes on the floor. Green and black stripes. He put it on - it looked baggy on him - and left £100 with a note.

HEY DUDE SORRY
NEEDED THE SHIRT
HXXXX

*****

It was Monday morning 9 am. It had been raining overnight in Surbiton too. The gardens there showed off their glistening lawns in the low morning sunlight. Commuters packed themselves off to work in trains. Badged in Arthur's green and black shirt, Harry had joined the early ones at Brockley station and crossed paths in central London with those coming up from Surrey and beyond. Since it was still the school holidays, more than a few would be stopping at home

258

rather than making the journey to work. Cash-rich families might be flying out round now for a quick break overseas before term started. Where would be good in April? Some years back, the three of them had gone to Barbados around this time, to a beach hotel that safely gated out the locals. Steve had been annoyed when Marianne and Harry had gone for a walk into the nearby town, where the people had been keen to chat and even persuaded them to try out some of their food. He had paid a fortune, Steve said, so that everything was laid on at the hotel. He himself had been water-skiing that morning. Harry was conscious he was hungry. He hadn't eaten since leaving Frank's the day before. Presumably, there would be some Granola sitting in a cupboard at home. They still had a home so far as he was aware; but, when that changed, he had enough money in the bank to rent somewhere. Plus there was the £100,000 cash he was carrying. He was the cash-rich one right now. He didn't think he'd go back to escorting, he could do better than that. There was a regular flow of cars going into the centre of Surbiton, but Marianne's was still on the forecourt even though she was due at work that day. Perhaps she was ill, perhaps the car had finally died. He was definitely going to drive the Maserati while he still had the chance, licence or no licence. He wondered what Adele's car was doing there too.

Inside, he found Adele in the hall, calling up the stairs. Turning round, she seemed taken aback to find him there.

'Oh, hi, Harry.' Adele, for whom everything always fitted into place, didn't seem to know what to do with him.

Marianne's voice came down the stairs. She was saying she wouldn't be long.

Standing there, watching Adele grasp the bannister, Harry tried to make sense of things. 'What's going on?'

Her reply seemed addressed more to herself than to him.

259

'I wish I knew. I haven't a clue.'

'Well, what are you doing here?'

His sharpness of tone made Adele pay him attention, which was how it should be. It was after all his home, not hers. '"What am I doing?" Oh, I'm sorry, Harry. I had a phone call from your mum half an hour ago.'

'Why isn't she at work?' He squeezed the black bag's handle.

'It sounded like she needed someone here, so I rushed over.'

'Is she all right?'

'She seemed upset. The thing is, Harry, I can't stay long. Martin's coming round any moment to pick up the boys and take them down to Dorset for a few days. I woke them up and told them there was a bit of an emergency here and that I was going to have to come over, but there's no way they'll get ready by themselves. I'll never hear the last of it if they're still in the bathroom when he comes.'

Harry didn't understand. 'Why is she upset?'

'She's heard from your dad.'

'Dad? Is he OK? Did they speak?'

'I don't know. All I know is she's going to Burford. She's upstairs packing.'

'Burford? You mean Auntie Sarah's?'

'That's what it sounded like.'

Harry sat down, trying to work this out, making sure the bag stayed close to him. 'Maybe she's finally had enough. Maybe it was something he said. Mind you, it's hard to think of anything he hasn't said already.'

'All marriages have an undercurrent of bickering, Harry. That's what keeps them ticking over.'

'Right. Did Martin ever call you a cunt, Adele?'

'No, Martin would never do that.'

'I really thought they would get on OK. All the money stuff and everything, it felt like it brought them back together. I never thought they'd split.'

'What money stuff?'

Harry wasn't sure how to reply. He'd assumed Marianne confided all their family problems in Adele, and that would have to include something this big. How, after all, could she help without knowing? But it seemed he was wrong, she didn't know. His phone bleeped, a text arrived. He replied.

'That wasn't your dad, was it?'

'No. Adele, why do you think Dad left?'

'Well, it's all tied up with the job, isn't it? He'd invested his life in that place; so, not getting the top job must have been crushing for him.'

'You could be right.'

She took hold of his hand. 'You need to understand, Harry, people can react unpredictably, really badly, when they come up against a crisis like this. Sometimes they just can't face up to it.'

'Can't face up to it? What? You mean they top themselves?'

'No. Well, not necessarily. It's just that you need to prepare yourself for whatever's coming.'

'Dad would never do that. All his life, he has been focused on making something of himself. Right from the start, from being the first in his family to go to university, then qualifying as a solicitor and getting to be a partner, he has done all that by himself, with no help from anybody else. You don't think he's going to top himself and let those bastards think they've won, do you? It's not going to happen, I promise you.'

'I'm sure you're right.' She squeezed his hand before letting it go. 'Just take care.' She shivered, then looked at her watch. 'God, it's cold. I can't afford to hang around much longer.'

'You go. I'm here.'

'I know.' Adele smiled at him, then turned to call up the stairs. 'Maz? Harry's here.'

A suitcase ran along the oak floor upstairs. They looked up to see Marianne at the balcony. 'Oh, Harry. Good.' The suitcase was the big red one usually used only for holidays. She started to bump it down the stairs. Harry dashed up to take it quietly off her. Once they were all at ground level, Adele asked if she had everything she needed.

'I think so.'

'Keys? Cash? Credit cards?'

'Check.'

'Cigarettes?'

'Of course. Top of the list. I couldn't manage without them.'

'For fuck's sake, Mum! What's going on? And what's happened to Dad?'

'Sorry, darling. He's turned up in Burford of all places. He's been staying at the Bay Tree there. It's way too expensive. He's obviously lost his marbles.'

'So he hasn't killed himself?'

'He wouldn't do that.'

'I know. But is he OK?'

'No-one could have helped. But he'll be all right.'

'And you're going up there now?'

'Yep. Bob's looking after him at the moment.'

'Bob?'

'Yes. Don't worry, Dad was fine when I suggested it.' She tipped her suitcase onto its wheels. 'I was waiting until I knew a bit more before calling you. I know you've got a lot on.'

'I understand.'

'You can come now if you want?'

'No, it's probably better if it's just you. I'll stay here and see off the bailiffs.'

'All right, but mind you get out of the way when the wrecking ball comes crashing in.'

'Think of all the money you wasted on that wet room. You wouldn't have spent that if you'd known.'

'I would, you know.'

They loaded up the car and Harry kissed Marianne goodbye. As they watched her drive off, Adele wrapped her arm round Harry, still in Arthur's shirt.

'I have to go now. You going to be all right?'

'Yep.'

'I'll come round this evening.'

'It's OK. I'll be fine by myself.'

'I know. You're a good lad, Harry.'

They were distracted by the sight of a bicycle racing up the drive, its yellow-shirted rider straining out of his saddle. He braked to stop right in front of them.

'What on earth?' exclaimed Adele. 'What are you doing here? You're supposed to be back home, getting ready to go to Dorset.'

'I know. It's just you said it was an emergency, so I thought I'd come up and see what was going on.' The rider turned to Harry, his face a mixture of excitement and concern. 'Hey, Harry.'

'Hey, Jake.'

Lightning Source UK Ltd.
Milton Keynes UK
UKOW06f0701210616

276699UK00012B/275/P